ERASED!

ERASED!

A COMEDY

Chris Payne

authorHOUSE®

AuthorHouse™
1663 Liberty Drive
Bloomington, IN 47403
www.authorhouse.com
Phone: 1-800-839-8640

This book is a work of fiction. All the people in it are imaginary. Any similarity between any character in the story and any real person, living or dead, is purely unintentional and coincidental.

Published by AuthorHouse   08/21/2012

ISBN: 978-1-4772-2338-3 (sc)
ISBN: 978-1-4772-2339-0 (e)

Also by Chris Payne

Leaving the Eurozone—How a country can escape the tyranny of the Euro and go back to its own currency. (With Jeremy Cripps) 2012

Encounters with a Fat Chemist—Teaching at a University in Northern Cyprus
Published by Authorhouse Inc. 2012

To my dear Loydz

"The injustice done to an individual is sometimes of service to the public."
- Junius (18th century polemicist.)

CONTENTS

ONE

As he began the last day of his life, Morton Alamein Scregg, the Principal of Upton Faldwell Community College, known as 'Big Al' to those he was used to referring to as 'my' staff, was feeling particularly chipper. 'His' college, for he regarded the place as his own personal possession, was a 1950's establishment which had been hastily thrown up to provide day-release further education to the apprentices and typists of the Ford factory which had been erected on an industrial estate on the edge of Faldwell Upton, a new town created during more optimistic times on the site of, and to the complete ruination of, the medieval villages of Faldwell and Upton.

UFCC was where Scregg exerted quasi-monarchical authority over his subjects and where he could strut unchecked as the sovereign lord of his little domain. One of the reasons why he was so chipper was because today was an interview day and he liked interview days, not least because it gave him the opportunity to contradict and slap down his sycophantic lieutenants and to weigh up the nervous applicants for those preferred academic qualities which he esteemed most highly. His successful candidates, those with the very finest academic potential among the shortlisted applicants were, amazingly, always young, female and a long way from home, and therefore in need of paternal protection. To Scregg's mind these were the paramount attributes of a further education lecturer.

Occasionally one of his underlings might dare risk his temper by questioning his finely-honed scholastic judgement by asking, for example,

"Why choose someone with a rubbish degree and no experience? She was by far the worst."

This dangerous affront would immediately provoke a furious response.

"Because I say so!! She smells nice!!"

He had also won a most satisfactory row over breakfast with Mrs. Scregg. Mandy Scregg had gone silent after one of his tirades, reflecting on just why she had married him in the first place. But then again, having been one of those day-release typists who had been elevated to the college front desk in tribute to her friendly voluptuousness, she was well aware of the limitations of a career at the factory, especially now that jobs there had all but dried up and eligible potential consorts with regular salaries and big houses in the suburbs were pretty thin on the ground. So when the first Mrs Scregg had decamped with a toy boy from Gambia, Mandy was in pole position to replace her. Morton Scregg might well be, she regularly consoled herself, a repulsive old fart, but he was a rich, or at least well-off, repulsive old fart. And there was always the occasional inconsequential flirtation with the window cleaner or even a student at her husband's own college to add a little leavening of excitement to the tedium of her life as a stay-at-home wife.

Scregg's smug mood continued as he got into his new top-of-the-range Ford, a perk of the job as leading educator of the few remaining Ford apprentices. Ford had, for years, supplied a couple of cars a year for the student mechanics to practise on. These new vehicles were immediately taken over by the Principal and one of his deputies. For Morton Scregg, with impeccable logic, reasoned that the students would learn better on a used car than a new one fresh from the factory. So at the beginning of the autumn term, when Ford made their annual munificent gift for the good of the students, Morton Scregg would trade in his year-old Ford to be worked on by the trainee mechanics and take the new one for himself. The same deal was also available for one of the two female vice principals, who was also able to get a new car, which Scregg would sell to her for a very good price indeed.

As he drove through the September sunshine, he briefly went through a mental list of his onerous duties for the day. This morning, he had promised himself, he would be giving old Braithwaite, the Head of Science and Tourism, a bollocking he would remember for a long time. The old loony was forever dithering about retirement. How better to tip him over the edge than by a thoroughly undeserved dressing down? That should make his mind up for him. He had always hated Braithwaite, 'one of the old school', with an Oxford degree and proper real world experience. Scregg thought him too superior by half, too full of himself. After that, there would be the usual lunch, served up by the Catering Department, under a chef who could be relied upon to lay on a good spread for Principal Scregg and his friends and professional colleagues. The afternoon would be the interviews. He rather liked the sound of that little Miss Lucinda Whatsit with, what was it, a degree in communications from Stockport Polytechnic? From the photograph, she looked as though she would make a very good teacher indeed. Put her in Braithwaite's old office across the corridor. Nice and near.

He saw the college ahead, so he switched on his headlights and blew his horn several times to clear the way to his parking spot of the dozen or so untidy students standing around smoking. "Fucking layabouts", he muttered under his breath, "why do we bother?"

Safely parked and car locked, he glared at the smoking students as if to warn them off doing any damage. Not an unreasonable precaution. One of his more undesirable duties was attending, on an almost weekly basis, Mondays usually, the local magistrates' court, as character reference for any UFCC students who had run foul of the local constabulary over the weekend.

He opened the door to his office, his mood of well-being now having completely dissipated.

"Tell Braithwaite to be here at eleven!" he barked at Cheryl, his secretary.

"And coffee, please, my dear?"

His day always started by his going through his mail.

For the next hour, he would open it and sort it into a number of piles. On each letter he wrote "Action this day—MAS." which, he had read, was the way Churchill used to do it when he was running the war. Then he called Cheryl.

"These for Jones. These for Morgan-Pugh. These for Cloughe. These for Braithwaite, if the old bugger can still see to read. These for Thomas . . ." and pushed them into Cheryl's hands.

The major task of the morning accomplished, he then turned his attention to lunch and phoned the kitchen.

"What are you doing today, Mario? I have some important guests from Ford."

"The students will be getting beef burger and chips. But for special, top-table guests we have a starter of carpaccio of Serrano ham with truffle and rocket salad, followed by a simple beef bordelaise and a coupe colonel dessert."

"The wine?"

"Very good, Principal! Very nice Beaujolais. Good vintage!! You'll like it."

The morning's work all but complete, he was about to turn to his drinks cabinet when Cheryl gently knocked the door.

"Doctor Braithwaite, Principal."

"Don't call him 'Doctor'! 'Mister' will do. Where do you think we are? Some poncy Oxford college?"

A stooped tremulous man in his early sixties shuffled in.

"Come in Braithwaite! Dont sit!! This isn't a social visit. Just look at the state of you!! Can't you even dress yourself properly? You look a mess! And they tell me you went to Oxford!! If your posh Oxford friends could see you now!! . . ."

And he went on at poor Braithwaite in this vein for the next twenty minutes. Once Braithwaite had left the room, Scregg said to himself, "I need a drink", and turned to his cabinet for the first gin and tonic of the day. But, he cautioned himself, better not have too many. There'll be a lot to drink at lunch and then the interviews. Don't want some disgruntled failed candidate making allegations about interviewers smelling of drink.

The lunch was, as promised, very *haute cuisine*. A little too much wine but, as Scregg always said, "you have to put on a show for the sort of people we entertain here. These are managers from Ford! Our real bosses!! They expect a good turnout."

Gin and tonics before, wine during, and brandy afterwards was his standard lunch operating procedure and Scregg had enough contacts and buddies from local commerce and industry to be sure that SOP would be strictly adhered to, five days a week. Other lunch guests would be drawn from the twenty or thirty senior college personnel, including the finance officer, who fancied himself, pretentiously, as a wine buff, the two women vice-principals, the registrar, some deans, assistant principals and a few favoured heads of department. But not, of course, Braithwaite, who had never been invited once.

There was a lunch rota of these panjandrums of the college and at every lunch, two, never more, ordinary teachers would also be invited for the meal. Not, of course, for the gin before lunch, and certainly not for the after-lunch drinking party, but, for the meal itself, a couple of token peasants were roped in to give the occasion a patina of democracy. This gesture of magnanimity was perceived by Scregg as a royal honour bestowed on a deserving toiler in the engine room of his little realm. The toilers themselves, not unsurprisingly, did not quite see it that way. As common wisdom had it—going to one of the lunches will not advance your career, but one minor slip-up can see the end of it. For it was commonly put about by Principal Scregg and indeed, all of his fellow principals, that there existed a national blacklist of all those college lecturers who had offended against someone important in some slight, maybe even near-imperceptible, way and, as a result, would never again succeed at any college interview, The blacklisted victim, it was commonly threatened by the principals' mafia, would effectively be sentenced to see out their entire career in the same college at the same rank without any possible hope of transfer or advancement. The royal banquet was not therefore any sort of pleasurable social event for the two teachers who had drawn the short straws. It was a dangerous minefield where their whole futures could be extinguished by a single injudicious comment.

Having no alternative but to obey the summons to the less well-lubricated part of the ceremony in the upstairs college restaurant, Ken Grassmann, humble senior lecturer in technical drawing, found himself seated at lunch between Sonia Lyttel, newly-appointed Assistant Lecturer in General Studies and Kathleen Cloughe, Vice Principal for International Development, Student Affairs and Academic Quality.

Sonia Lyttel was exactly Scregg's type—young, pretty and full-figured, almost a younger version of Mandy Scregg herself, before Mrs Scregg had given up the groves of academe for domesticity and wifedom. Grassmann asked Sonia Lyttel what she did, given that there was little doubt about why she was there.

"I'm new. I teach gen. studs. Sorry, General Studies."

"And what does that entail?"

"Mostly I am on the basic literacy and numeracy programmes. I'm new, so I get a lot of classes of welders and bricklayers."

VP Cloughe cut in, "I wrote that syllabus! It was approved by the college Academic Quality Committee! Aren't you supposed to be doing Macbeth this term?"

"Well, yes," Sonia went on, "according to the syllabus. But first, I need to get them to be able to write their names and addresses. What do you do, Ken?"

"Oh me, technical drawing. All on computer these days. Staring a new course 'Technical Drawing for Housewives'. I'm the course leader".

"Sounds interesting. Maybe I'll take it. If I ever become a housewife."

"If you ever become a houswfie. You are obviously Scregg's blue-eyed girl, getting a lunch invite so soon after starting."

"Well, he has been very nice to me."

I bet he has, thought Ken Grassmann.

Eventually lunch was over and the assembled diners, got, or in some cases, staggered or lurched to their feet. The Principal was in a mood of post-prandial expansiveness so generous that he was even prepared to greet his minions as near-equals.

"Grassmann! Tell me, how is that Drawing for Haufraus course going?" he said, chuckling at his own humour. "Would it suit the memsahib? Gets a bit bored in the house all day!"

"I am sure Mrs Scregg would enjoy it very much."

And with that, unstable after a bottle of French wine, three gins and tonics and a large brandy, Principal Scregg swung around to launch himself down the stairs and go back to his office on the ground floor, his coterie in his train.

Unfortunately, the delicious starter of ham and rocket salad had been rather generously anointed with olive oil and, during its passage from kitchen to table, quite a lot of the oil had spilt on to the top step of the staircase at precisely the point where Morton Scregg now placed his unbalanced foot. Which meant that Principal Scregg's terminal experience consisted of his sliding down the stairs to the very bottom, the back of his head beating a tom-tom rat-tat-tat as it collided with each step.

When Morton Alamein Scregg BA, FRSA reached the bottom of the stairwell, he was, quite definitely, stone dead.

The ensuing commotion meant that the joyous news of the conveyance of Principal Scregg to the afterlife did not take long to get around. First the screaming ambulance arrived, shortly followed by the college doctor and then the Faldwell Upton police whose job it was to push back the growing crowd of rubber-necking students and to cordon off the college drive.

"Nothing to see! Go back to your classes!" implored the Registrar in vain.

But no one took much notice. The students were pushed back by the constables, who enjoyed pushing students back. The chance of a little, non-too-gentle pushing around of student layabouts was a much more enjoyable way of spending an afternoon than sorting out domestic disputes on the council estate or sitting in front of a computer at the station. Eventually, though, the sheer weight of students who had come to celebrate the sudden turn of events, was, Sergeant Knacker realised, likely to turn the situation nasty. The police were now heavily outnumbered which forced the Sergeant to the not illogical conclusion that discretion is the better part of valour. So he adroitly switched his mood from aggression to magnanimity, told his men to pull back and gently advised the students that they could stay where they were.

After a little while, a hospital trolley was pushed out of the college front door, strapped on to which was a body bag containing the mortal remains of the late Principal Scregg. A few disrespectful students at the back started clapping and there were even one or two cheers, but, all in all, the late Morton Scregg's final exit from Upton Faldwell Community College was conducted with nearly as much respect as tradition and convention require.

When the ambulance had gone and the doctor had gone back to his surgery for his usual Wednesday afternoon tryst with one of his lady patients and after the police had removed the tape and had gone back to their computers and after the students had gone home, for there would be no further classes today after such a momentous happening, Ken Grassmann found himself alone in the college forecourt with the stark realisation that he, Ken Grassmann, senior lecturer in technical drawing, had been the one chosen by divine fate to hear the great man's final words.

"Would it suit the memsahib? Gets a bit bored in the house all day!"

Yes, that was what he had said. Principal Scregg's final utterance. How appropriate, how unselfish, that his final thoughts on this earth would be concern for his wife, the tender Mrs Mandy Scregg, now prematurely widowed and alone after an all-too-short few years of connubial bliss.

Ken was still deep in these profound and respectful thoughts when he became aware that a colleague had suddenly popped up beside him. It was Lawson Baines, a fellow senior lecturer, but in French and German. Lawson was Ken's main crony in a college where one chose one's friends and confidantes from one's own rank. It being England, even a place like a community college was still unspokenly class conscious, where every small nuance of social difference was instinctively observed. Indeed, UFCC was the English class system in miniature, with its finely delineated gradations of rank from the regal principal at the top, right down to the lowly untouchables who did the essential work of keeping the college clean and functioning.

This class system had, albeit unconsciously, always been made much of by the late Principal in his state-of-the union address to the entire college personnel at the start of the academic year. He would go through a list of standard platitudes about the college being a family, and everyone in it being equally important. The same speech had been made year after year and had become traditional. He always spoke about 'all working together for the good of the students' and 'we will all sweat a little more freely during this difficult first few weeks'. Nor did he ever omit 'my door is always open to anyone in the whole college'. This last remark, which Scregg would bellow as he thumped the table, never failed to bring suppressed cynical guffaws from all those who had known him long enough.

So Ken and Lawson, both being long passed-over senior lecturers, formed a natural alliance together with a few other long-standing UFCC 'old sweats'.

"Nasty business," said Lawson.

"I never thought the old bastard would go so quick. Makes you think."

"Too right. Later than you think. Fancy a pint?"

"But it's only three o'clock. Besides, I've got City and Guilds Tech. Drawing for Typists at four."

"Cancel the class. Put a note on the board. Nobody'll be there. Day like this, they'll all have gone home".

"I suppose you're right. What the hell. He's not going to come back to haunt us, is he?"

Within ten minutes, desks cleared and work over for the day, Ken and Lawson were in the local college pub, *'The Ford Zodiac'*, named after the famous Ford car in honour of the town's leading employer, but known to students and lecturers alike as the 'Stranglers Arms'.

"Should rename this place. Mark of respect. 'The Dead Scregg!' Good name for it."

"Like they do with college libraries!"

"Exactly. No point in naming a library after him. He was all for closing the college library down to save money."

"Agreed. I never saw him read anything. On the other hand, a pub, that's different. Just right for an old pisshead like him."

"I don't like to speak ill of the dead. But in his case, I think we can make an honourable exception."

The pub was full. Not often did Mike the Landlord have a full house mid-afternoon on a Wednesday. Usually it would be quiet—just the odd alcoholic from business studies or the nursing care course and that would be about it. But today the Stranglers Arms was overflowing with happy drinkers, celebrating the sudden festivities. The landlord had already put up a sign 'Principal Morton Scregg 1948-2005. RIP. Donations for a wreath'. The tin beneath it was empty.

A group of students and assistant lecturers started singing and stamping their feet.

> *"He's dead! He's dead! The fucking bastard's dead!!"*
> *"He's dead! He's dead! The fucking bastard's dead!!"*

The landlord moved in quickly.

"Now, now, lads," he chided, "keep it down. Whatever would he say if he heard you? He never approved of swearing."

"Sorry," said one of the drunken singers, "we won't say 'fucking' ".

"That's better. Bit of respect."

"Pity that, fucking was about the only thing he was any good at."

"So," began Lawson Baines, "the two big questions. No three."

"First, who is going to be our new master? Two, who will get his new car? Almost brand new. Not even run in."

"And three?"

"Just coming to that. C, who is going to console the lovely Mandy?"

"All right. The apostolic succession. It's bound to one of the bitches, isn't it?

He meant, of course, the two female vice principals.

Kathleen Cloughe had the magnificent title of Vice-Principal for International Development, Student Affairs and Academic Quality. She was a thin, chain-smoking, peroxided little harridan devoid, as far as anyone could tell, of all human qualities save personal ambition. Her speech was a high-speed barrage of T-shirt slogans—"it's bums on seats", "if you can't stand the heat get out of the kitchen", "I work hard and I play hard", "if you're not part of the solution, you're part of the problem" and the like. She could keep this up for hours, never once pausing for thought. No one had ever heard her construct a full sentence. All she seemed capable of uttering was a string of tired old clichés which she spouted as if they were the latest management-speak or arcane philosophical profundities.

Then there was Melys Morgan-Pugh, Vice-Principal for Operations, Industrial Liaison and Academic Protocol. She was posh Welsh but she had ironed out her valleys accent into an approximation of Oxfordian English. She was big and fat and considered herself a model of cosmopolitan sophistication on the basis of her once having had a fling with a Bosnian lounge lizard while on holiday in

Fuenteventura. Her speech tended to the languidly superior as she described, as she was wont to do, her personal moral excellence as an avid instant supporter of anything vaguely trendy or left-wing.

Actually, these two women had done most of Scregg's real, college work for him, leaving him free to his preferred pursuits of drinking and fornication. They were referred to in private, because of their disparities of size and shape, as 'Stan' and 'Olly', although more often, the terms used by the ordinary teachers in private were 'Little Bitch' and 'Big Bitch'. Each would, quite happily, have slit the other's throat for the new vacancy. Or, to be more precise, each would, quite happily, have slit the other's throat. Either would have made a perfectly suitable new principal. They both had, after all, the entire set of necessary qualities for advancement to the top job—they were both vain, self-important, ambitious bullies.

"So, it's going to be one of the bitches? You could be right."

"Not much choice. A toss-up between anthrax and cholera."

"Someone from outside, do you think?"

"Could be. A compromise between two evils?"

"Problem with an outsider is that, one, they are almost certain to be just as bad. No-one gets to be an FE principal without being a complete shit."

"What you say, my friend, is undoubtedly true. But a new guy will, at least, leave us alone until he finds his feet."

"On the other hand, remember, there's something to be said for the devil you know. While the new guy finds his feet, the two bitches will be up to all sorts of stupidity."

"So we're fucked both ways."

"Looks like it. Your round."

Ken struggled to the bar which was now at bursting point. The landlord was in heaven, where, of course, he would not be meeting Scregg, who had gone elsewhere.

Back with the pints, Ken took up the thread.

"I wonder where the old bastard is now."

"If there is life after death, then he is certainly down below. He's probably already got himself a cushy number as chief stoker, excused duties."

"Ha! Ha! I can't see a well-managed place like hell putting up with him for long."

"There was that theory that teachers go straight to hell when they die because they have already done their time in purgatory."

"That's what worries me. Think what hell must be like."

"Something like Technical Drawing for Fishmongers 24 hours a day, I should imagine."

"And Scregg standing over you with the hot irons."

"So, on to more interesting items. What about Scregg's new motor?"

"College property. Probably go to someone on the board of governors. Or the director of education. One of his mates."

"They're probably getting it registered in a new name even as we speak."

"No point in hanging about. It's a very nice vehicle. Someone will already have his eye on it."

"Not for the likes of us, that's for sure."

"Then there is the very interesting question of what will happen to the lovely Mandy."

"Oh, I think a few weeks of grieving, for appearance's sake, and then a new life with her inheritance."

"Was she, you know, up to it with anyone else?"

"If she was, she was very discreet. Odd rumour, of course. There was that student from the second year course in the history of football."

"Yes, I remember. Last year. Seen chatting her up and next day got expelled."

"Probably nothing in it. She'd be stupid to risk anything. Scregg was worth a bob or two."

"All bets are off now though!"

"Too true! Let's await developments. Another pint?"

"Why not? I cancelled my evening class as well."

Mandy Scregg had been very busy when the call had come. She had taken a long hot bath followed by a thorough creaming and oiling with her many fragrant unguents and she had just settled down with the boxed set of 'Sex and the City'. Out of sense of delicacy, the Registrar, who had been chosen to convey the bad news, came in person and rang the front door bell. Actually, this had been one of the late Principal's few concessions to decorum and humanity. One must not, never, ever inform someone of the death of a close relative on college premises by phone or email, he had decreed. It must always, he insisted, be in person. It was duly recorded in college minutes. The rule applied whenever the nearest and dearest was a spouse or parent or a child of the unfortunate deceased. It specifically excluded siblings, live-in partners, grandparents etc. who could be phoned or emailed with the fateful news. It was a rare human moment from the recently departed Big Al.

On hearing the news, Mrs Scregg immediately, without a moment's pause, composed her features into the standard expression of shock and distress as she had seen it done numerous times on the telly. After a few minutes of embarrassment while Mandy summoned up tears and sobs by her favourite device of thinking about poor little doggies at Christmas, the Registrar excused himself with a small benediction

". ., if there's anything we . . . . we are just a phone call away . . . help with the arrangements . . . very sorry . . . he was a fine man . . .".

When he had gone, Mandy pulled herself together, wiped her eyes and opened a bottle of wine. She too, recalled Scregg's last words as he took his final drive to his destiny.

She would now be able to recall them forever more. What were they now? Ah yes, she remembered.

"And that's final!!" he had shouted before he slammed the car door shut.

And so indeed it had been for him.

Over the next week or so, there would be, she knew, much to do. There would be the selling of the house, not to mention all that paperwork with the life insurance. The widow's pension to be sorted out. The furniture to sell. And where would she go? Time to think of myself, she thought, I have been far too unselfish for too long. It's about time I put myself first. Would she be able to keep the car? And what about the stuff in her late husband's office? Oh yes, the Registrar had said that he would take care of that.

Then there was the funeral. She would need a new outfit. Hair! And a manicure! She would need to look her best. The Mayor and all the council would be there.

In the following couple of weeks people spoke well of her. "She's taking it very well . . . keeping busy . . . she's being very brave . . .".

The newly-widowed Mandy Sandra Scregg, née Boggsworth, would, indeed, be keeping herself busy. There was a whole new exciting life opening up for her and a nice little pot of the late Principal's money to live it with.

TWO

Ken and Lawson stayed on at the pub for a yet another drink or two, occasionally raising the odd jeering ironic toast to their recently departed boss but mostly, just getting mildly plastered.

"Do you remember", Lawson slurred, "when we discussed killing the old bastard with that copper who used to be in one of my classes?"

"'Sright!" Ken remembered. "The nine-nine-nine course!! Talking Foreign for Plod!"

"I think it was called 'French for Public Servants.'"

"Yer right! French for Public whatsits. Yes."

"Well," said Lawson. "Do you remember what he said?"

"No."

"He said that if you are going to do someone in, you're going to get caught."

"So?"

"He said that the police always look for three things. And they are motive, opportunity and association!"

"So, if we wanted to kill him, we would be straight in the frame because we have all three!"

"One," Lawson Baines went on. "Motive. No question. Everybody in the college had a motive."

"What about the other two?"

"Well, opportunity. Not really much opportunity to do the old shit in."

"True. What was the third?"

"Association. Do we have any connection with the dead one? No question."

"We'd have been picked up straight away."

"What do you get for murder these days? Mitigating circumstances. What, ten years? Might be worth it."

"Something like that," said Ken.

"Remember what else he said?" said Lawson. "The best weapon is a hammer. A quick bash of the skull and then throw the hammer in the river. No, er, thingies. Forensics."

"Don't they have like, DNA, these days?"

"Well, yes. That could be a problem. Still, worth bearing in mind for the next lunatic they dump on us."

"We'll see. Pity it was an accident. I'd have liked to kill him myself. Would have been worth doing ten. Out after seven with a criminal CV."

"We should have done something with that idea of yours. You know, wait until he was drunk and then tip off the local traffic police when he tried to drive home. That was a good idea."

"True. But didn't our bluebottle friend tell us that the superintendent would never prosecute any of his friends unless he actually hit something?"

"Yes, I remember now. Wasn't that the time when the local top coppers used to come and get pissed at the college Christmas dinner?"

At that moment, who should they see pushing her slender way through the drunken crowd but new Assistant Lecturer, Sonia Lyttel.

"Hello again," she greeted Ken. "Remember me from lunch?"

"Course I remember you. Join us. This is Lawson Baines from the Modern Languages Department."

"Hi."

"Get you a drink?"

"Thanks, I'd love one. White wine spritzer, if I may?"

"Sure thing."

As Ken was waiting at the packed bar, he glanced back to where Lawson Baines was smalltalking the comely new arrival. Baines looked up at Ken's glance and raised his eyebrows in that 'what are you doing with such a lovely, you dirty dog' sort of way which men use on such occasions.

"Have you two been in here since lunch?" inquired the fair Sonia.

"Just about. Classes cancelled. Everybody else seems to be drinking like New Year's Eve. No point in pissing out on a good marty. Sorry, missing out on a good party."

"I think you were right the first time."

"Anyway, what brings you here? I wouldn't have thought the Stranglers would be your sort of den of iniquity?"

"Just like you really. A girl doesn't like to piss out on a good marty."

"So you are pleased to see the back of him as well?"

"I sure am."

"But I thought you were flavour of the month, getting invited to the royal banquet an' all?"

"Well, it's a long story. But I'll tell you. Morton Scregg was trying to be extra nice to me after he jumped on me in the room where they store the old books."

"What, the old goat attacked you?"

"Well, yes. Nothing I couldn't handle but I got cross and threatened to go to the lecturer's union."

"Which wouldn't have done you much good."

"I didn't know that then. But he does know from my application that my father works for a national paper."

"So, he backed off?

"Yes. I told him I'd tell my dad and he suddenly came over all apologetic. Mind you, he did rip my new blouse. Cost me twenty five pounds."

"Yes, that's the Big Al we all knew and detested."

"It wouldn't have made any difference if I'd gone to the union?"

"Not a jot. It was Scregg who appointed the union rep. And guess who she is?

"Who?"

"Vice Principal Melys Morgan-Pugh. Known to all and sundry as 'Big Bitch'."

"So not very democratic then?"

"It's democracy, my sweet, but not as we know it."

Ken got, or rather dragged himself, up.

"Must go. Cheryl will be clocking off. She can drive me home."

"Didn't you know? All the offices were closed by order of the Registrar. All the staff were sent home. Mark of respect."

"Shit", thought Ken. "Here I am rat-arsed and she's taken the car. Still, better go. Can't get too pissed. She doesn't think it dignified in a senior lecturer."

"Goodnight Lawson. Goodnight Sonia."

"Goodnight, Ken." He could have sworn that Sonia held his gaze just a nanosecond longer than formal etiquette requires. Or it could have been a trick of the light, more likely.

And indeed his little ten-year-old Toyota (He never bought Ford now, on principle.) was no longer in its customary place in the car park where he had left it only that morning when he had dropped off his wife, Cheryl, the Principal's secretary, on the morning of this momentous day.

Having no alternative, he turned around and walked slowly down to the bus station, where there was, fortunately, a gentlemen's lavatory where he could discharge a goodly quantity of the Stranglers Arms' best four-star 'Old England' strong ale.

A cold wait at the bus station and he got into the warmth of the bus which took him the couple of miles to the Hawthorn Gardens Estate where he and Cheryl owned ten per cent of a 1970's semi-detached. Then there was a quarter mile walk past the lighted windows of his neighbours, who regularly monitored, in standard British suburban fashion, the schedules of all the other estate dwellers for the slightest sign of deviation from respectable behaviour.

Before he even reached his front door, Ken Grassmann had already been tried and found guilty at the bar of Tennyson Avenue, Hawthorn Gardens' opinion for several serious transgressions of the austere suburban code. One, he was walking, when he should have been driving. Two, his wife had driven home alone. Three, he had not taught his Wednesday evening class because it was not yet 9.30. Finally, and most seriously of all, he had been drinking!! These charges, in direct violation of all that was held most sacred by the inhabitants of the estate, had already, by some mysterious process of thought transference, been communicated to every single household in Tennyson Avenue and would stay on file forever. The Grassmanns would need to spend considerable time and energies over the next decades pleading their mitigations and explanations for their gross dereliction of those high standards of order and respectability which define the English suburban *petite bourgeoisie*. As he got out his key in the gathering crepescular gloom, Ken could smell the censorious eyes of his fellow estate inmates watching his every move and passing on from house to house the news of his fall from grace by his outrageous departure from all civilised norms.

He expected anger when he opened the door and he was not disappointed.

"You've been drinking!!"—the traditional opening gambit of the offended wife.

"Why not? There were no classes. Everyone else was down at the pub. It was such a happy day. You should have joined us."

"Someone had to stay behind and look after things. There were reporters from the paper. You should have been there!"

"Whatever for? They would only have asked me what happened? Who cares? The old bastard's dead. Let's be happy about that."

"Happy!!!" she exploded, "HAPPY!!"

She was open-mouthed with incredulity,

"You are happy because your employer is dead? Happy, how can you be happy on a day like this?!"

She was now into her familiar indignant stride.

"And where were you? Down the pub!! Down the pub when you should have been there to help me cope. I had things to do. Reporters to talk to. They are bringing a television crew!! And you were down pub, drinking!! Drinking!!"

She was now in full flow, which as Ken Grassmann knew from long experience, it would be better to ignore and let the storm blow itself. Then she would sulk for a few days, or, if he were lucky, there would even be a few weeks when she would not speak to him at all. But now she was building up to one of her famous furious tirades when she could scream for at least an hour, much to the entertainment of the denizens of Tennyson Avenue.

"You!! You should have been there!! You should have!! You should have been there!! Why weren't you? I was there and I had to sort out all the problems!"

What these problems were, she did not explain, except to keep repeating how she had had to speak to the local newspaper.

"So, you are going to get your name in the paper!! Big deal!!" said the husband, who was now completely sober and prepared to move on to anger himself.

"How can you come home, smelling of drink and say that you are happy because some poor man who never did you a bad turn in his life, was dead! Never a bad turn! In his life!!"

"Scregg never did a bad turn in his life!! Where have you been? The man was worse than Hitler! He was a megalomaniac! He was a thief, a drunk and a lecher!"

"You should talk about drinking! Spending all day in the pub!"

"The whole fucking college spent all day in the pub! Everybody was celebrating because everybody hated him!"

"Well, I didn't go drinking before the poor man was cold! And there's no need to swear. No need for it. No need at all! No bloody need!!"

"You should have come down the pub with everyone else. You missed a really good time!"

"How can you talk like that!! HOW CAN YOU!! Have you no respect!!"

"I certainly have none for that old bastard. He deserved it."

She was now incandescent.

"After all he did for you!! After all he did for you!!"

"What the fuck do you mean—after all he did for me?"

"He promoted you to senior lecturer when he didn't have to. Don't you know that?"

"What do you mean,—didn't have to? I'd been an ordinary lecturer for twelve long fucking years. I was due a promotion. I'd earned it."

"Earned it? Earned it? He gave it to you because I got it for you, you stupid man!!"

"What do you mean?"

And then the penny dropped.

"You mean you and him?"

"What do you think I mean? Your senior lectureship was 'for services rendered' as you might say!! You should be grateful. He was good to both of us, in his way."

"When was the, er, first time?"

"Just before your promotion, three years ago. So there. Now you know."

"And just how long were you up to it?"

"Oh, it's mostly in the past now. Mostly in the past. He moved on. Younger stuff. Things started tailing off about a year after you were made up."

"Mostly?"

"Yes, mostly! Just the odd quickie in the office to keep him sweet. For our benefit, remember, our benefit. Means nothing. Nothing at all. I thought you'd be grateful. He said you'd appreciate what I was doing for you."

Appreciate? thought the wronged husband. Did the bastard expect me to be grateful. For fucking my wife?

"He was only using you, you stupid bitch!"

But one thing was true in what she had said. Big Al had never actually done him a direct bad turn that he had known about although his every instinct told him just how dishonest and duplicitous Scregg had been. And there had been lots of hints and rumours about Scregg and his 'favours'. Poor Ken had just never realised that he had been the one being fooled. He could have gone on for years never realising that he only held his job because his wife, whose faithfulness he had never once doubted, had fucked Principal Scregg and she had been paid off by her husband's promotion. Ken wondered how many of the college personnel had known about the arrangement? Had he been a laughing stock—every newcomer being taken on one side and initiated into the secret of the Principal's secretary and the wife of the senior lecturer in mechanical drawing, and what the *quid pro quo* had been?

He sat down heavily.

"No more," he thought. "No more."

The day had been full of surprises already. After Scregg's sudden demise, he had been happy. Now, suddenly, things had returned to their regular miserable. Worse even. His wife was a whore who would allow that old monster to fuck her so that he could live on the Hawthorn Gardens Estate and drive a ten-year-old car and do a crappy job, which he hated, teaching rudimentary basic skills to smelly, moronic adolescents who would never use them. There had to be, there just had to be, a better life than this.

Clearly a lot of decisions were going to be made very quickly. He wondered, in passing, how many other domestic dramas would be catalysed by the termination of the late Principal's life. His would not, he was sure, be the only one for whom Scregg's terminal experience had forced on them a sudden existential realisation of exactly what sort of a hell they had made for themselves by a Faustian pact with UFCC and its evil leader.

He came to the first decision immediately.

"Right, you bitch!! You and me. We are through!! Through! I want a divorce and I want it now!! I will pack a bag and stay in a hotel. Then tomorrow I'll put things in motion. It's over. Now fuck off!"

"But Ken, darling," wheedled Cheryl the Adulteress. "I only did it for us. I never enjoyed it. I was only thinking of you and me. It's never going to happen again. Can't we be friends, sweetie?"

He pushed her arm away.

"No, you lying bitch. We can't be friends. We can't be anything. I am leaving you!!"

Ten minutes later he was striding down to the bus stop with an overnight bag and a steely determination to rid himself of all the excess junk baggage which he had unconsciously accumulated during his life in Faldwell Upton—wife, job, career, and most of all, he screamed at the lace curtains of Tennyson Avenue, "THIS FUCKING ESTATE AND ALL THE TIGHT-ARSED SMALL MINDED WAGE SLAVES WHO ARE SLOWLY DYING HERE!!"

The next day he went into work as usual. The place was awash with gossip. He wondered if he had a walk-on role in it, especially since, he soon heard, Cheryl had not come in. Lawson Baines filled him in.

"Apparently, there has to be a coroner's inquest. Unusual circumstances of death. Normal procedure. It's at the Magistrate's Court next Monday morning. You were last to speak to him, so you'll likely be called. They say that if the body is released, funeral's likely to be next Friday, week tomorrow."

"Did it make the Chronicle? I haven't seen it yet."

"Here."

The local paper, *The Faldwell Upton Chronicle*, did indeed carry the story of the last moments of Morton Scregg. Indeed all the events of the previous afternoon were carried as a front page splash, easily the biggest story of the year for a small town paper which would expatiate at length on the golden weddings and tennis club suppers and scout swimming galas of the town. To say nothing of devoting at least two pages a week to the achievements, or lack thereof, of the town football club, renowned far and wide for having brought new meanings to words like 'pathetic' and 'dreadful'.

So the sudden death of the local college principal was a story the Chronicle's editor could only usually dream about and it was correspondingly given the full treatment—photos of speeding ambulances, pictures of the buildings, a full formal portrait and an orotund obituary lauding the late, great man, in which he was described as a sort of statesmanlike Churchillian figure who had effortlessly combined the intellect of Albert Einstein with the humanity of Nelson Mandela.

Ken read through this mush with a curled lip and then checked that they hadn't got the date wrong as well. It couldn't be April Fool's Day yet, surely?

Then there were the interviews, including one with a tearful Cheryl.

'Everyone is so shocked. It was so sudden. We all loved him so much, so very, very much. He was like a father to us all,' she was quoted.

Ken couldn't bear to read any more and dumped the local rag in the bin.

He was just about to start phoning around the flat-rental agencies when he was interrupted by the new office junior. She was carrying a formal looking letter.

"What a shame," she said. "Poor man. Sorry to hear about Mrs Grassmann, I hope she's better soon."

"Yes, she'll be OK," he said to her and "let's hope it's serious," he said to himself.

So news of their breakup hadn't yet gone around the college. Give it a couple of hours.

The letter was for him and was from the Court, requiring his attendance at the inquest to be held, as Lawson had predicted, the following Monday at 10.00am. He could expect to be called as a witness. Then he went back to searching for a bachelor pad and the little matter of teaching shelf stackers how to read a ruler and draw straight lines.

THREE

The inquest was duly held at the Magistrates Court, the worshipful Coroner presiding. It was fairly quick, given that the facts of the case had been laid out for all to see. First the college doctor was called to give evidence of cause of death, which was due to a cracked skull consistent with Scregg's banging his head repeatedly on the stairs leading down from the college restaurant.

"Tell us, Doctor," asked the Coroner. "Had the deceased been drinking?"

"Yes sir," replied the Doctor, "a quantity of alcohol was found to be present in the deceased's blood."

"How much? Do you have the figures?"

"About a hundred and fifty milligrammes per hundred millilitres of blood."

"So, that would be about twice the legal limit for driving a car?"

"Yes, sir, about that."

"So the deceased was completely unfit to drive a car, but not too unfit to drive a college? Is that right?"

"Indeed, sir."

When Ken was called, he was asked just a few routine questions about the lunch and the oil on the step and what Scregg's terminal mood had been. Then it was all quickly wrapped up with a verdict of accidental death and permission to release the body for the funeral.

All the participants at the inquest then spilled out of the Court including one nondescript man whom Ken had noticed at the corner of the public area. He had, at first, thought him to be a journalist from the Chronicle before he realised that the real Chronicle reporter was sitting in front of him. As Ken turned to go back up the road to the college, he felt a sudden tug on his sleeve. It was the nondescript.

"Let me introduce myself, sir."

"Yes?"

"Inspector Fordham, Faldwell Upton CID. I wonder if I might have a word?"

"Yes, of course. But right now I have a class to give."

"My card. Are you free this afternoon?"

"Any time after two."

"Thank you, sir. I'll see you then."

Inspector Fordham was prompt to the second. The other occupants of the staff room which Ken Grassmann shared were at class so he asked the Inspector to sit down, knowing they would not be disturbed for at least an hour.

"Good afternoon, Inspector. What can I do for you?"

"Well, sir," Fordham began, "as you might guess, it's about the late Mr. Scregg."

"Go on."

"Well, if you don't mind me saying so, you were not exactly a friend of his. Is that right?"

"He didn't have a lot of friends here. He wasn't liked."

"Quite, sir. I understand he wasn't very popular. Did he have any particular enemies?"

"More or less everybody who met him. He was a real nasty piece of work."

"But was there anybody who hated him enough to do him physical harm?"

"Of course there was!! Ha! Ha! Chance would have been a fine thing."

"Please be careful, Mister Grassmann, this is a very serious matter."

"Serious?"

"Yes, serious."

"Serious, as in criminal?"

"We are just making preliminary enquiries at the moment, sir. Just in case."

"What had the old boy been up to? Was he helping himself to the dinner money?"

"Like I said, sir, this is not a joking matter."

"So how can I help you? I don't have access to the college finances. You would need to ask the college finance officer about that."

"No we are not looking into any financial misconduct, sir. In any case, matters of that nature would be the responsibility of the fraud squad who would liaise with the financial people at County Hall."

"So it must be something personal. Don't tell me. Let me guess. One of the women lecturers has made a complaint. We all knew about his little, er, 'romances'."

"No, sir," continued Fordham with heavy patience, "it's not financial and it's not sexual. What we are looking into are the circumstances of how he came to fall down those stairs."

"I was there. He slipped on some olive oil. I saw it! It was an accident. The coroner said so. This morning. You were at the inquest."

"Well, sir, that's just it. We are wondering if it really was an accident, after all."

"You mean someone pushed him?"

"Could be, sir. Who knows? It wouldn't be the first time someone had disposed of some person they hated by pushing them down some steps."

Grassmann was now getting alarmed.

"I hope you are not suggesting that I pushed him?"

"No, sir, of course not. We are just making enquiries. Just a few more questions, if you don't mind."

"OK, go on."

"We came across a report from one of our officers from a few years back. Dated 1996. Do you remember PC Billings?"

"Never heard of him."

"Well, sir, I guess you've forgotten. Anyway, you were one of the teachers he met when he was here on one of your courses. Called, if my memory serves, 'French for Public Servants'.

"I don't remember your constable, or the course for that matter. It was years ago."

"Probably nothing, sir, but Billings wrote in his report that you, and another teacher, one Lawson Baines, spent a lot of time questioning him about how to murder your late Principal, Mr Scregg."

"If you say so."

"I do say so. In fact, Billings's report was quite explicit. He even wrote that you had discussed with him, and I quote . ."

Here Fordham pulled a piece of paper from his inside pocket and started to read.

. .'subject talked about using a hammer to kill his boss, the principal of the college . . ."

"But that was just fantasising. We didn't intend to actually do him in."

"I am sure, sir. But, you understand, we have to be absolutely sure that the late Mr Scregg's death really was a genuine accident."

"How could he have been murdered? We all saw him fall. The coroner said it was an accident."

"Why do you say 'murdered', sir? I never said he'd been murdered."

"Just a slip of the tongue."

"A Freudian slip, perhaps, sir? Well, as you will understand, we will be talking to everyone who was at the scene at the time. Normal police procedure. Perhaps you could let me know who else was there?"

"Yes, it was after lunch, so all the lunch guests were there. I am sure the Catering Department will have a list."

"Was Mister Baines, your friend, also there?"

"No, he wasn't invited."

"But Miss Lyttel? She was there?"

"She was there. Sat next to me, as it happens."

Inspector Fordham was writing furiously.

"Not much longer now, sir. Can we talk about last Wednesday afternoon?"

"What about last Wednesday afternoon?"

"Is it true that immediately after Mr. Scregg had met with his unfortunate death, you and Mr. Baines went straight to *The Ford Zodiac* public house?"

"With a lot of other people."

"Not very respectful of you, was it, sir?"

"No-one had much respect for Scregg. It was an afternoon off. All classes were cancelled."

"Quite, sir."

"About what time would you have got to the aforesaid public house, Mr. Grassmann?"

"Oh, I don't know. About half three, I suppose."

"Actually, you were timed entering the licensed premises at exactly three nineteen pm. CCTV. You were there a long time. It was five twenty five when you left."

"What the hell is this all about?"

"All in good time, sir."

"Can you tell me please, sir, exactly what you and Mr. Baines talked about in the two hours you were together in the bar of *The Ford Zodiac*?"

"Oh, you know what pub conversation is like. We talked about Scregg, of course. I told Baines what had happened and how I'd been the last to speak to Scregg. We discussed the dire state of Faldwell Upton Football Club. We discussed the economy. We discussed the size of the barmaid's chest. Do I really have to explain to you what pub talk is all about? You must have been to a pub or two yourself in your time."

Fordham ignored this outburst and pressed on.

"Did you and Mr. Baines discuss killing the late Mr. Scregg?"

"I don't think so. The accident had done that for us."

Fordham went back to his notebook.

"According to a witness, you were heard discussing with Mr Baines, and here I quote . . . 'what do you get for murder these days' and . . . 'I'd have liked to kill him myself'. Did you and Baines say those things, Mr Grassmann?"

"I may have done. I was fairly drunk. But it hardly means I actually did it, does it."

"My job, sir, is just to get at the facts. Can we just go back to your conversation with Mr. Baines?"

"First can you tell me who was listening in to our private conversation?"

"I'm afraid I can't reveal the source of my information, sir. Police confidentiality."

"Police invasion of privacy, more like it. If you can't have a private conversation without the police listening in, we're in a very bad state indeed."

"Some may see it that way, sir. But without good police information, who knows what might happen? Our job is to keep the country safe for people like you."

"Thank you, Inspector, for that civics lecture. You and I are going to have to disagree about the limits of police powers and when they are being overstepped."

"Actually, sir, if I might correct you. Your discussion about killing Mr Scregg was not exactly private. It was in a public house and anyone could have heard it."

"So not much of a conspiracy then?"

"Either that, sir, or a bit of over-confidence. I am afraid that I will probably need to speak to you again. Do you live at 115 Tennyson Avenue, Hawthorn Gardens Estate?"

"Yes. No. I've moved. My new address is . . ."

And here Ken had to refer to his new apartment rental agreement to get his address and post code.

"I see, sir. One last question. When you were joined by Miss Lyttel at, let me see, 4.55pm, did you discuss the killing of Mr Scregg with her as well?"

"I keep trying to tell you. There was no killing of Scregg. He died accidentally."

"Officially, at least. But we have to be completely sure. Sorry to take up your time, sir. All normal police procedure. If you've nothing to hide, you've nothing to fear."

With that, Inspector Fordham departed, no doubt to 'proceed with his inquiries' elsewhere.

Then who should pop her head around the office door than the young and pretty Miss Sonia Lyttel herself.

"Sorry about Wednesday night," said Ken. "A bit pissed."

"Not to worry. Occupational hazard, I gather."

"Yes, it's only the demon drink that keeps us lecturers sane. One needs some narcotic to dull the pain of our daily struggle with the malign forces of darkness and ignorance. It has to be alcohol—we can't afford anything stronger on our wages."

"I've only been in the game for a couple of years, but I am starting to realise what we are up against."

"So young and already so cynical!"

"It makes you cynical. One of my present classes is the "Back to Work" thing which some bright spark thought up to get government money. The syllabus says we should be reading Hamlet. What I spend most of the time doing is showing them how to cash their housing benefit cheques."

"Makes you cry, I know. That's why we drink."

"Who was that I just saw leaving your office?"

"That, my dear Sonia, was Inspector Nick Fordham MBE, a detective from the Faldwell Upton nick!"

"So Nick from the nick!!"

"Yes, very good."

"What did he want?"

"Well, what Inspector Fordham wants is a collar, a tug. He wants someone in the frame for killing old Scregg. I was first on his interview list. He'll be talking to you as well. Everyone who was at Scregg's last supper. He wants to find someone to play the role of Judas."

"But it was an accident!"

"Of course it was. I know that, you know that. Probably even Scregg up the in the clouds knows it. Problem is, Fordham doesn't believe us. He thinks someone, i.e. me, bumped him off. And, what is more, he has recorded evidence of me and Baines saying what a good idea it would be."

"But that means nothing, surely?"

"Could be. He'll be back after he's spoken to you and the others who were at lunch."

"Given that you and me were the only ones who hadn't tanked up on gin before, I am not sure he's going to get many coherent answers."

"And you were right at the back of the bunch as we came out."

"No I didn't see anything. The first I knew was when people started shouting."

"Don't worry. I don't think I'm going to need an alibi."

"So, I just popped around to invite you to share a glass at the Stranglers, if you're free."

"Bugger! I would love to but I've got wall-to-wall classes for the rest of the day. Tomorrow? Wednesday?"

"Work really is the curse of the drinking classes. Maybe Thursday?"

"About 4pm?"

"Perfect! I'll pick you up."

The next day, as expected, Fordham reappeared in Ken Grassmann's office, having done the rounds of the *dramatis personae* of the Scregg 'case', as Fordham now thought of it. Overnight, their perceptions of each other had undergone a transformation. Fordham had now convinced himself that Grassmann was a violent murderer hiding a black and devious soul hidden beneath a carapace of bumbling academic innocence. It had been given to Fordham to crack that carapace and expose the senior lecturer for the cunning vicious criminal whom he, Fordham, and only he, because he possessed a unique insight not given to most mortals, knew him to be.

Grassmann, who had begun by thinking Fordham to be a nondescript, a nonentity, now perceived in the rat-like features of the policeman, a dangerous adversary, a predator species who would pin the putative murder on to him by fair means or foul. The stakes were high for both men, now that the battle lines had been drawn and they were now, metaphorically, circling each other warily. For Fordham, there was the kudos of career success and another scout badge on the slippery pole of professional advancement. Failure to solve the Scregg case and his career would be set back. If he made a real hash of it by, for example, mishandling the planting of evidence, all that would be left would be ignominious disgrace. For Grassmann, there was everything at risk—not least his liberty.

So when Fordham started his second round of questions, Ken Grassmann was less flippant and more alert than he had been the day before.

"Tell me, Mr Grassmann, were you the one standing next to Scregg when he fell?"

"Yes, I was."

"According to several reliable witnesses, you were not at his side. You were actually standing just behind him."

"It could be. He was near enough to be speaking to me when he fell."

"Or was pushed."

"I didn't push him. I told you. It was an accident. The coroner agrees."

"But you could have pushed him. You were in a position to push him."

"Maybe I was. But I didn't."

"No one saw his last step because you were obstructing their view."

"So no-one saw me push him either?"

"Are you admitting that you pushed him?"

"Don't be stupid. I didn't push him. End of story."

Fordham changed tack.

"Did you know that we had a complaint about you from one of your neighbours?"

"Really?"

"Yes, really."

"Go on."

"Well, it appears that last Wednesday, the very day, you will recall, when your late employer met his death, possibly at your hands, you caused a nuisance in Tennyson Avenue. It appears you were drunk and abusive."

"The residents of Tennyson Avenue deserve all the abuse they get. But yes, I did shout at them and yes, I had been to the Stranglers Arms before going home, as your Big Brother cameras have already told you. Charge me with being drunk and contemptuous and I'll plead guilty."

"You're missing the point, Mr Grassmann. It's the reason why you were drunk and contemptuous which interests us. Isn't it true that you have just broken up with your wife?"

"That's not a criminal offence."

"No, not a criminal offence, Mr Grassmann, but it does give us a motive! We spoke to your neighbours. They report hearing a furious row at your house last Wednesday night. From all accounts you and Mrs Grassmann were going at it hammer and tongs. A couple of them wanted to call our officers."

"Am I the only one who has ever had a row with his missus? Is this really police business?"

"According to the neighbours, you threatened Mrs Grassmann with violence. You are a violent man, Mr Grassmann!"

"Do you believe them? Do you not think it possible that they might have exaggerated for dramatic effect? Sort of embroidering their story?"

"Yes, but the main point is the reason for your row. According to quite a few of your colleagues here, your wife and Mr Scregg were lovers and the row at 115 Tennyson Avenue was because you had only just found out."

"But if I'd only just found out, why kill Scregg before I'd found out?"

"You know what I think, Mr Grassmann?"

"No, what do you think, Inspector Fordham?"

"I think that you found out about the affair before that lunch last Wednesday and you saw a sudden opportunity to do in your love rival and you took it. A risky strategy but you might have got away with it since no-one saw you strike the fatal blow and push Mr Scregg down the steps."

"But, I keep telling you. I did not push him. He slipped because he was having difficulty standing up straight and that was because he was three quarters pissed. As usual."

"We also spoke to Mrs Grassmann, your dear Cheryl, who was, I understand, Mr Scregg's personal secretary and mistress. She is prepared to swear that you were often violent towards her and only sought comfort from Scregg as a refuge from your behaviour."

Fordham wasn't finished.

"It's not looking good for you, Ken, boy. It's not looking good at all. I think you'd better come down to the station with me. Don't worry, there'll be a lawyer present. We'll be looking at quite a few charges. Murder for starters, then conspiracy with Baines, then domestic violence against your wife. We're going to throw the book at you."

Down at the police station, Fordham kept going over the exact same questions which he had asked Ken Grassmann at the college, getting gradually more frustrated when his prisoner would not deviate from his story.

After about three hours, the lawyer asked for a private meeting with his client.

"One question. I'm your lawyer. You didn't do it, did you?"

"Of course I didn't. The coroner's verdict was completely fair. And, let's be straight. I never laid a hand on my wife, soon to be ex-wife. She's lying. Well, you know, a woman scorned *et cetera*."

"Good, Fordham has nothing or he'd have charged you by now. He's just trying his luck. Give me ten minutes."

With that, the lawyer left the interview room to explain the workings of the British statutory rules of evidence to a bemused Fordham. After a few minutes Fordham returned.

"Thank you for helping us with our inquiries, Mr Grassmann. You are free to go now. There will be no charges at the present time. We may need to speak to you again."

And it was over. He just got back to college for the end of evening classes. A few lecturers were still there. They all crowded around him. Some slapped his back.

"You got off!!"

"I didn't do it!"

"Yeah, right! But you could have done it and you would still have got off! That's brilliant!"

"He's right", said Lawson Baines, "it doesn't matter whether you did it or not, the old bastard is dead and you are not going to go to jail for it!! That's what I call a real result! Stranglers?"

"Why not?"

Of course, the news of Grassmann's arrest did not go unnoticed. Cheryl and her fellow secretaries saw the police car waiting with flashing lights outside the main door of the college and were quick to call the Chronicle and local TV.

That evening, the local television station made Ken's arrest their lead story.

"Police are still following up the sudden death last week of the Principal of Upton Faldwell College. A man was arrested this afternoon. He is believed to be 45 years old and a member of the college staff. He was later released without charge."

Short of spelling his name out, the local telly had just about totally identified him to the whole world and in addition, declared him guilty as charged.

Ken was still in the pub when the broadcast came on.

"Hey, Ken, you're famous!! Headlines on the telly!!"

Which probably meant that there would be reporters already camped outside his new apartment. And that is exactly what did happen. The landlord phoned him late.

"Can't have it, Mr Grassmann. Can't have it. You'll have to go. Can't have criminals and reporters. Looks bad. Never be able to let my flats if they know there's a criminal living here. A murderer!!"

"But I'm not a murderer, Mr Ozalay. They let me go. They questioned me and then they let me go."

"I'm sorry, Mr Grassmann. It just looks too bad for my business. I'll return your deposit in the morning."

"What about the month's rent I paid last Saturday?"

"Sorry, Mr Grassmann, I think I am going to have to keep that. I think I deserve it for what I have had to put up with from you. You've brought shame on my apartments."

"Then fuck you, Ozalay."

"No call for bad language, Mr Grassmann. No call at all. I knew you were a bad lot as soon as I clapped eyes on you. Now all this cursing and swearing."

Fortunately, Ken's personal belongings had not yet been unpacked. Some were in suitcases and boxes, some were in his office and some were still back at Tennyson Avenue. Just another small problem. Among many.

In fact, when word had got around the landlords and rental agencies of Faldwell Upton, all of whom owned TV sets, Ken could find no-one prepared to harbour this unconvicted alleged murderer, with the result that he had to travel to the county town, some twelve miles away, before he was able to get a new place. This time he rented under a false name, Kelvin Greenwood, so that he could possibly avoid the reporters, who were avid to pursue what was, for them, the biggest story of the year so far in this small parochial community. To commute from his new abode he would need his car, which Cheryl was still using. He could not see the justice of her keeping the car for her short trip to the college when he had to make a twenty-four mile round trip every day. Since the vehicle was registered and taxed in his name, he had no compunction in liberating it from the college car park for his own use. Cheryl did subsequently report its theft to the police but Fordham was unimpressed when she told him that Ken himself had most likely reclaimed it.

"He'll only get that crooked greasy lawyer to say that it was his all along and why are we harassing poor Mr Grassmann," he decided. A sensible tactical withdrawal for Fordham, given the lawyer's delight in making formal representations to the Police Complaints Commission.

Friday, as Fridays always do, arrived and with it the occasion of the interment of Morton Alamein Scregg, late Principal of Upton Faldwell Community College. There was to be a cast of thousands for a service to be held in the impressive Faldwell Parish Church, in which the late Morton Scregg had married both Mrs Scregg's.

Leading the congregation and resplendent in scarlet mayoral robes was His Worship Councillor Charles Fanshawe, who, as owner of the town's largest shop, was considered part of the aristocracy of this small borough. The Education Committee were all there, together with the local MP, for whom this funeral was a welcome diversion from a police investigation into his expenses claims. There was a delegation from the County Council and music was provided by the town band, the Faldwell Upton Silver Prize Band, who greeted the mourners with their soft rendition of 'Wake me up before you go go,' one of the late Principal's particular favourites.

Naturally, all the college surviving bigwigs were in place, Vice, Assistant and Deputy Principals, Deans, various people who held titles with 'Director of' in them. The teaching body, those working lecturers whose fate and guidance had been in the hands of the late Mr Scregg, had also been invited, as had all the college administration. All had declined, except those women, teachers and clerical staff alike, including Cheryl Grassmann, whose favours they had once generously lavished upon the deceased. In fact, a dispassionate external observer would have been able to discern the lineage of the Principal's erotic career from the ages and the facial expressions of those women present. Lovers past and present were in attendance, some to express a little grief and respect, the majority, those older, discarded, grim-faced ones, to confirm for themselves that the old goat really was dead and buried as they had, in most cases fervently, wished for once their own sell-by dates had been exceeded and he had moved on.

Fordham was there with his boss, the Superintendent, chief drinking mate and golfing buddy of the departed.

"So, Fordham, you think there might have been some funny business over Scregg?"

"I'm sure of it, sir. That Grassmann's a nasty little sod. He's up to something. I know it."

"You'll need more than that. I see you brought him in and had to let him go?"

"That greasy little lawyer's fault. Threatened to go to the PCC."

"I'm sorry to have to tell you, Fordham, that that is the law as it stands and we have to follow it."

"Of course, sir, of course. It's just that we are fighting the war against crime with one hand tied behind our backs."

"What would you like to see instead? Bang up every 'nasty little sod' you take a dislike to?"

"Well. sir, you've got admit that's not such a bad idea. It would clear up the crime rate pretty damn quick."

"Maybe, Fordham. But rules is rules and you shouldn't risk your career over this case. It's not worth it."

"I know, sir, but I know he's guilty. Guilty as hell."

"Well, you can't prove it, so there it is. Let it go. Drop it. You need to get out more. There's a home match tomorrow. Go to that. Bound to be a bit of action. Make you feel better. Beat up a few young tearaways. It'll take your mind off things."

"If you say so, sir."

"I do, Fordham, I do. Case closed. Accidental verdict. Consider that an order."

"Yes, sir."

Fordham sulked through the rest of the funeral service, at the same time scrutinising the congregation for some clue as to whoever else might be in on the plot. He could see no one who could possibly have been a likely suspect amid the tearful women and the aspirants for the succession.

"But," he vowed silently, "I'll get the little bastard. Yes, I'll get the little bastard. Whatever the Super might say." His first big murder case and it had been snatched away from him! He seethed at the injustice of life.

Meanwhile, as Fordham was wallowing in self-pity, the funeral rituals were being enacted in that relaxed demotic way by which the Church of England stage-manages life's signal events. Vice Principal Cloughe read a lesson—Psalm 23, of course. Then Vice Principal Morgan-Pugh gave a well over-the-top eulogy which praised the late Principal as a mighty figure of history—like a Schweitzer or a Kennedy, with an intellect so incisive and a vision so far-reaching, that his automatic apotheosis to an immediate seat at God's right hand would be the very least of his richly deserved afterlife honours. Even the Superintendent could not completely stifle a laugh.

The undoubted star of the show was the grieving widow herself. Beautifully kitted out in a figure-hugging black Givenchy dress with hurriedly bought high-end accessories and top-notch perfume to match. (She had watched the first ten minutes of 'Breakfast at Tiffany's' at least a hundred times.) Her hair and manicure, every accoutrement, even down to her underwear, were perfect for her big day. No expense—Scregg would not need it any more, would he?—had been spared on her buying spree in Bond Street.

"After all," she consoled herself. "I'm a widow now. I need to take care of myself."

It is difficult to be sure which part of the ceremony she enjoyed most, the dressing up, her fine theatrical performance as the grieving widow, or, and here she smiled a private smile to herself, the looks on the faces of those losers in love's game? By which she meant those cast-off former mistresses of her late husband who were now sitting forlornly in the mourners' pews while she, the lottery winner, was arrayed in the finest raiment while being simultaneously lauded with tributes and sympathy.

"Life is cruel," she mused. "At least it is for them."

The body had been placed in a cardboard coffin, in tribute to Scregg's professed green credentials as someone who had once been to a conference on the environment and therefore did not believe in unnecessary waste. Not, of course, that he really did give a stuff about the environment, but, he had realised, a prominent public figure like himself needed to be associated with at least one good cause and eco-environmental green-ness was the one cause where you got easy approval without needing to do very much or to spend much money.

The coffin was finally laid in the ground to the plangent sounds of the Silver Band's rendition of 'Don't cry for me, Argentina' which was the cue for Mandy Scregg to do her well-rehearsed act of falling and sobbing at the graveside, during which display the mourners looked on with typical British embarrassment. Then back to the County Arms for a buffet lunch and, much to the delight of Scregg's old cronies, a free bar. The Widow Scregg, now miraculously recovered from the distraught grief she had flaunted at the cemetery, was shaking hands and accepting condolences.

"Thank you for coming."

"Very sad. He was a good man."

"Thank you. You're very kind."

The Superintendent, never a man to pass up free drinks, drank his fill, said his goodbyes and got into the waiting police car with Fordham. He slumped back into the seat and uttered Scregg's true authentic epitaph.

"You know, Fordham? I always hated the bastard. Never paid his round at the club. Thought he was God's gift to women. Fancied himself as a clever bugger."

"Then why did you play golf with him? I thought he was a friend of yours."

"Yes, he was a friend. But I always hated him. But, in this town, he was important. And that's where you get your friends from."

FOUR

Over the next few weeks of the autumn term, Ken Grassmann's life underwent a sharp change of direction. There were the regular daily awkwardnesses every time he bumped into his wife Cheryl. But those moments of discomfort gradually declined in embarrassment level as he came to realise, not entirely without significant relief, that her bitter sulk as the wronged wife meant that she would keep up the silent treatment for months to come. When they had been married and living together, even the smallest infraction of what she considered her due respect would have been greeted by an indeterminately long silence. So a major offence, such as he had committed by walking out, would not come in at much less than six months or even a year, given that even his mere raising of a quizzical eyebrow during one of her frequent tirades would result in instant door slamming and a bitter, two-day, self-pitying sulk. Her record sulk, whose cause he had never been able to figure out, was a good four months of total excommunication without a word being exchanged between them, during which time he slept in the spare room. But that was before the life-changing events of what he was now starting to look back on as 'liberation' Wednesday. Where once her temper tantrums and sullen silences would have weakened and depressed his spirit, he now found himself grateful for this adolescent aspect of her character—it did at least mean that the obsequies of their marriage and the divvying up of the marital property could be done without any pretence at being 'civilised' or 'mature'.

There was the divorce, uncontested of course, which was conducted relatively easily in the County Court. Then the division of the property. The joint account was split down the middle and Cheryl got the ten percent of the house not owned by the building society and which she immediately sold. Ken himself took the car and his own few effects. After the final bills had come in, he had only a few paltry pounds left to show for his twelve years of Cheryl's sulks, tempers and now, adulteries. And, what is more, she would probably want maintenance as well.

"Don't worry," his lawyer assured him. "That is one of the finest achievements of feminism. These days they are expected to earn for themselves."

So Ken, freed from the bitter clutches of the rapacious, dishonest Cheryl, soon found himself spending more and more time with Sonia Lyttel. So much so that they soon came to be recognised in the college as, to use that unflattering phrase, an 'item'.

Lawson Baines urged caution.

"Don't want to jump out of the frying pan into the fire, old boy. She might be young and good-looking but you're still on the rebound. Give it a year at least."

"We'll see. No hurry."

But he was definitely getting in deeper and when they started spending weekends together, he realised a milestone corner had been turned in the relationship.

It was one wintry Sunday morning, when the pillow talk turned to the events of four months previously and

Scregg's promotion to glory, as the Salvation Army so quaintly describe the concluding human experience.

"I was wondering. Does that inspector fellow still call you in for questioning?" asked Sonia.

"No, not since the funeral. I'm hoping he's given up."

"I don't think he's the giving-up type. I wouldn't be surprised if he is keeping an eye on you."

"No, surely he's got better things to do? Even a place like this has crime. There must be all sorts of stuff to keep him busy. Anyway, I still live a very blameless life. Just like before the trouble."

"Yes, but most of the local crime is small-scale. Small time house breaking, a bit of domestic violence, shop-lifting. That sort of thing. You were his sniff of the big time. Murder, that'll look good on his record. Much better than locking up drunks and car thieves, I'd have thought," Sonia went on.

"Maybe. I was probably a disappointment to him. He thought he'd got a murderer and all he had was me. I never killed anyone in my life. Just in the wrong place at the wrong time."

"But he thinks you did it, even if you didn't. He's definitely going to bear a grudge towards you. Aren't you worried he might fix you up with something to get his own back."

"I think the phrase is 'fit me up' not 'fix me up'. That's what they always say on the telly. You fit someone up when you plant evidence on them for a crime they didn't commit. Fixing up is when you, well, fix someone up with a date."

"Sorry, I am not familiar with criminal slang. But seriously, aren't you worried Fordham's going to do something like that to you. Fit you up."

"Yes, I am, as it happens. I don't trust the bastard, not an inch. But it's difficult to see what he can do."

"Be careful. And don't ever drive home from the Stranglers. His lads with the breathalysers have probably been told to keep a lookout for you as well."

Sonia was gently reminding him that the hanging judges of the local magistrates' bench regularly handed out six month prison sentences for drink-drivers who were one milligram over the legal limit on a first offence. And if the Faldwell Upton police stopped you, you would certainly prove to be over the limit, whatever the pharmacological facts of the case might be.

"Life has certainly been better for most people since Scregg went. Can't argue with that. Well, maybe not for Cheryl."

Cheryl had, in fact, been transferred to the secretaryship of the new Principal, Kathleen Cloughe, known as 'Cloughie' or 'Old Bighead', in honour of the famous football coach of the same name. For Vice Principal Cloughe had duly become Principal Cloughe and her Welsh rival, predictably bitter in defeat, was spending most of her time on the road between interviews for a principal's job at whatever community college could be persuaded of her sterling qualities.

Principal Cloughe was possessed of a temper and self-importance quite in keeping with her new rank. She liked to think of herself as a tough manager. One of her favourite phrases, repeated frequently, was "I'm tough, I am. Don't mess with me." Which is an admirable enough attitude for the governor of a high security prison but is not exactly a declaration of academic or scholastic excellence for the leader of an educational establishment, even one as far removed from intellectual eminence as Upton Faldwell Community College. But, until Cloughie found her feet and morphed into the traditional unhinged megalomania of the standard FE college principal, things were indeed better for the regular staff of the place. Given, of course, her virtually autocratic position, and remembering the oft-quoted Actonian dictum that power tends to corrupt while absolute power corrupts absolutely, none of the old sweats of the college expected this short intermission of peace and co-operation to be much prolonged before normality, in the form of bullying macho management, returned with a vengeance.

For poor Cheryl, the former Mrs Grassmann, work with the new boss was not too taxing, although she was missing those employment side benefits which she had occasionally enjoyed under, literally, former Principal Scregg. Madame Cloughe was not known to be a sexual person. Indeed, she oozed an aggressive asexual neutrality. Had Cheryl been so inclined though, she might have found some job satisfaction in her new position, given that Kathleen Cloughe's real sexual personality was not one of genuine asexuality but actually one of severe Sapphic repression.

"You know what Lawson said to me when I got out of the police station?" Ken was saying to Sonia. "He said that I had done everyone a real good turn by doing in old Scregg. Even he thought I had pushed the old bastard down the stairs."

"What if you had? What if you had actually killed him? Deliberately. What if Fordham had got it right? Supposing you really had bumped him off. Where would that leave us?"

"About where we are now, I suppose. But I just couldn't. I just couldn't. I didn't do it and Fordham was trying to frame me."

"Is that another piece of telly slang?"

"Of course, 'fit up', 'frame', 'grass'. I know it all, me."

"Right", said Sonia. "This is the situation. You didn't murder Scregg but you don't mind if someone else murdered him. But you were still blamed for it because you could have murdered him, but you didn't."

"That's about it, yes."

"But the upshot of it is that everyone is happy because Scregg was removed, whoever did it. So whether you killed him or not, the final result is the same. The old so-and-so has gone. Everybody benefits, except you, . . us, because we got nothing for it."

"I could stand a better chance of promotion under Cloughie than I ever did under Scregg."

"I doubt that. She hates men. Likes to see them humiliated," said Sonia. "I'm tough, me!!" she mimicked. "No my dear, your career prospects remain unchanged as before at roundabout exactly nil, zero, zilch."

"So I'll need to wait for a similar accident to befall Cloughie?"

"Could be a long time. She's a tough old bird, as she keeps telling us. Lightning doesn't strike twice."

"Ah well, we can dream. Time for breakfast?"

Sunday breakfast, the only day with enough time for a cooked breakfast and a long leisurely read of the Sunday heavyweight papaers, was a high-spot of the week and a time for gentle daydreaming.

"I wonder how many other of our fellow lecturers feel better now Scregg has gone?" Ken pondered.

"Most of them, I would think."

"A lot of them actually think I did actually do him in and got away with it. I keep telling them it was an accident and you know what they say?"

"What?"

"Yeah, right, nice one, Ken! That's what they say."

"Should organise a collection for you. Get some money back for all those lawyers' fees and the divorce."

"That's a point. British justice does not come cheap."

"You should have got compensation for all that police harassment. As it was, you'll be paying until you retire. That's certainly not fair. After all you did for them, too."

"Remember, I did nothing. If he hadn't got pissed and fallen down the stairs, none of this would have happened."

"Still, it does seem a shame that you should finish up paying all the costs, one way or another. You did see that Mandy Scregg was left nearly half a million? Even Cloughie got a promotion out of it. But you got nothing except a big bill."

"Given Mandy Scregg's taste in clothes, half a million won't go far."

"Still, there should be some way of getting your money back."

"I could write a book—'The Life and Times of Morton Alamein Scregg'," said Ken.

"A horror story? I can't see that selling."

"You know what I'm thinking?" Ken continued. "I'm thinking that the situation at Upton Faldwell College can't be all that different from elsewhere. Look, I've known a lot of further education college principals. And, give or take, they were all pretty much the same. Not as bad as Scregg, obviously, no-one could be, but pretty similar. Some were drunks, some helped themselves to college funds, most of them were bullies and liars. That comes with the territory. Just think though, all around the country right now, at this very minute, there must be thousands of lecturers who've read about Scregg in *The Times Educational Supplement* and thought 'Why, please God, why can't that happen here?'"

"All those thousands of poor devils, just waiting for a benign God to arrange a little accident?" Sonia asked.

"But it doesn't have to be an accident. You said so yourself. The outcome would have been the same whether I'd pushed him or he'd just slipped down the stairs because he was drunk. Makes no difference. Same result."

"These things can't be arranged, unfortunately. But there must be a lot of money in it for someone who can do it."

"It would have been much cheaper to pay a hitman to take him out instead of all those fees to those lawyers."

"I am sure hitmen come more expensive than that."

"Ha! Ha! We could have set up a fund like a Christmas Club. Everyone who hated the old shit could have put a fiver a week into a fund at the building society. When we had enough we could hire some James Bond type to 'take him out'."

"More criminal slang?"

"I got that from an Al Pacino film."

"We could even have said it was for something like Greenpeace. Then we could have got him to pay into it himself!!!"

By now, both were laughing uproariously. They got on with their Sunday. It was not until later when they remembered the morning conversation.

"I am sure there is an idea for a business here." said Sonia.

"You mean some sort of online advice service for coping with college principals who have Hitler complexes?" said Ken.

"Could be. Like counselling? Doesn't sound very exciting."

"True. Anyway the local medics do a roaring trade already. Rumour has it that every chemist within two miles of the college gets regular deliveries of extra Valium."

"What we really need to do is to offer a service to remove their bosses."

"A private assassin?"

"Exactly! Instead of getting bankrupted for pushing Scregg down the steps, you could now be sitting in a nice little bit of hedge," pointed out Sonia.

"I think you mean 'wedge'. You said 'hedge'."

"'Hedge', 'wedge', you know what I mean. A nice little payoff for you, for your service to suffering humanity," continued Sonia. "What about if you had really done him in? You could have cashed in the Christmas Club and we could now be sitting on a beach in the sun."

"I don't think I could actually do him in."

"Why not? Is it worse to do him in and risk going to jail or not to do him in and get a police record anyway? You can be sure that your little brush with the law will not have gone unnoticed in the close-knit world of community colleges. Imagine the discussion if you were ever to get an interview for head of department or principal lecturer. Not that you'll ever get through the door. What principal is ever going to be stupid enough to interview you now? Maybe just the odd nutter who is interested in seeing what a real-life murderer actually looks like."

"But I'm not a murderer. I never killed him."

"Get real, my dear. Every single college principal in this country knows you are guilty as charged. Whether you did it or not. Aren't they always telling us they keep a blacklist?"

"So that's it. Career over?"

"I would guess. What college is going to touch you now? I wouldn't be surprised if Cloughie herself wasn't looking around for a way to ease you out. You are definitely a threat now. Think, if you really did Scregg in, she's bound to be wondering if you are going to be doing the same to her, isn't she?"

"And she thinks I could have done it, even though I didn't."

"Exactly. We need a Plan B."

"Career change? I don't think I could do anything else. Lecturing is all I've ever done."

"Let's face it. You are poison as far as other colleges are concerned and Cloughie will be putting you up for compulsory early retirement as soon as she can. If she doesn't find an excuse for making you redundant first, that is"

"Almost makes me wish I had done it now."

"Especially if they'd collected a fund for you."

They were now on to the mind-lubricating second glass of Tesco Red.

"A professional hit man probably makes a lot more money than a lecturer in mechanical drawing. Better lifestyle too, I shouldn't wonder."

"Might be a nice line of work. Short working hours, cosmopolitan life, lots of money." said Sonia.

"Certainly better than Upton Faldwell Community College. I wonder how you get into that sort of job."

"Not a job, my dear, a profession. Jobs are what we have, someone who provides a much-needed public service has a profession."

"We could advertise," said Ken, with a sudden increase in interest.

"Where, on telly, like those lawyers? Whatsit, ambulance chasers? We could make a commercial—Contact Grassman and Lyttel right now if you want someone rubbed out!!"

"I think we need to be a bit more subtle than that. Anyway advertising on TV is expensive. We don't have a big budget."

"So we'd be working the cheap end of the assassination market. 'We will wipe out that irritating problem, at a special bargain price!!' Doesn't sound quite right."

"No, but if someone wants someone else rubbed out, price is not going to be a problem, is it?"

"Getting away with it would be the problem," said Sonia.

"Thinking how Fordham tried to pin Scregg on me when I was completely innocent, if I'd actually done it, he would soon have me stitched up," said Ken.

"No darling, think. What did that copper say? It's all about motive, opportunity and association. You were only questioned because you had all three. If you'd been at the back of the group, where I was, he'd never have thought of you."

"I still had a motive though, didn't I?"

"But so did lots of people. Cheryl might have been fucking him, but at some time or another he fucked most of the married women in the college. There were lots of people with the same motive. No, it's having all three that gets you questioned. And then if he can break your story, only then are you done."

"Which means," said Ken, "that if you don't have motive or association, there is a good chance you could get away with it."

"Professional assassin. I wonder how many people are already doing it right now and making a good living at it?"

"Probably plenty. Thousands of people go missing every year. Just a moment." Ken turned to his laptop computer.

"It's here," he said. "Nearly two hundred thousand go missing in the UK every year. In the States it's two thousand a day!"

"Most of those will be innocent. You know, escaping bad homes, losing their memory, accidents."

"Yes, but a fair proportion must be murdered. Bodies destroyed."

"You're right. There must be a nice little niche market in there."

"Let's assume, for the sake of argument, that only one per cent of those two hundred thousand is murdered, that still means two thousand unsolved murders every year. That's a big industry."

"Not just unsolved but unknown to the police."

Ken went back to his computer.

"Look," he said. "The number of recorded homicides in the UK each year is only about six, seven hundred. That's official murders. In reality, there must be an awful lot which never come to light."

"And that means that you have a pretty good chance of getting away with it."

"If they were all like Scregg, I would be saying Hallelujah. Trouble is, most murder victims don't deserve it," said Ken.

"Yes," Sonia agreed, "a lot of decent people must be being done in by some real bastards."

"What is needed is a service for eliminating the Scregg's of this world and not the decent folk. At a price, of course."

"We could advertise, like you said," said Sonia.

"Another problem I see," said Ken, "is that we only got to know what Scregg was like over a period of time. How do we know that, say, the principal of some college is the sort of monster Scregg was?"

"For a college principal, the odds are in favour. But you just couldn't go around only knocking off college principals now, could you? Even Fordham would soon see a pattern."

"Yes, he's stupid, but not that stupid," agreed Ken.

"Which means that we would have to offer our service to the wider community. The world, after all, is full to the brim with Scregg types whose removal would definitely be in the public good. I can think of a dozen people right now whose deaths would bring the sun out."

"So, how would we know which was which?"

"Difficult. We would only want to rub out the shits and the bastards, not decent people. So we would need a code of conduct. An ethical position."

"But there's another problem. Suppose someone comes to us and says that his boss is making everyone's life a misery. How would we know whether he was telling the truth or he was the bastard himself? He was the one doing the buggering up of other people's lives?"

"I see the point. If we are going to make a success of this business it has to be quick-in-quick-out. Not much time for researching the target to see whether the client was right."

"We are going to need some research, that's true. The papers are full of stories about wronged wives and husbands who bump off their other half and then get caught."

"Bound to get caught. They forget the three basic rules—motive, association and opportunity. That's why domestics are so easy to solve. The cops just go straight to the spouse. Job done."

"Yes, and in a marital there's never any way of telling who was right and who was wrong. When it's marital, it's usually six of one and half a dozen of the other."

"I think we should stay away from marital contracts. Too problematical."

"Same applies to other parts of the bumping-off business. Think, if Scregg had been able to get rid of people on the quiet, who knows what he might have done?" Sonia reminded Ken.

"That is certainly true. If there had been an assassination service for the general public, Scregg would have used it himself and we'd have been at old Braithwaite's funeral years ago. By the way, speaking of Braithwaite, did you hear what he's been telling everyone? He's been going around saying that he can now take his retirement and now that Scregg's dead he can die happy himself."

"Oh, bless him!" said Sonia.

"So, back to our plan. We need to be able to offer a quick disposal service for all those poor sods out there who are in daily contact with some monster and will pay good money to get rid of him."

"Yes, I agree. Governments do it all the time and if governments do it, then certainly big companies must be doing it," said Sonia.

"You mean real-life James Bond figures? Oh-Oh-Seven, licensed to kill?"

"Probably a lot less glamorous. But Ian Fleming based his stories on fact. He was a spy himself in the war. James

Bond is probably based on reality with a bit more sex and exotic locations. Oh, and fancy cars, of course."

"Whereas we would be in cold wet Faldwell Upton with a ten-year-old Toyota."

"Got to start somewhere," put in Sonia.

"Governments have people rubbed out all the time. You read about it occasionally, like that umbrella case with that Bulgarian spy."

"Yes, and there's always the odd dodgy looking car accident."

"Do you remember? No, you're too young," Ken said. "But apparently there was some cabinet minister in the early sixties who was shagging some model at the same time she was having it away with a spy from the Russian embassy. Never got into the papers until they were forced to go public and they couldn't keep it quiet any longer."

"So?" asked Sonia.

"What I am saying is that governments and big businesses can cover these things up. But there must be a lot going on we don't hear about. Somebody standing in the way of some important deal? If he's the problem, then that's how it works. Bang! Problem solved." said Ken.

"But it's not available to all of us. They have laws to control us. That's what laws are for. Us, controlling the people who don't matter."

"While they get on with taking everything for themselves."

"So, a private little assassination business is a blow for the little man!"

"Quite right. Killing the people who make our ordinary everyday lives miseries. It's a blow for democracy. That's how I see it," concluded Ken.

"I think we are moving towards a business plan," said Sonia.

"Right. We offer a removal service. People we, or someone else, can't abide, who make decent people's lives a misery."

"Yes, for a fee, remember, for a fee."

"Quite, we are not going to be a charity."

"So, what sort of people?"

"What sort? Let me see. The Scregg's of this world, all the bullying managers, obviously. Then there's all those people running businesses who rip people off, incompetent tradesmen, who overcharge, like the plumber who does a job at your house, charges hundreds and leaves the job not done. He can go on the list."

"And those planning jobsworths at the town hall.

"Of course. What about the immigration department? All of them, I would have thought."

"Right on. Especially those people on the immigration desk at Heathrow who can hardly speak English and then interrogate you as if you were a car bomber."

"Not to mention a fair number of the local police. Especially the ones who tell you that you are committing some offence whatever you are doing, because there is always something they can do you for."

"The cops I hate most are those who arrest someone and bang them up, fingerprints an' all, just because they have fought off some little thug trying to rob them."

"Because it's easier to get your arrest quota up by going for the law-abiding citizen than chasing down some criminal."

"Traffic wardens, car clampers?"

"Sadistic nurses, incompetent doctors. The list is endless."

"Politicians?"

"Almost all of them, I would think."

"So our business plan is that we offer this service on a customised basis, one case at a time."

"What do we charge?"

"Tricky. What we are offering is a bespoke service which will involve a fair amount of research, not to say travelling."

"Yes, we can't give our jobs up yet."

"Why should we? Two harmless, college lecturers in some out-of-the-way college. What could be a better cover? And, what is more, with evening classes and so on, we can often be free during the day."

"No, I think we'll need to negotiate the fees separately each time."

"Supposing we really had done the Scregg job. What would we have charged for that, do you think?"

"Well, given that there must have been at least two hundred people who would happily have pushed him down the stairs themselves, then, let us say, a hundred quid per, makes twenty grand."

"That sounds about right."

"Here's an idea. We could offer a deferred payments plan. People could save up monthly until they had enough in their account to have the job done. Like saving up for cosmetic surgery."

"That's another on the list. Cosmetic surgeons who mess up. But deferred payments might be OK except that they would have to have saved up the full amount before we do the job or they wouldn't pay the balance. Anyway, we don't want to make it too complicated. Just quick-in-quick-out like you said. All in cash, half before, half after. No names. We have to be careful."

"Remember, we are not just in this for the money. We are also a charity, an altruistic organisation devoted to good works. Which means that if there is some very deserving victim who can't afford top whack then we have to adjust our fees accordingly."

"What shall we call our little company?"

"Something like 'Ken and Sonia—Purveyors of Bumping Off to the Gentry'?"

"Or a joke title even—'You're Killing Me!!'?"

"Maybe 'Assassinations are Us!'"

"No, something a little more professional, I think. After all, we are going to be serious professional people, offering a proper professional service. We need to be a limited company."

"Right. What about 'Conflict Deletion Services Ltd.'? Nice and anonymous."

"Perfect!"

"The next thing is a business plan. Mission statement, corporate objectives, policies etc."

Actually the drafting of the business plan was quite easy. CDS Ltd. would offer

> *'. . the very highest standards of conflict deletion based on complete client confidentiality and leading to permanent client satisfaction based on a terminal successful outcome of the negotiation process.'*

"Beautiful," said Ken, "I knew your English degree would come in useful one day. I like 'terminal'. Just the right hint of what we offer."

"And now," said Sonia, "just how do we make ourselves known?"

"Advertising. We could put classified ads in small magazines, such as *Private Eye* and see what kind of response we get."

"Good idea. Let's draft something."

So, what duly appeared in several small publications was a carefully worded invitation. They both considered it a masterpiece of subtlety. It read:

> *'Problems in the workplace? Maybe you have been ripped off by a company or your local council? Whatever your problem, it is probably a breakdown of human communication. We can*

> *help. We offer a full professional service for conflict deletion by negotiating on behalf of the aggrieved party and securing a permanent termination to the dispute.'* Plus email address.

"Maybe we should join the British Association of Counselling as well? Sort of, get respectable," offered Sonia.

"Maybe, there might be some good business there. A final solution to some of their more difficult cases?"

"Just one question, before we start," asked Sonia. "Is what we are proposing to do entirely ethical?"

"Well, we won't take a penny unless we finish the job to the customer's satisfaction, if that's what you mean?"

"No, that's not what I mean. I mean, killing people, is that fair?"

"Not legally, no, I don't suppose it is. But at the way things are set up now, governments and rich people can kill us, just when they want to. Look at the way governments send people to die in wars to protect business profits. Look at the way companies sell all sorts of poisons to ordinary people. Look at the way the cops kill people in the street and never get prosecuted. I am sorry, my darling, ethics shouldn't just work one way. All our little business will do is help tilt the balance the other way just a bit."

"Rubbing out someone like Scregg is one thing, but I wouldn't like any innocent people to get killed."

"Yes, I think we're going to have to be very careful. Which is why we can't do domestics. I know we are missing out on a big share of the market because the world is full of violent husbands and shrewish wives but we must stay neutral at all times. We have to maintain our standards as a public service."

"Yes, we must stay professional. With the very highest ethical standards. And never, ever, let our feelings or emotions get the better of us."

"Quite right. Once we have approved a client's case, so that we can be sure they are right about someone, then we just do the job. Stay cold. Just do it. If we get emotionally involved, then we are probably done for."

FIVE

The advert was placed and it duly appeared as a small classified ads. in some small-circulation weeklies. Ken and Sonia went back to their duties at the college and awaited replies. They did not have to wait long before a rag-bag of wild emails started to show up on a daily basis. Many of them were spam—advertising of all sorts of things from colonic irrigation to funeral plans. Here and there was the odd serious-sounding plea from a wronged wife or some poor soul who had been ripped off by a plumber or a travel company. Most of the messages were simply deleted.

"We can't write back to everyone, can we? No point in drawing unnecessary attention to ourselves," advised Ken.

"Quite right. There may be some genuine possible customers in there, but it's difficult to tell."

Still, they considered each message on its merits until one day Sonia had a eureka moment.

"I think this looks promising." she said and read out the message,

> "... 'I am a lady in a difficult situation with my member of parliament because of some financial malpractice. I am seeking some way to retrieve

some of the money he has embezzled from my family. I have tried the usual avenues such as lawyers and formal complaints but because of his position, he is always able to block any move I try to make. Can you please meet with me to discuss whether you are able to take my case on and make some progress where I have failed? My phone number is . . . .'"

"Sounds promising," agreed Ken, "let's write back." They wrote,

'Thank you very much for your message. It is indeed possible that we may be able to help in your case. We need to meet to discuss the details of how we can help you. Signed CDS Ltd.'

And Sonia phoned. A woman's voice answered. She sounded guarded, even apprehensive.

"I can't talk about it on the phone. But I've tried everything else. I am getting desperate. Can you meet me in London?"

"Day after tomorrow? After lunch?"

"Sounds good. Two pm. Starbucks Leicester Square?"

"How will I recognise you?"

"I'll be wearing a long green coat. And a silver silk scarf."

"I'll be there. Looking forward to it."

Sonia was very excited.

"It looks like we're on," she said.

"You go," said Ken. "It might be easier to get her to talk to a woman. If I am going to be the one to do the job, it's better she doesn't know about me."

"Yes and you have a class. It's my day off."

"Right," said Ken, "a couple of practical points. First, let us not use our own names. I rented my flat as Kelvin

Greenwood. Let us get a name for you. How does Sophie Liston sound? Same initials, always a good idea."

"Yes, Sohpie Liston. Yes, I like that."

"Right, if it looks like we are in business, let's register the company. And we need business cards and some advertising bumf."

"You'll take care of that, Ken?"

"It's Kelvin now. I'll get the cards printed tomorrow so you can give one to our first client."

Sonia was up bright and early for the first day of her new career as one half of a latter-day Bonnie and Clyde. She dressed in a standard business suit instead of the usual jeans and T-shirt, the standard outfit of the junior college lecturer. Looking as much like a member of the yuppie class as she could, she got a day return ticket to Euston station, in good time to get to Starbucks in Leicester Square. She had intended to arrive early so that she could observe the arrival of her guest and maybe get some impression of her before the woman could compose herself for the meeting. People look different when they are moving because their attention is diverted. However much they may try to disguise the inner structure of their personalities, they can never, when in motion, completely give themselves over to self-presentation. So a person walking gives unconscious clues about themselves which are not visible when they are sitting face-to-face and they can concentrate on their public persona. A stoop, a slouch, head up or down, even the speed they walk at, tell a lot about a person.

But Sonia was disappointed. Although she had arrived at Starbucks at 1.30pm, a good thirty minutes early, already waiting was a lady wearing a green coat and a silver silk Hermés scarf. She was an attractive, full-figured, handsome woman in her mid-fifties. In less intense lighting she could have passed for a glamorous woman at least ten years younger. But even at her worst, for she was now grim-faced and unsmiling, she was still striking and chic. Her hair was well coiffured and her makeup had been carefully and expertly applied. Sonia/Sophie took in her shoes (Gucci), her handbag (Mulberry) and her watch (a Cartier Tank Française), those three absolute standards of female style and economic status. And Sophie was quite sure that her substantial emerald earrings would not have been imitation costume jewellery. So affluent did this woman look and so out of place did she appear in a coffee bar, that Sophie/Sonia wondered whether they should maybe have been meeting for tea at the Ritz, a milieu which would, no doubt, have been one in which this stylish woman would have been more at home.

"Hello, I'm Sophie Liston from Conflict Deletion Services. Thank you for your phone call. I hope we can help."

"Good afternoon," began the elegant woman. "You can call me Isabel for the time being."

"Go on," urged Sonia.

The woman, Isabel, reached into her Mulberry tote bag and extracted a thick sheaf of papers, contained in a manila folder and bound by a rubber band. They appeared to include correspondence and press cuttings and many other documents. Isabel banged the file down on the table and put her hand on top of it.

"Before we go any further, I will need to know what sort of service you are offering and exactly how you go about things."

Sonia was cautious in her reply.

"Well," Sonia said, "we can negotiate between parties to a dispute using well-known conflict deletion techniques. We are not lawyers or marriage guidance counsellors and in fact, we don't handle marital disputes at all."

"What sort of clients do you work with, then?"

Sonia improvised.

"Professional people, mainly. We tend to specialise in disputes where one person, usually our client, feels disadvantaged in dealings with someone who is causing them distress or worse. Our last client was a senior member of the education profession. We were able to arbitrate a very satisfactory settlement of the problems."

"Do you mean that you are just like those lawyers I have been too? Always writing letters and setting up meetings. And always at my expense! And what expense! Imagine how much a lawyer can run up in five years!"

"Is that how long you've been trying to get settlement?"

"Longer, actually. It started before then. But I have spent five years at least, trying to sort these problems out," said Isabel.

"Look," she continued, "I don't need another lawyer, or a social worker or anyone who wants to get me to sit round a table and 'talk the problem through'." She sneered this last phrase.

"So," sympathised Sonia, "you want some action and you are through with talking?"

"You've got it," said Isabel. "Forgive me asking, but aren't you a little young for this sort of work? I take it you are some kind of counsellor."

"No, I'm not a counsellor. We don't have counsellors and we don't ask people to sit round a table and talk things out. That's not what we do at all." explained Sonia.

"Then, what do you do?" countered Isabel.

"Before I come to that," countered Sonia, "let me ask you a question. Why did you come to us?"

"I saw your ad. I thought I've tried everything else. What do I have to lose? It's only a phone call."

"So, Isabel, you're desperate. Is that right? Wit's end?"

"Wit's end."

"Was there any part of our advert which particularly struck you?" asked Sonia.

"Not really. Do you have it with you?" asked Isabel.

"Yes," said Sonia. "I've got it here."

Isabel re-read the advert. And then she looked up.

"Yes, that's what I saw. You say 'terminal'. Are you really able to solve a major problem like mine and make it permanent?"

"Well, certainly permanent," said Sonia, "although we prefer the word 'terminal'."

"Terminal, as in, er, terminal? Finished? Terminated for ever?"

"You could say that," replied Sonia. "We find that the most serious and most distressing conflicts are usually the result of a single individual, often someone a little disturbed. What usually happens is that when we remove that person from the situation, the conflict is automatically resolved."

"That would be wonderful," said Isabel, her eyes lighting up with delight. "If only you could remove that one person who is causing so much unhappiness, you would find so many people who would be grateful."

"Well, that's exactly what we specialise in doing."

"Would I have to be involved?"

"Not at all. As soon as we have the contract and your deposit, you can leave everything to us. After everything is over and the person you want removed is finally eliminated from your life, then we take the second half of the payment. You are completely separate from the whole business."

"How long does it all take?"

"Depends, really. It's the research which takes the time. We have to carefully check the background of the person we are intending to delete. One reason for that is to avoid the possibility that the client may actually be the one who is responsible for the bad situation and not the other way around. If that happens then we return the deposit and call the job off."

"That's fair," agreed Isabel. "What is it all going to cost?"

"Again, our fees are variable," said Sonia. "We like to see ourselves as a necessary social service. Something that should be on the National Health Service, but isn't. So we place our fees accordingly, related to what the client can afford. And, Isabel, if that is your real name, you don't exactly look as if you are on social security."

"Money is not a real problem," said Isabel, "and yes, my name is not Isabel. Money would be even less of a problem if the person I am thinking of were to go on to a better place, as it were."

"Well, depending on the facts of the case, we can give you a very rough estimate. In your case, we are looking at something like twenty thousand."

"Pounds?"

"Yes, twenty thousand pounds. Sterling."

"More than I expected," said Isabel.

"Well that's our price. If it's not worth it to you, then we can end this conversation right here and now. But just how much do the lawyers cost? How much will you be spending in the future and getting nothing for it? It sounds a lot of money but we do a thorough permanent job. You will be happier afterwards. But it's up to you. Remember, we will be taking a lot of risks."

"How do you want paying?"

"Ten thousand will set the wheels in motion. Cash, of course. Look, take a week or so to think about it. Here's my card."

"'Sophie Liston, Conflict Deletion'," read out the fragrant Isabel. "How do I contact you?"

"Call that number or email at that address. Then we'll arrange a second meeting."

"Here? Next week?"

"No, different place. Different time and day. No patterns. By the way," said Sonia/Sophie, "do you want to tell me your real name, so we can start researching?"

"OK, then," conceded Isabel. "I am Arabella Bruce-Bubbson. Lady Bruce-Bubbson actually, wife of Sir James Bruce-Bubbson MP and he's a real pig."

"We don't do marital disputes," said Sonia. "I told you that up front. Is he the target?"

"If you knew him as well as I do, you wouldn't be quite so squeamish."

"OK, we'll think about it. Next week?"

"Next week."

"So," said Sonia, when she was back home, "Arabella Bruce-Bubbson is our client. And, guess what, her husband, Sir James, is our target."

"I thought we were not going to do marital?"

"Well, yes. But I told her that we would need to research her case before we could take her on."

"So, let's do some research."

They googled 'James Bruce-Bubbson' and started to find out about the man what had driven his wife to wanting him terminated. The usual biographical details came up—education at a top public school and then Oxford at a rich man's college; a career in an investment bank; a safe conservative seat; public service with a number of worthy public bodies; a knighthood as an MP's long-service medal; a flat in Belgravia and a manorial pad in Sussex; membership of White's and the MCC; hobbies: field sports etc . . . etc . . .

"Couldn't be more typical. Bog-standard Tory MP. What did she call him?" asked Ken.

"She called him a pig. And she said we wouldn't be squeamish about terminating him if we knew him better."

"So, what is it, do you think?" said Ken.

"Given his background and his write up in *Who's Who*, it's either gay bars or S&M."

"Both of which are kinky enough for the Sunday papers, but hardly execution reasons."

"Hardly," agreed Sonia, "and certainly not enough for Lady Arabella to risk her life style, flat in Belgravia, country house and all that."

"So, what could it be? Drugs? Money laundering?"

"Who knows? Let's look further. So far we've only been looking at the recent stuff about him. Let's go back to the older stuff further back in Google."

They combed through the back pages of Google and found nothing exceptional, except that he was once in a spot of bother over a planning application near his country pile.

"If that's all he's done, he's blameless. With this record he could run for Pope."

"Not quite, he's definitely C of E. He's even a Church Commissioner on top of his other good works. But she said he's a pig. She definitely said pig. There must be something. She was definitely looking worried. Like she was at the end of her tether. She said she was at her wits' end," said Sonia.

"Well, unless we want to kiss twenty grand goodbye, we are going to have to turn her down."

"The only way. It could be that she is not being exactly straight herself. Maybe she has a toy boy and she wants her husband out of the way. Maybe she just wants to get her hands on his money."

"Why don't you phone her and ask for a hint?" suggested Ken.

"About all we can do in the circumstances. Wait a minute, I don't have a number. She will have to phone us."

"So that's the end of that then."

But Arabella Bruce-Bubbson did phone. The very next day.

"Hello. Sophie? Any news?"

"We are still looking. Can you give us a hint? Sort of point us in the right direction?"

"When are you next in London? We could meet up."

"Good idea. What about the cafe at the V&A? Thursday? Three thirty pm?" said Sonia.

"I'll be there."

Once again Sonia made the day trip to London, straight after her early morning class, 'Basic Literacy for Graduates.'

As before, Arabella was waiting.

"Are you on?" asked Arabella urgently.

"Hold on," said Sonia. "We don't know what this is all about. Look, cards on table, we have done an Internet search and, frankly, we can't find a thing about your husband, apart from what a wonderful pillar of society he is. If this is just between you and him, then, well, as we said before, we don't do marital. I can see that the lefties and Trots would probably not be too heartbroken if he fell under a bus, but we're not political either. He wasn't screwing his researchers was he? We read about these things in the papers."

"Of course he screwed his researchers. It's part of the job. All MP's screw their researchers unless they are too useless or too gay or too gaga. It's one of the perks. That's why all those girls go straight into politics the moment they graduate, to get screwed by an MP. I should imagine it's a notch on the suspender belt to most of them."

"Didn't you mind?"

"Of course I minded at first until I realised what the game is. We MP's wives have to learn to turn a blind eye and make our own private arrangements. Party conferences are a good place to start when the husbands are all drunk in secret meetings playing politics and there are lots of young boys on the prowl for neglected wives."

"So it's not marital."

"No, I told you. It is more serious than that."

"I am sorry, Arabella. I can call you Arabella?"

Arabella nodded.

"I am sorry, but you are going to have to give us some more. A hint. Point us in the right direction."

"OK," conceded Arabella. "Why don't you start by looking at the Malabar case from June 1992?"

Sonia made notes.

"And here," said Arabella, as she handed over an envelope containing papers, "I've made some photocopies you might be interested in."

"I need a phone number so that we can confirm contracts and so on," said Sonia.

"Look, never say anything on the phone," warned Arabella. "James is always telling me. The police tap everybody's phone all the time. And emails. Apparently it's easy these days with computers and things. That's how they catch terrorists and those dirty old men with pictures of children."

"I thought phone hacking was against the law." said Sonia.

"My dear child," replied Arabella patronisingly. "How little you know. Phone hacking is against the law for you, or for me for that matter, but it's not against the law for the people who really matter. Every single phone call and email is automatically stored and searched through. So be careful, if you are getting into the sort of trade I think you are getting into."

"Right," said Sonia, chastened.

"What's more," added Arabella, "we must be careful where and how we meet. They also search all the film from those TV cameras you see everywhere."

"Do you mean that we are being watched, even now?"

"Almost certainly. I'm the wife of a prominent MP. They're bound to be tracking me."

"But surely they can't track everyone? Millions of cameras, emails, phone calls? How can they do that?"

"They do it with very big computers hidden away. And then they tell you and anyone who asks that we are very strict about privacy and human rights and they make a big fuss about it as if they only do spying in places like Russia, not here. But they have the technology and since they have the technology, they use it. Obvious really. No point in knowing how to do it and then not doing it."

"How do you know all this?" asked Sonia.

"James was on the Commons Security Committee for years. He was sworn to secrecy but one night we had a row and it turned out he knew all about my little private meetings with various useful young men from the local constituency association. It appears he had recordings of phone calls and photographs. There was no email in those days. It seems that as the wife of an important MP, I was a potential security risk, so they had to keep an eye on me. Or so they said. I've always been very careful since."

"Is this part of the reason you came to me?"

"Sort of. Look up 'Malabar' and read the photocopies in there. Look, I must rush, you never know who's watching. If you are still interested, send me a postcard from Bournemouth or somewhere. Just write 'Wish you were here', and no signature and then I'll know you're up for it. Be sure to cover your tracks. Burn letters and any records after reading. Put nothing on your computer—they know how to look at what's on your computer. They put some sort hidden program in it by remote control that you don't know about and it sends messages back to their own big computer tucked away in Wales or somewhere. It tells them what you've been doing while you've been online. Actually, hand written letters are the safest way of passing on information these days. Ironic isn't it? Here's an idea. Join your local art appreciation society so that you always have a good reason for meeting at the National Gallery where there are always crowds of people. I'll join one as well. That's how we can communicate."

Then Arabella swept up her sheepskin overcoat, slapped down a note for the coffee, picked up her Louis Vuitton bag, turned abruptly on her heels and disappeared, leaving Sonia with a spinning head at the masterclass in practical spymongering which she had just been privileged to attend. Was Arabella some sort of double agent, setting her up, for some reason, Sonia pondered. Much to talk about back at HQ in Faldwell Upton.

She read the enclosures from the envelope on the train back home. They were all about some case she couldn't fully remember when some gangster had been bringing in girls from abroad and getting them fast-tracked through immigration using official contacts. She wondered if the 'contacts' included the hated Sir James. But it was nothing, just hearsay. Was Arabella taunting her, she wondered? What if she wanted out of the clutches of Sir James in favour of one of her toy boys and immediately dismissed the idea. She was wealthy in her own right—her father owned half of Yorkshire. Which was not half bad for a man who had started life as a black marketeer after the Second World War and had finished up in the House of Lords where a good proportion of its membership had received monetary favours from him at one time or another. So Sonia surmised that Lady Arabella could quite easily have divorced the husband she loathed. So why did she plead lack of funds? Twenty grand would have been pocket change for her, the cost of a few decent handbags.

No, it had to be something else. Blackmail, over Arabella's paramours? Possibly, although it would appear that the Bruce-Bubbson's, both man and wife, were members of that aristrocratic class not possessed of a sense of sexual shame. Sonia still did not know the truth from the documents she had been given. As soon as she arrived home, she went straight to her computer and typed 'Malabar case' into Google. But, just before she hit the RETURN key, she suddenly remembered Arabella's warning. No, she thought, googling the Malabar case would have to wait until she was at college and she could safely use a computer in the students' computer laboratory.

SIX

Ken and Sonia began their research on the Malabar case. It proved to be one of those stories which surface from time to time in the British media and which are strung out over a teasing few weeks before they disappear from view. When one of these stories emerges, there is never enough real detail in any single newspaper report for the ordinary reader to form a coherent overall picture of exactly what the reporter is getting at. Those writing the story can only hint very carefully what is really happening when they don't have enough cast-iron verifiable facts to be explicit, even when they are sure of the real truth. That is because there exist all sorts of official proscriptions to make it more or less impossible for the casual reader ever to be properly informed until the full story finally breaks, if it ever does break. Until the story is out in the open and the ruling establishment can no longer keep it under wraps, the severity of the various secrets regulations and the ruinous penalties inflicted on unsuccessful libel defendants mean that the follower of the story has to try to piece the facts together from oblique hints and sly innuendos. Sometimes the hints will take the form of a careful, clever, juxtaposition of speculative articles and seemingly unrelated photographs, suitably placed so that the perceptive reader might get a useful clue about what is really going on. In most cases though, the retributive threats, implied or real, from on high, are sufficient to frighten the investigative journalist into dropping the story until it duly gets forgotten. Very, very, occasionally, though, the story will have a will of its own and the affair can erupt into a full-blown public scandal such as happened to John Profumo and Jeremy Thorpe. The fear of revelations of what goes on in the murky world of politics, particularly where it slops over into the grey areas of business and official secrecy, is the reason why governments are so paranoid about the necessity of keeping the public as ill-informed as possible.

So it was with the Malabar case, officially long since consigned to the history books. As far as Sonia and Ken could make out, it had featured some unspecified, but certainly corrupt, dealings by one Mehmet Malabar who had, as far as they could discern, been on very good terms with a lot of the bigwigs at the top end of the ruling Conservative party. From what they could make out, reading between the lines, Mehmet Malabar was some sort of fixer who could arrange things, usually illegal, for important people, at, of course, an important price. Included in the ancient clippings were well-hidden hints about drugs and 'parties'.

One sentence in a column of the time, caught Sonia's eye—

> ' . . . *Sir James Bruce-Bubbson MP, the leading childrens' charity organiser, was at a party last night given by pharmaceutical magnate Sir . . . .* "

which was notable for being entirely out of context with the rest of the piece. And another sentence—

> ". . *James Bruce-Bubbson has enlisted the support of millionaire Mehmet Malabar in his campaign to stamp out trafficking in children . . .*".

The machinations of Malabar and his famous connections had all the makings, it appeared, to have developed into a serious scandal, had not Malabar done a bunk to his home in Northern Cyprus which effectively put him outside the reach of most of the world's jurisdictions. But not before he had relieved, one way or another, but usually by blackmail, it was subtly hinted in contemporary newspaper reports, a goodly number of the British ruling class of a great deal of their money. There had been calls from some members of the opposition party for a public enquiry into why Malabar had been allowed to escape and had not been arrested in time, but, again, the reporter carefully but legally suggested, the calls never got party backing because some leaders of the opposition party were among Malabar's victims. There were even some dark murmurings that he had been helped in his flight by well-connected senior members of the security community.

"Look at this one," said Sonia, "on the very day that Malabar skipped the country, there was a picture of our boy James in *The Daily Telegraph*. On the same page."

Yes, there it was, a large front-page photograph with a caption 'Sir James Bruce-Bubbson MP Chairman of the Commons Security Committee and his wife Arabella, daughter of Yorkshire businessman, Cavendish Rowbottom, return from their Mediterranean holiday.'

"Why put that picture there?"

"To tell us something they can't write. Must be."

Let's go back to those things she gave you. When they looked at Arabella's documents a second time, things started falling into place. Most of the photocopies Arabella had given Sonia were about child exploitation and drug smuggling. Now things were starting to make sense.

"Look at the key words—'parties', 'pharmaceutical', 'children', 'child trafficking'. What are they trying to tell us?"

"Yes, and the photograph. If anyone could have stopped Malabar absconding it must be the Chairman of the Commons Security Committee."

"It's nice to know our country is safe in their hands."

"Let's google Cavendish Rowbottom."

There was not much online about the famous self-made multi-millionaire, except that his own career was, somehow, in curious synchronicity with that of the disgraced Mr. Malabar.

"Look, he sold a majority of his holding in Rowbottom Metals just four months after Malabar left. And, so the *Financial Times* has it, for a good deal less than it was worth. He was made a lord in the next honours list"

"That's interesting. After he had got into the Lords, The FT wrote '. . the new Lord Rowbottom is the father of Arabella Bruce-Bubbson, the wife of Sir James Bruce-Bubbson MP, who did much to calm last year's furore over the Malabar affair . . . .'

"So it appears that Rowbottom took a haircut, presumably to pay Malabar for what, blackmail?. And got a peerage for his efforts."

"Christ, what a mess it must have been!" said Ken, "But why should Arabella want Jimbo rubbed out now?"

"She did say she had been in dispute for at least five years. And this must be it, apart from the motive."

"Look at the clues—'parties' equals orgies, right? And 'pharmaceutical' well, that's probably drugs. And then all this emphasis on children? Prostitution?"

"Could be," agreed Sonia.

"So, her father loses an awful lot of money and her husband may, I only say 'may', be involved with child sex and orgies or something and there are a lot of drugs around."

"Meanwhile Malabar is hiding out in Cyprus where no-one can reach him."

"So far. But if they could ever get jurisdiction in Cyprus, say after a resolution of the partition which they're always talking about, then Malabar might find himself in a court over here and have something interesting to tell the world."

"And Jim will go down?"

"So, the fragrant Arabella, whose daddy has paid heavily for Jim's indiscretions already, will be both financially ruined and disgraced as well."

"What's the betting that she's done that calculation and she's been looking around for a hitman for a while?"

"Makes sense. If hubby is disgraced and a lot of people come looking for restitution, or revenge, there's not going to be a lot left for her."

"More than that. She could even be some sort of accessory. Such as employing illegal servants, underage maybe, something like that."

"So it makes sense to eliminate him now before Malabar can appear in court. She needs an unfortunate accident. She can then play the grieving widow like Mandy Scregg and quietly take her fortune and go and live somewhere nice. They say the Cayman Islands makes a very nice bolt hole. Maybe if Malabar is arrested they won't be able to keep a lid on things this time."

"Oh dear," said Sonia," look what I've found. In this gossip column.

> '. . . *Bruce-Bubbson country house up for sale . .'*
> dated last year."

"I wonder if Malabar is still putting the squeeze on our titled couple?"

"Could be. Or his 'pharmaceutical' habits have become too expensive."

"Either way, we have a problem. Do we take the job or not? Why, is not our business, really, is it?"

"True", agreed Sonia, "they both sound pretty unsavoury. All that posh front and a shitty story in the background."

"As my mother used to say, 'fur coat and no knickers'."

"I think 'no knickers' is how Arabella Bruce-Bubbson spends most of her life."

"Why don't we take the job? We have to start somewhere. Jimbo is obviously just as bad as Scregg. We have our own ethical position to maintain. We are, after all, only knight crusaders dedicated to ridding the world of its undesirables. And James Bruce-Bubbson is certainly one of those. We would be neglecting our duty if we chickened out of this one," explained Ken.

"Quite," Sonia confirmed. "Ours is indeed a noble, saintly calling."

"The problem we have now is getting paid. First thing is to confirm with her that the job is on. Send her the postcard. Then fix up a meeting at the National Gallery where she makes the first payment."

"Suppose she doesn't pay up the second half of the cash?" asked Sonia.

"Yes, I've thought about that. So here's what we do. Tell her that we are expecting the second ten grand exactly one week after the job. Then, just before you get up to go, or she gets up to go, pull out your mobile phone and very obviously switch it off. Then she will think we've been recording everything. She'll get the message. Send her that postcard and fix up another meeting."

Sonia got a picture postcard of a rural scene in the Lake District which she had left over from her last holiday, scrawled on it 'Wish you were here' with a box number to reply to and addressed it to 'Lady A. Bruce-Bubbson' at her Belgravia address. Then the pair drove thirty miles to the nearest city and posted it. Two days later she got a letter with an SW1 postmark. Inside was a single sheet on which was typed 'Ven245Tue'.

"Well," said Sonia, "it looks like we are on. She wants to see me next Tuesday at the National Gallery Venetian Room, 2.45 pm."

"I'll believe it's on it when we are counting the money."

"Have you given any thought to how we are actually going, er, to push him down the greasy stairs?"

"Some," said Ken. "I have a bit of an idea. Try to ask her where he is going to be this month. Whether he has any plans to travel. Make it sound casual. Oh, and don't forget the mobile phone trick."

"No, course not. I'll phone you straight after I've seen her."

"Yes, and I'll cover your Tuesday classes. No point in worrying Braithwaite with a staff absence he doesn't need to know about."

"Absolutely. He wouldn't care. He's demob happy anyway."

Sonia made her way to the Venetian Room at the National Gallery and sat down beside Arabella who was already waiting. Neither woman looked at the other.

"Hello Sophie," said Arabella.

"Hello Arabella. We're on. It's twenty grand. Ten today. Ten more one week after delivery."

"Which will be when?"

"About a month. Is that OK?"

"Sounds fine."

"Have you got the money?"

"I don't carry that much around with me."

"But you can get it. Today?"

"I need an hour. Impressionist Room. Four pm?"

"Four o'clock.", Sophie/Sonia confirmed, "and I need a little information to help with the job."

"What's that?"

"Will Sir James be doing any travelling in the next month?"

"I think he's going on some trade mission jaunt to the States. An excuse to take his researcher, I shouldn't wonder."

"Can you get me the date?"

"Is that when it will happen?" asked Arabella.

"Maybe. You really don't want to know," said Sophie/Sonia. "It'll be in the papers when it's been done. Read about it and pay us. Then you'll be free."

"Right. Four o'clock."

An hour later Sonia and Arabella met in the Impressionist Room of the National Gallery. Arabella sat close beside Sonia and swiftly placed a package between them.

"When the job has been completed to your satisfaction, we will meet just the one more time and you will pay me the other ten."

"How do you know I won't cheat you and not pay you?" asked Arabella.

"Two reasons," said Sonia. "One, you know now what kind of business we are in."

"And two?" inquired Arabella.

"Two," replied Sonia. "I think you have more to lose than we do."

As she said this, she pulled out her mobile phone and made a very ostentatious gesture of switching it off.

"I don't want any more blackmail. I've had enough of that."

"Don't worry. We are conflict deletion specialists, not blackmailers. It's in our interest to do a job quickly and then go for complete closure."

"So why record me?" said Arabella.

"Just a little insurance. No more."

With that Sonia got up, put the envelope in her bag and walked away to the tube and back to Faldwell Upton.

On the train she went to the toilet to count the money. It was all there.

A few days later, Sonia and Ken went to their post office box and found a letter addressed to 'Sophie'. In it was a clipping from the previous day's Financial Times about a forthcoming parliamentary visit to the United States Congress by a delegation of MP's led by Sir James Bruce-Bubbson.

"Nothing else?" asked Ken.

"No, nothing else. It looks like she means it."

"So, now we must deliver. How are you going to do it?"

"I think we need a trip to Heathrow Airport," said Ken.

At that little piece of Hell which is called London's Heathrow Airport, Ken started to make his plans. He carefully calculated distances, parking, how much time would be spent getting from a VIP car to the lounge until he was satisfied that all his calculations were correct. Now it was just a matter of waiting for the big day. Ken was nervous, not because he was about to break one of organised religion's stricter commandments but that he would botch the job and they would not get paid. Another brief letter from Arabella had determined the flight number and, Ken estimated, the approximate time when the delegation would arrive at Heathrow.

Ken was wearing a thick coat, a scarf and a baseball cap to which he had added a pair of thick spectacles. His disguise looked natural enough for a CCTV camera, he reckoned. He travelled to Heathrow by underground and went to the main concourse where he knew the MP's would be arriving before going to the VIP lounge two floors up. He carefully chose a spot where he would look inconspicuous and where he could observe the comings and goings of the ground floor car park. When the MP's car drove up and its occupants, two men and two women, had been decanted, Ken took the lift up the departures lounge where, he knew, those four would soon be heading. He then stationed himself at the end of the catwalk with his back to the departures hall and awaited the arrival of the four travellers. As they exited from the doors of the lift, Ken walked forward and shouted out, as if in surprise,

"It's Sir James, isn't it?"

"Actually, yes, it is."

"Sir James! I really must thank you! You're my MP! You remember. You did that favour for me with the social security."

"I'm sorry. I'm in rather a hurry."

"No, Sir James, I really owe you. You did me a really good turn. I'm really grateful."

"Please, why don't you call my office. I must get on."

"But, Sir James, I haven't thanked you. My missus, she's . . ."

"Why don't you three go on?"

Sir James motioned to his travelling companions, making his big mistake.

"Constituency business. I'll only be a moment."

The other three passengers continued into the departures hall until Sir James and Ken were, for only a moment, together alone on the high walkway, some fifty feet above the concrete of the Heathrow car park. Ken suddenly bent down and with one deft heave, tipped the surprised Sir James over the rail to the ground below. Ken then strolled nonchalantly back into the lift shaft and, arriving at the ground floor, divested himself of spectacles, baseball cap and scarf in a rubbish bin in the Gents before getting on the tube back to central London and the main line train back to Faldwell Upton.

"Job done," he announced to Sonia.

"Well done, I'm so proud of you. I've been watching it on telly."

"Now, let's get paid."

Arabella's note arrived two days later after news of the mysterious accidental death of her husband had faded from the front page.

> 'Dear Sophie,' it read, 'Thank you so much for your kind words. It is very kind of you to remember me at this difficult time. The funeral service is to be Monday next at St Joseph's. I know you will want to pay your last respects. A. B-B.'

St Joseph's was quite full. Many of the faces were well-known and Sonia recognised some of them. She had dressed for the occasion and even passed for one of the many House of Commons researchers who had also shown up. After the service and cremation Arabella took her on one side.

"Here," she said. "My husband would have wanted you to have this," and pressed a small parcel into Sonia's hands.

"That was very kind of him," replied Sonia. "What are you going to do now?"

"Well," said Arabella. "My poor papa's getting on a bit, you know. I'll probably be spending a bit of time looking after him. We may well go abroad. He needs to be somewhere warm."

"That's a good plan," agreed Sonia. "They say the Cayman Islands are very nice. And quiet, of course."

"Yes," said Arabella. "After all I have been through, it may well be the Cayman Islands."

"Do you think you'll ever get married again?"

"No, I don't think that's a very good idea. Do you?"

SEVEN

With the first contract successfully completed to everyone's satisfaction, Conflict Deletion Services Ltd. could now be considered a going concern. Sonia and Ken stepped up the advertising to take in a few specialist small publications in the business world, figuring, not unreasonably, that while they might attract the occasional disgruntled MP's wife by national general advertising, it is among the community of small businesses that the richest seam of megalomaniacs, bullies, thieves and sociopaths will be found.

The directors of CDS Ltd. were both agreed.

"We can't expect a Bruce-Bubbson every week," said Ken.

"If only."

"So we are going to have to aim lower. Move down-market to a wider clientele."

"Indeed, it's what a lot of companies do when they want to make more money. Move out of a niche market serving just the AB1's and go for a more mass appeal," said Sonia.

"Where did you get that?" asked Ken, seriously impressed.

"Open University course in business management," replied Sonia.

"Well, keep it up, it could be useful."

"So that translates as more jobs at a lower rate."

"Not too low, of course. We are offering an elite service."

"It's a good idea, but aren't we forgetting the cardinal rule of crime?"

"What's that?" asked Ken.

"Do it once, do it big, do it fast, do it alone," answered Sonia.

"Good point. Maybe if we just did small turnover, say one job a month. Minimum fee, five thousand?"

"Let's try that."

They also put a bit more thought into their advertising, which now included some nice glossy brochures with the face of a happy mother and child on the front. And some sunbeams.

"Don't you think it looks like advertising for a hospice or a cancer charity?"

"Yes, it does," said Sonia. "That's the point, image association."

"Oh that's all too clever for a technical drawing teacher like me."

But they did do some re-phrasing of their adverts online and in those small specialist publications they favoured, including *White Van Man, Pit Bull Terrier Breeder* and *Abattoir Weekly*. Out went words like 'careful' and 'caring' and more explicit phrases were brought in. Phrases like 'all our services are executed to your specification' and 'permanent, terminal problem removal at a competitive cost' were inserted instead.

As a result of these small modifications to the business plan, the replies to the adverts were from fewer lost souls in search of a shoulder to cry on and more from genuine seekers after a final problem solution and removal.

"At this rate, we could do one a week." said Ken.

"Let's see how it goes. It looks as if it is going to pay better than the classroom," Sonia reminded him.

They went through the replies from the first week's adverts until they decided on Job Number 2, from a Mr Singh in Birmingham.

> 'Can you really get rid of problems with people as quickly and easily as you say? I am owning a fish and chip shop and I am being always terrorised by a man who does very bad car clamping. My clients need to park outside my premises for 15-20 mins. When they do, he comes and clamps them. It has happened four times this month. So far. Every time he clamps them he demands £400 or £500 before he is letting them have their car back. My customers are leaving me. I can see him and his gang waiting for someone to stop outside my shop. He drives around the town every night looking for cars to clamp. A lot of other businesses are losing money as well as me and we are happy to be paying good money to get this so-and-so off our backs. We have been going to the police but they say they can do nothing because he is not breaking laws. They tell us that if we do anything against him, they will arrest us for breech of the piece. He is also a local counsiler. Please email back.'

The next day, Ken emailed Mr Singh.

> 'Dear Mr Singh. We can certainly help with your problem. Our business is to solve problems of this sort when the normal negotiation process has broken down. Our service is completely

confidential and leads to a permanent solution to our client's problem. We do not use conventional discussion or counselling techniques. Instead we seek a total removal of the disputant from the client situation, so that our client can look forward to a peaceful and worry-free future.

Let us meet at New Street Station tomorrow at 4.00 pm, if that is convenient to you. Please bring as much information about your adversary as you can e.g. name, address, photo if poss. I will be in Costa Coffee, reading *The Daily Telegraph* and wearing a dark blue jacket.'

Ken and Sonia were now using the college email exclusively, remembering how easily email traffic can be traced and monitored. They reckoned that the college would be a reasonable cover for their new business, given that what they were doing was actually against the law. Although, of course, they preferred to see themselves as righting a few wrongs which the official legal code was happy to ignore. Mr Singh's case certainly sounded like one of those.

Ken got to New Street Station early and waited. Singh was ten minutes late and Ken was just about to get up and go when a breathless Sikh man came in.

"Sorry I'm late," he said. "I had to pick up my children from school."

Ken came straight to the point.

"Tell me everything. Who is bothering you, how he does it, what it's costing you? The lot."

Singh began his story about how some local gangster called Manny Boyden was terrorising the local shop keepers by clamping cars after dark when the only shops open are convenience stores, off-licences, chip shops, takeaways—a lot of them run by small, very hard-working, Asian businessmen. What Boyden did, according to Singh, was to cruise the streets looking for someone who had stopped on a yellow line outside a shop, thinking it would be safe to stop there for a minute or two. Then Boyden's men would clamp the car and call for a tow truck. If the car owner could catch them before the car was towed away, the owner would get off with just paying a couple of hundred pounds. If the owner was inside the shop for more than five minutes, he was likely to find his car had been towed away and he would need to retrieve it from a private pound at a cost of up to five hundred pounds.

"What have you done about it so far?" asked Ken.

"Well, Mr.?"

"Greenwood," said Ken Grassmann. "Call me Kelvin Greenwood."

"Well, Mr Kelvin, we formed a group of us. Mostly businessmen with small shops. First we went to the police."

"What did they do?"

"It was all very puzzling, Mr Kelvin. The police said they could do nothing because what this bad man is doing is within the law."

"What?"

"Yes, Mr Boyden is being legal. We spoke to the senior officer, an inspector."

"Not called Fordham, was he?"

"No, I don't think so, Mr Kelvin. Why do you ask?"

"Oh, nothing. Go on."

"Well, the inspector, he told us that he must keep the streets empty so all the traffic will flow free without problem. Mr. Kelvin, there is no traffic in the evening. Apart from our shops, the town is as dead as the doornail. It all started when they painted yellow lines on every road."

"So the police were not very helpful?"

"Not only that, Mr Kelvin, they warned us ourselves. The inspector said that he would record our meeting but we must not try to settle the dispute with Mr Boyden on our own. He said that we would be taking the law into our own hands and he would never tolerate it. He told us that he would be keeping an eye on us and if there was any trouble with Mr Boyden, he would know who had caused it. Mr. Kelvin, this surprised us very much. When we were in school in India, we were always taught that the English policemen are the best in the world, the most honest, the very best at catching evil men and keeping law and order. It has been a great disappointment to us all."

"Did you do anything else?" asked Ken/Kelvin.

"Yes, we did," continued Mr Singh. "We then went to see Mr. Clifton Parker, who is our member of parliament."

"What did he say?"

"He said he would write to the chief constable and find out what was happening."

"Did he?"

"Yes. He did. He also said that we should speak to our local council as he was not in a position to do anything about it. He said that roads were the responsibility of the council."

"What did they say?"

"Oh, Mr Kelvin, they were quite useless. They said that the chief constable had made a policy of 'zero tolerance' for road parking and his yellow line scheme had been very successful. They said that Mr Boyden was a legal businessman who was assisting the council in helping the police to keep the streets safe for the good of the whole community. You know, Mr Kelvin, I wonder if maybe, the council are not being completely honest. Is it good for them that every business like mine to have to close because of this one bad man?"

"Do you think the council is getting money from Boyden?"

"That I don't know, Mr Kelvin, but if this problem is not solved soon, we will have to shut down and go back to India. I do not want to do that, Mr Kelvin. My children were born here. You are our last hope. As soon as I read your advertisement in *Small Shopkeeper*, I thought you are the sort of service that we need."

"Do you have any details? What happens when a car is picked up by Boyden?"

"His place is a compound on the industrial estate. The cars go there and the owners have to take a taxi or a bus to get there."

"What happens to the cars if they are not collected."

"They say he sells them for scrap. They say that sometimes Councillor Jones buys them."

"Councillor Jones?"

So, that was the racket. All neatly tied up—chief constable, local police, councillors, MP. As long as they are all in it, the poor victims have nowhere to turn.

"Well, Mr Singh," explained Ken. "I think I can remove Boyden from your life. It will be expensive and once he is gone, they will find someone else to do it. But we can give them a warning. They may not be quite so keen to do it to you a second time. Can you and your friends afford twenty thousand?"

"For something as important as this, yes, we can, Mr Kelvin."

"Don't tell a soul what you are doing. Don't phone me and only use this email. We will meet again in two weeks time. I will need half the money up front and a half after you have seen the last of Mr Boyden."

"Thank you so much, Mr Kelvin. You are an honest man, I know. I feel I can trust you."

Ken and Sonia discussed the plan.

"Trip to Birmingham. We'll need the car for a quick getaway."

False plates were a precaution they had foreseen. But since they were intending to do the job in the early morning, it seemed a wise thing to change them. In case they were spotted.

They drove to the West Midlands in the early hours. Sonia/Sophie, as agreed, was dropped off at Singh's shop which Singh opened for her. He silently and swiftly passed over half of the money for the job.

"When?" Singh asked.

"Now."

"Good."

They had calculated that Boyden would be the first to arrive at his compound. His workers worked evenings doing their clamping, so he did not expect them to be there. Ken was waiting for him like an impatient car owner. Boyden was a large, ugly man with a vast belly, a bald head, an earring, a couple of piercings and copious tattoos carrying messages both aggressive and sentimental—'MUM', 'HATE' etc.

"You've got my car." said Ken.

"Shouldn't park where you shouldn't then. That's what happens when you break the law."

"All right. Let's get it over with. How much?"

"Which is it?"

Ken looked at the confiscated cars and chose one at the far side away from the entrance and not visible from the road.

"That one. The red Fiesta."

"Five hundred."

"Five fucking hundred!" said Ken, in mock horror.

"Take it or leave it. Don't collect it in three days, I'll sell it."

"Is that legal?"

"If you want to argue, you can go and ask the council."

"It's worth more than five hundred. I've no choice."

"Don't take credit cards. Credit cards extra twenty quid. For the administration. Cash."

"Ken reached into his wallet and handed over five hundred in cash. Boyden stuck it in his pocket and went to his wall where there were lots of sets of keys. He picked up one set and walked over to the red Fiesta. It was when Boyden bent down to unlock the wheel clamp that Ken hit him as hard as he could with the iron bar which Ken had carefully hidden down the back of his shirt. Boyden's skull shattered with a satisfying crack and he fell down as dead as Scregg and Bruce-Bubbson.

Ken then moved quickly. The first thing he did was to lock the gate to the compound so that anyone arriving would think it was still closed. Then he retrieved his money before carefully dragging Boyden's body over to the large commercial jack where cars are lifted up so that their undersides can be worked on. He switched on the electricity and sent the jack to its highest. Then he placed Boyden's inert body beneath it and switched the electricity off again. The jack came crashing down on the dead body of the late Mr Boyden, removing all evidence of a skull cracked by malice aforethought. Ken then calmly walked back to his car, being careful to lock up the compound as he left. Sonia was waiting for him around the corner in their car with its false number plates.

They stopped three miles down the road in a wooded lay-by where Ken changed his clothes completely, dumping the disguise, which bore, no doubt, traces of Boyden's DNA, in a roadside bin. They then threw the murder weapon into a river so that all traces of the dead man's brain tissue would be washed away. After that, they went back to tell Singh the good news and collect the other half of their well-earned reward. Which Singh was only too happy to give them.

"You are a very wonderful man, Mr Kelvin. If I ever need another favour like this, I will certainly call you again. I will tell all my friends."

"No please don't do that, Mr Singh. Let this just be our secret, shall we? Goodbye."

The first editions of the local paper were coming out. They bought one for its glorious headline—'LOCAL SCRAP DEALER DIES IN FREAK ACCIDENT'.

What it is to be so useful to one's fellow man.

On the way back from the West Midlands, Ken and Sonia stopped for breakfast at a hotel which also had a cybercafé where they could log into the emails. They were careful only to use an American email address, which would be much more difficult for the British authorities to get access to, should the worst come to the worst. Half a dozen messages were waiting.

"What a lot of unhappy people there are," reflected Sonia.

"And how they can't get any sort of justice. Coming to us must be the last resort."

"The more I hear their stories, the more I am convinced that what we are doing is the right thing."

Among the messages was a regular. They had ignored the man several times because they could not quite understand what he was on about. He was, he said, long pensioned off and retired and he was in some sort of dispute with his local county council. But he did not write well and it was not at all clear what he really wanted.

"Maybe we should take him a bit more seriously. He's obviously desperate." Ken said.

"OK, let's look at his case next."

They went back over his emails and tried to piece together the story of Malcolm Hobbson, widower and retired pensioner who was living in a large village near the south coast. As far as the two could make out, Mr Hobbson was angry that he had been cheated out of his field by a firm of property developers who had bought his field from him as agricultural land and then it had suddenly become worth a hundred times more after it had been redesignated for building development. This is a common trick of planning departments and there could be no doubt that Mr Hobbson had a case. In fact, there were probably thousands of people up and down the land who had been cheated in the same way. The main problem was where to fix the main part of the blame. Was it the council planners? Or the developer? Or the local councillors? Or all of them?

Ken and Sonia also had other, more immediate, practical problems. One of the most pressing of these was what to do with all that cash they were starting to pile up.

"Nobody uses cash anymore. It's a bit out of date, these days. How do we dry-clean it? asked Sonia.

"'Launder', my darling, not 'dry-clean'. The correct technical term for hiding hot money is 'launder'."

"OK, then, clever clogs, how do we 'launder' all that cash."

A major problem. They now had nearly forty thousand in cash from two jobs. For college lecturers, that was something like all the money in the world. It was certainly more than either of them had ever seen in one place at one time in their entire lives. At the present moment it was nestling in a shoe box in the loft. But if their business was going to go from strength to strength, as it showed every promise of doing, then deciding on a safe haven for their honest earnings would soon become an urgent priority. They considered possibilities.

"We could put it in a number of different accounts, say a thousand at a time. Go round the banks."

"A lot of work. We would need forty different accounts already."

"We could use some for everyday living and gradually build up our salaries as savings."

"But that would be slow. If we are getting tens of thousands in, we couldn't hide it that quickly."

"Foreign bank accounts?"

"Possible. But we'd have to show our passports."

"Aren't there all sorts of foreign banks in London? Indian? Lebanese? There can't be too much checking there. All those dodgy eastern businessmen. Don't tell me that our government checks up on them."

They solved the problem of where to put the money by a piecemeal strategy until they could find some better way. They opened a number of bank accounts around Faldwell Upton and the county town a few miles away. They kept some back to feed into the domestic accounts and they also bought gold sovereigns, a few at a time, for cash at a number of London coin dealers. They were tempted to splash out on a new car but resisted the temptation as being likely to draw attention to themselves. But, they reckoned, they might put a deposit down on a house with a suitably large mortgage.

They reflected that money laundering was quite a problem in today's wired-up global world. Imagine they thought, the headaches of surplus money if they were ever to graduate to the first division of serious criminals.

"Well," Ken reflected, "too much is certainly an easier problem than too little."

"Let's look at poor Mr Hobbson.", said Sonia.

"Yes, indeed, he could be another winner."

They made the trip to the south coast from Faldwell Upton and booked into a modest three star hotel. They had toyed with the idea of staying in the £500 a night Presidential Suite in the six-star Hotel Grande which they could now well afford, but they soon rejected the idea for two very obvious reasons. They would, without necessarily consciously realising it, look out of place in the Presidential Suite. However hard they tried to disguise the fact that they were low paid college lecturers, that finely-honed English skill for instantly placing a stranger at their exact position on the class ladder would guarantee that staying there, outside their natural ambience, would be a sure way to attract attention. The second reason was that of natural coincidence. It is a well-documented fact that whenever you are in a new, strange place, you will always meet someone who knows you. So Ken and Sonia's sojourn by the sea was, to all the world, not a business meeting with the hapless Malcolm Hobbson, but a break from the arduous duties of college lecturing.

They drove out to see their next client at a pub in the small town or rather, large village, where he lived.

"Not your local," Ken had advised him. "Somewhere you are not known. If anyone asks who we are, we are your niece and her husband visiting from London."

They sat in a quiet corner of *'The Frog and Bucket'* and ate Cornish pasties and chips, washed down with pints of Shipman's Old Vindictive Ale.

"Don't like this pub, "said Malcolm Hobbson. "I'd rather be in my own local. I usually go to *The Doctor Crippen.* Just down the road. Goes back to the middle ages. More character."

"This is business," reminded Ken. "We're not here for a pub crawl. Tell me about your problems."

"Well, it's a long story," began Hobbson, settling back. "I reckon I've been cheated."

"How's that?"

Malcolm Hobbson began his story.

"Well, I used to own this field behind my house. About an acre and 'alf. No, three quarters. Nearer two acre. It were mine and my brother's but then he died and he had no children, so I got it all."

"When was that, Malcolm?"

"Oh, about four year ago, he died."

"Tell us about the land. Where was it?"

"Well, that's it, you see. It were not far from the centre of Blackbird Neston. It were right in the centre before they started building houses round it. My dad, he's been gone forty year now, he allus said it would be worth something someday. He got it from his father hundred year ago when the place were just a few cottages. Not like it is now."

Ken and Sonia could guess what Blackbird Neston would be like now, if it was anything like the rest of southern England where all the old medieval villages had become expensive dormitories for the Chelsea Tractor set.

"So, did you try to sell it?" asked Sonia.

"I did. I went to Mr Wetherington, in the High Street. He sells land. Biggest estate agent in the county. Well, he comes and looks at it and says that it's not worth very much but I would probably get a few thousand as grazing land."

"So why didn't you sell it through him?"

"Well, it'd been grazing land in the past but they been building houses all around it for years. Started building up the village about thirty year ago. By now, my little two acres is completely surrounded. No way anyone could graze any cattle on there. No way in or out. Just a path across it and a gate into the road. But you can't drive the animals down the road because it's full of cars these days."

"What did you do next?"

"I asked Mr Wetherington why we couldn't sell the land for houses. Makes sense. Houses all around. Land can't be used for anything else."

"What did Wetheringham say?"

"Wetherington. What he said was that the land would need something called rescheduling to be converted from agricultural land to housing. But if we could get that, the value would go up quite a lot. From ten thousand to a lot more."

"Did you go to see the planning department?"

"I did. I made an appointment to see Mr Tranley, who is the Chief Planning Officer. He told me that it was up to the council to give permission for rescheduling but I could make an application. Said I would need a solicitor. So I went down to the solicitors and told him I wanted to make a rescheduling of my land."

"What did he do?"

"He charged me an arm and a leg and got Wetherington to do a valuation."

"What was the value he came up with?"

"Wetherington gave a valuation of ten thousand as agricultural land and over a million if they sold it for houses."

"And then?"

"I thought things would be OK but then I got a letter from Tranley saying that permission had been refused."

"Did they give a reason?"

"They said something about greenbelt. I couldn't understand it."

"Did you appeal the decision?"

"Well, I asked Mr. Wetherington and he said that we could appeal but in his experience, no-one ever won an appeal for rescheduling. And it would be very expensive. So we did nothing."

"So you've still got your land?"

"No, about six weeks after I spoke to Mr. Tranley, I got an offer on it. Right out of the blue."

"What sort of offer?"

"Well, it was from some fancy lawyer in Bristol. They said they were willing to buy up land which had been refused planning permission for redevelopment at more than the going rate. They offered me hundred thousand for it."

"Did you ask anybody what you should do?"

"Of course. I went straight round to Mr Wetherington and he said I should take the offer because we couldn't get any further with the application."

"Did your own solicitor advise you to sell as well?"

"He did that. So, I took his advice."

"Why did you come to us then?"

"Well, about six months after I had sold it, I suddenly saw that they had put twelve of them, 'executive dwellings' on it. I went to Wetherington and he said that some builder from Bristol had made an application which had been approved. I reckon I was swindled, Mr Greenwood, I was swindled."

"Sounds like it." agreed Ken. "Who do you think was in on it?"

"Dunno, it could be any of them. Tranley, the council, could be any of them."

"What about Wetherington? Could he be in on it?"

"Maybe, but I don't think so. I been dealing with him for forty year. And his father before him. He's always been honest with me."

"So why did you come to us?"

"Well, I thought you might be able to do something. What was it, 'conflict deletion'?"

"Well, I have to tell you, Mr. Hobbson, I don't think we can get your money back for you. They have stitched you up good and proper. Your best bet would be to try to get some sort of investigation. Maybe go to the police or you could sue them."

"No, I want justice. Money's not important. I want someone to pay."

"Well, Mr. Hobbson, if it's revenge, then that really is something we can help with. We do offer a service which will provide a little satisfaction. It's not completely legal, if you get my drift, but we are able to terminate a bad situation in what we like to think of as a just manner."

"They've cheated me! I don't mind if I swing for that Tranley."

"No need for that, Mr. Hobbson, we can eliminate him from your life without anything coming back on to you. After all, you don't want to be doing time at your stage of life now, do you?"

"Permanent, you say? Tranley? How much will it cost me?"

"As much as it is worth to you, Mr. Hobbson. We'll talk about it at our next meeting."

"When?"

"Tomorrow. Different pub. Twelve o'clock."

"What about *The Pig and Dustbin*, on the other side of the village?"

"Until twelve tomorrow then."

Ken and Sonia went back to their hotel to make plans.

"It's a neat little conspiracy," declared Sonia.

"Very smooth," Ken agreed. "Wetherington finds the victim with land to sell and the Council Planning Committee turn it down on Tranley's orders. Then they have a connection who buys the land cheap and sells it on to a developer for the market price after Tranley and Wetherington have fixed the planning permission. They're all in on it—Wetherington, Tranley, planning department, council, solicitors, police, the lot. They've taken Hobbson for about nine hundred thousand and he doesn't realise what has happened. Not properly, anyway."

"Bog standard planning con. Goes on whenever and wherever there's a bent council, dodgy lawyers and a planning officer on the take."

"So just about everywhere then?"

"Ain't that the truth? Who was it said that corruption and local government go together like horse and carriage?"

"So who do we rub out? There's a big cast list."

"Wetherington or Tranley. Has to be one of those two. Probably Tranley. Hobbson likes Wetherington. Thinks he's honest. If we eliminate Wetherington, Hobbson might think we'd got the wrong man. Then he might start talking."

"But no-one will miss a chief planning officer and Hobbson obviously hates him."

"Looks like Tranley's our man. What about the price?"

"I'm thinking five for this. Ten is too much, anything less is too little. Old Hobbson probably has five grand in a sock under the bed."

"So, let's research Tranley."

First they did a computer search on the district council's planning history. Some interesting facts showed up-particularly a sequence of prosecutions of planning officers over the years. Indeed, the impression given was that junior planning officers were taking it in turns to spend a few months at the county jail. But never Tranley himself. He was getting away with it time after time. There was even a four-year-old clipping from the local paper showing Tranley at a party with the mayor on Tranley's boat. The party seemed to be a coming-out party for one of Tranley's lieutenants.

A quick look in the phone book showed Tranley's address. He was the owner of a large hotel on the sea front.

"Tranley's done well for himself," observed Sonia. "Big hotel, big boat, expensive friends. Amazing what you can do on a town hall civil servant's wages."

Next stop was the district council offices where Tranley worked. They asked their way to the Planning Department where they could take a look at their quarry.

"My name is Jim Green and this is my wife Valerie," said Ken to the receptionist. "Can we see a planning officer please? We need some advice about making a planning application."

A moment later they were face-to-face with Tranley. He was a well-dressed furtive-looking man with slicked back hair and a slim moustache. He could have been a used-car salesman. Ken and Sonia asked a few empty questions as if they were real local residents. Their main reason for being there was to take a look at their next target.

Back at their hotel, Ken and Sonia worked up their plan. The next day they met Hobbson again.

"Look," said Ken, "this is the situation."

He then explained to Hobbson the conspiracy which had cheated Hobbson out of the fair price for his land and how Tranley appeared to be the ringleader.

"The so-and-so!" said Hobbson, "What can I do?"

"Well," said Ken, "you can try to sue him, but from our reading of the setup, they'll all close ranks. All of them, police, council, planning officers, all of them. Proving a conspiracy is difficult. And if you make too much trouble or ask too many questions, they will find some way to get back at you. Those people always get away with it."

"What about all those young fellows who went to jail?"

"Yes," replied Ken. "Tranley uses his underlings to take the fall for him. Whenever there are any charges, Tranley gives them a very good character reference in court. They always plead guilty and only get a few months inside. First offence, mitigating circumstances etc. No doubt they get released with a very nice coming-out gift for their inconvenience."

"Why?"

"Well," explained Ken, "it would look strange if there were never any prosecutions in the planning department. Every planning department in the world has at least one member away in jail for fraud. So Tranley and the local cops have to invent some minor fraud every couple of years or so for appearance's sake. The poor fellow who draws the short straw does a few months inside and then gets looked after. Six months for a hundred grand? Some will take it."

"So, what will you do for me?" asked Hobbson.

"Well," replied Ken, "if you pay us five thousand, half now, half later, we will kill Tranley."

"Kill him? Really kill him?"

"Yes, kill him."

"That sounds wonderful!"

Hobbson duly paid the deposit and they made arrangements for the final payoff. The plan was put in motion. Sonia and Ken had decided, this time, to use the classic 'damsel in distress' routine.

Two days later, they were waiting in a quiet road along which, they had found out, was where Tranley often went to meet his girlfriend, the wife of one of his junior officials temporarily working a short term, well-paid contract in the county jail. Tranley was returning from his *rendez-vous* when he passed a parked car with its bonnet raised. A skimpily dressed Sonia was bending over the engine. Ken was behind the hedge with a hammer. Tranley, ever the Sir Galahad, screeched to a halt and reversed back to help.

"It's Valerie, isn't it? You came to my office the other day. Anything I can do to help a pretty lady?" he asked.

"Oh, my knight in shining armour!" said Sonia. "Just when I'd given up hope."

Tranley smiled hard and bent over the open engine.

"It's the igniti . . . ." was as far as he got before the bonnet came crashing down heavily on top of him. A hefty tap with the hammer for good measure and Tranley suddenly found himself Chief Planning Officer in the world to come.

Ken and Sonia moved swiftly to cover their crime. First they laid out the lifeless body of Tranley on his side. Then they drove his car over him so that the end of the rear hydraulic shock absorber was situated directly over his head. Finally they let the air out of the adjacent tyre so that yet more damage was done to Tranley's insensate head as it was crushed by the rear suspension. Then they opened Tranley's car boot and put the car-jack at the side of the car so that it would look as if the victim had been trying to change a tyre. Not a perfect job of covering their crime, but good enough to pass for an accident if the forensic examiner were not too observant.

It was now almost dark, so they were sure Tranley's body would not be discovered until the next day. Only one final task remained and that was to go the lane behind Wetherington's office and dispose of the hammer in one of the dustbins there, after carefully wiping it clean of their own fingerprints.

"Oh dear," said Hobbson, as he handed over rest of the money. "It couldn't have happened to a better man."

Ken and Sonia went back to their modest hotel, ate dinner at an Indian restaurant, slept the sleep of the just and checked out the following morning.

EIGHT

Ken and Sonia got back from their south coast break inspired to return to their altruistic calling with new enthusiasm. They were starting to feel that warm inner satisfaction which only comes from doing a worthwhile job for one's fellow man. Once back in the college computer laboratory, which was starting to become their office, they looked at the emails which had been accumulating over the week they had been away. By now they were getting two or three calls a day. A lot of them were the sort of crank message which they soon came to recognise. A crank or loony has a special way of writing and expressing himself, usually with a lot of capitals and individual grammar. Possible sensible enquiries were more serious and reflective. Nevertheless, there were enough troubled souls out there to provide a steady stream of correspondence.

"All this sadness," said Sonia, "and only us to provide any sort of justice."

"All those people who are being ripped off, bullied, cheated. I could get quite emotional."

"Yes, I've been thinking." said Sonia. "We've done OK so far. We've only been in business for a couple of months and already we are making a steady living. We should be doing a lot more regular work. Not just the rich like Arabella thingy but ordinary people. Isn't that why we chose this vocation in the first place? To help people?"

"That's true." agreed Ken. "Just because someone can't pay thousands, it doesn't mean they don't deserve a decent service. We are working for the good of the community when all's said and done."

"The Arabella's of this world can afford top class termination professionals. But what about Joe Ordinary? We could be his only hope."

"Right," said Ken, "so let's do more, what's that Latin phrase you use, pro something."

"*Pro bono publico*. For the public good," said Sonia.

"Right. Now where do we start? Here's another of those car rental things."

Ken started reading.

> 'Dear sirs, I don't know if you know that car rental companies are stealing people money in all sorts bad ways. I rented car from Birdas Car rentals July. When I took the car back they say I scratch it. they charge me £514 for repair. I told them I hit nothing and they said I must have because they had report from when I'de picked it up and they said it not scratches then. I told them no scratches now but they said yes there are take a look. I don't know how scratches got there. I could hardly see them and I am sure it cost me less than £500 to get repaire. I said i not going to pay but they said it had already been paid from credit card but if I have complain I must write law dipartment at Birdas head office. Ying Chang (Student)'

"The famous 'false damage scam'," said Sonia. "We've heard that before."

"I would guess they're all at it."

"That's the third car rental firm we've had a complaint about."

"Let me see. Birdas, we had two complaints about them. And one each from URent Car Rentals and MetroRentaMota. Times must be tough in the vehicle rental business if they've got to do a sideline in credit card fraud."

"Let's go back."

They trawled through the old emails to find the other scam victims.

"Yes, it's the same every time. The punter picks up a car for rent and hands over his credit card. When he turns the car back in, they, e.g. Birdas Rentals, discover some imaginary scratch and then charge him an arm and a leg for the so-called repair. They already have his card number so it's then down to the customer to get his own back. Which, of course, he can't do because the car rental company has its own mechanics reports and their fancy lawyers. They don't expect any trouble because it is too expensive. Would you spend thousands going to court for five hundred?"

"They could go to the police."

"I can't see the police being interested. Those car rental companies are well-established businesses. Why should the cops go to all the trouble? It's not big enough. They probably think it's half a dozen of one and six of the other. Too much work for them. They know the punter will just go away in the end. The most the cops are going to do is tell the company to be careful who they cheat."

"Which probably explains why the victims are usually temporary visitors like this Ying Chang. Probably a rich student passing through."

"And why all our victims were ripped off at airports. Leaving the country."

"Think the police are in on it?"

"Could be. The odd free car loan for our gallant boys in blue."

"So this one is definitely *pro bono publico*."

"Looks like it. Let's write back to Mr Ying Chang. We'll tell him that we can't get his money back but he will be very happy with the outcome."

"And let's start researching Birdas Car Rentals."

Birdas Car Rentals was owned by a Mr Birdas, actually Oliver Kitchener Birdas, a plutocratic businessman who owned a manorial pile near Henley. The company taxes were filed in Luxembourg and the head office was in Jersey.

"Getting to him is going to be tricky," observed Sonia.

"Yes, but think of the benefits to the human race if we can eliminate him. Definitely worth the risk."

"True, but how?"

They mulled over the question for a couple of weeks. It was something to think about when they were teaching their classes. Classroom boredom is a traditional occupational hazard for the journeyman teacher.

"Car accident?"

"Nah! Real people might get killed."

"Drowning? His yacht in Jersey?"

"Getting close is difficult. Then the getaway. They'll have all the boats and airports watched."

"Pushed off a roof?"

"Possible, but difficult to get him on to a roof."

"Electrocution—wire his desk to the mains, so that when he sits down he makes contact?"

"A lot of work. Anyway, we'd need to get into his house or office."

"I could try to get a job as a cleaner and get in that way."

"Difficult. And remember, we're not getting paid for this one."

After a fortnight of ideas thought up and rejected for some reason or other, usually their impracticality, Ken had a brainwave.

"Look, love," he said to Sonia, "Who's that biology lecturer who fancies you? What's his name? Benkins or Jenkins?"

"You mean Benskin," said Sonia, "I try to stay away from him. Every time I have to talk to him, he tells me what he wants to do to me in the chemistry cupboard. Dirty bugger. He's married to a very nice woman. Why do you ask?"

"Well, it's Benskin who might just know what sort of poison we can use on Birdas of Birdas Rentals. And he will tell you if you move the conversation around and promise him his way with you. You don't have to deliver, of course."

"I don't intend to. He lays a finger on me and I'm off to the union with sexual harassment charges."

"You won't get very far there. After Morgan-Pugh left, Cloughie made Benskin union rep. So you'd need to go directly to Cloughie if you wanted to make a complaint. Then it would be official. And that would certainly draw attention to us."

"So you're asking me to go into the chemistry cupboard with him."

"No, just play him along a bit. Should be easy. What we need is some info. About poisons. If he can give you a lethal sample then all the better. Butter him up. Most women can do that. He must be growing all sorts of dangerous things in that lab of his."

"What do I do, ask him straight out? Like 'where can I get a decent fatal poison, Mr. Benskin?'"

"No, love, you can do it. Be joking like. Say something like—'you must have some interesting things here. Are any of them poisonous? I am safe aren't I? You're not going to feed me some sort of aphrodisiac, are you?' That sort of thing. He won't be able to resist bragging to you. All we need is the name of something."

"Then what?"

"Oh, I'm quite sure Birdas likes a drink at his local golf club or pub. Then I spike his drink, courtesy of Benskin."

Ken and Sonia met at home later.

"I've got it!" Sonia said triumphantly. "It's called dimethoxydi . . . something sulphate. Well, according to Benskin, this stuff kills a full-grown man in about an hour. Apparently it makes a colourless tasteless liquid. Just about perfect for poisoning someone. They use it for killing weeds."

"That sounds like Birdas. And what did you have to do for it?" asked Ken.

"Not too much, don't worry. I chatted him up, sort of softened him up and sort of hinted and then he pushed me towards the chemistry cupboard. You were right, he couldn't help bragging. I told him to turn his back for a moment—well a girl has her modesty, hasn't she? That's when I slipped some of this stuff into an envelope. After that it was plain sailing. He suddenly attacked me and I got all cross and told him he was a dirty old man who should be ashamed of himself and what would his wife think? He got a bit annoyed at that and called me a dirty little prick teaser. That's when I ripped my blouse and told him I'd scream. We won't have any trouble from him."

"Well, we'll put him on the backup list just in case."

The next plan was the implementation. A quick trip to the leafy suburbs of wealthy Oxfordshire and Birdas's local pub showed that Birdas never went there and no-one knew him at the golf club. But, it turned out, Birdas did support the local Conservative Association where he was putting in the spadework for a mention in a future honours list.

Perfect, thought Ken, and joined the Conservatives himself under a false name.

At the next meeting of Birdas's Conservative Association, Ken was there, pretending to be hanging on to every word of some imported politico who had been drafted in to lecture the faithful about free enterprise, the evils of socialism and the benefits of corporal punishment. Coffee was served halfway through the meeting which gave Ken an excellent opportunity to add his little bit of weed killer to Oliver Birdas's Nescafé. Ken had brought along sufficient dimethoxy . . whatsit sulphate to poison a small town and he was sorely tempted to pour all of it into the full coffee pot. But, on this occasion, caution wisely stayed his hand and he confined himself to poisoning the Birdas coffee only, reasoning that wiping out an entire Conservative Party Association branch, while desirable from the point of view of most decent folk, might, unfortunately, have the countervailing disadvantage of attracting the attention of Inspector Knacker. So sadly, after giving Birdas enough poison to kill him several times over, Ken reluctantly flushed the rest of it down a drain and disposed of the bottle some miles down the road on his drive back to Faldwell Upton where he arrived, tired but happy, in the small hours.

The next day, Ken and Sonia read the newspapers online and searched for Birdas. Sure enough, there was a small item on page 14 of the *Financial Times* about the demise of the founder of Birdas Car Rentals. Apparently he had been poisoned by a commercial weedkiller, available at all good supermarkets and DIY stores. No report about how it had happened, just that he had returned home from a Conservative Party meeting and been taken ill. Died in hospital. There was a tribute from the Conservative party chairman written by rentaquote ". . . fine man . . . blah . . . outstanding businessman . . . blah . . . great loss . . . blah . . .

blah, blah, blah . . .". What the real serious loss to the party was were all those donations from Mr Birdas which he had been making as a downpayment for his knighthood.

"So," said Sonia, "You can buy that poison at Tesco's. Could have saved myself all that trouble with Benskin. Still, it was quite amusing, leading him on like that."

Their musings were suddenly broken by a knock on the door. Outside was a large heavy man in his forties wearing jeans and a donkey jacket.

"Hello, I'm Bill. You must be Ken and Sonia?"

"Yes," said Ken guardedly. "How can we help you?"

"Can I come in? I need to talk to you. It's important."

"Not so fast. What do you want?"

"Well," began Bill. "I understand you run a little business?"

"So?"

"Well, I think I can help you." said Bill. "Let me in, I can't talk out here."

"OK, come in."

"Thank you."

Bill came in and Ken sat him down at the kitchen table.

"Now, what's this all about?"

"I think you and me are in the same line of work," said Bill.

"Go on."

"Well," continued Bill. "I have been watching your careers after I saw your advert in *Private Eye*."

"We do conflict deletion," said Sonia.

"Yeah. Nice name. Conflict deletion. Good one."

"We like it," said Ken.

"It's good."

"So, you said you could help us?" asked Ken.

"Right. I'm something in the conflict deletion business myself," said Bill. "In fact, I think I more or less invented it."

"You're not telling us that we are trespassing on your turf, are you? Because we can tell you that we have set up this business entirely in good faith. We saw a need, and just like good entrepreneurs, we set about filling it. A niche market with plenty of customers."

"No, no, don't get aereated," said Bill, in unmistakable Merseyside tones. "I really am on your side."

"So, tell us more," put in Sonia.

"Well, for a start, you are doing a number of things wrong. Sooner or later, Plod is going to come knocking on your door. You've been rather sloppy, here and there."

"Such as?"

"Well, that fellow on the south coast. Very untidy. If the cops wanted to make a case of it, they would be on to you in a flash."

"You know about Tranley?" asked Sonia incredulously.

"Of course. There's a sort of grapevine in this profession. Nothing happens without word getting around."

"So why didn't the cops trace us? Did they know?"

"Well, yes, they certainly know it was some kind of job by someone in 'conflict deletion'." Bill chuckled as he said the last phrase.

"So why did they leave us alone?" asked Ken.

"Could be several reasons. Shortage of manpower is what they always claim in public. But it could be that they didn't mind Tranley being rubbed out. You could have saved them doing it themselves. Or maybe they just didn't care. But seeing as how Tranley was in some sort of planning scam and the cops would be getting a bit of a bung from that, you killing Tranley would have cost them."

"All the more reason to come after us then, wasn't it?"

"Only if the officer in charge wasn't one of us."

"One of us?"

"Yes, one of us. Someone in the 'conflict deletion' game like you are and I am."

"So, let me get this straight," said Ken. "Are you saying that there are people all over the country doing this sort of thing and the police turn a blind eye?"

"A fair few, yes. You didn't think you were the only people to think of, er," and here Bill laughed out loud, "'conflict deletion'?"

"Including the police!" asked Sonia.

"Especially the police. Of course! Some of the best professional operatives are in the force."

"Why?" she asked. "Why would the police be, er, breaking the law like that."

"Obvious really isn't it? Some do it out of public duty because they get pissed off—Oops! Sorry, love—with letting scumbags get away with it when they know they're guilty. Some do it to supplement their wages."

"But they're paid well enough, surely?" asked Sonia.

"Ah, greed, my dear, pure greed. Not really the best of motives for our profession. But it takes all sorts."

"Don't they have to investigate, write reports, do post mortems. All that sort of thing?"

"Have you been watching too much telly? I know that's what happens on the detective shows. A murder in a pretty village and some pretty-boy photogenic inspector with a messed-up personal life who drinks too much and has been passed over for promotion because he uses unorthodox methods but is full of integrity? And he spends every working minute on one case. Is that how you think it works?"

"We don't know really," Ken replied.

"No, well, let me tell you. I was a copper myself for ten years. Most cases are shelved. Reports are written and if the crimes are not high-profile enough or the public doesn't get too worked up about them, because, maybe, children are involved, they just get forgotten about. Tomorrow there'll be another. It's like fraud. Financial fraud is big business because there are thousands doing it and all of them make millions. The Fraud Squad is three men and a dog and they get paid peanuts by comparison. And chances are that two out of those three are bent. You have to be simple-minded to get caught at fraud. Just look how those bankers get away with it."

"I spent years watching those police shows on telly. I really thought that was how it was," Ken said wistfully.

"No, my son, those police shows on the TV are just comfort material for the masses. So they can sleep soundly in their beds. Anybody who's got a grudge, or a score to settle, has to use a free enterprise operation like ours. It's like the National Health. You might get cured in time if you wait five years for your hernia to be fixed. But if you want a quick result, you have to go private."

Ken returned to the main business.

"So why are you here now?"

"Right," said Bill. "We think your operation needs a little streamlining. Efficiency planning, as they say in business colleges."

"We're listening," said Ken.

"Right, first thing. Stop advertising. You're drawing attention to yourselves. You don't need it."

"So how do we drum up business?"

"Well," explained Bill, "you might have noticed that you've been getting a lot of email business lately. Ever thought about where that comes from?"

"We thought it was from people answering our adverts."

"No, it isn't. We have been directing it to your email address. Those adverts will only raise one or two enquiries a month. Even if they were safe, they are a waste of money."

"We?" asked Sonia.

"Yes, 'we'. My organisation. We call ourselves ERASED—the European Really Appropriate Summary

Execution and Deletion company. You will need to be members. We can't have people working outside our code of practice. That wouldn't be safe for any of us. I'm here to sign you up. Well, not exactly 'sign up' but at least tell you of the benefits."

"And if we don't join?"

"Silly question. What do you think we do for a living?"

"Gotcha," said Ken. "What was that about a code of practice?"

"A code of practice which protects our members by only doing jobs the authorities won't get too upset about."

"Which are?"

"First, only erase the scumbags. No decent people. Don't overcharge. Only charge what a person can afford. We may be killers but we're not greedy. Third, no maritals or domestics. Too messy. Nothing people like more than some juicy marital scandal on page three of *The Daily Telegraph*. Obviously no kids, teenagers etc. You can see our code of practice on our website. A long list. It's important that we stick to doing things in a principled way. We did think of making members swear an oath but that sounds too much like the Boy Scouts. We saw that you are already following most of our guidelines, so we reckoned you'd be the sort of people who should belong in ERASED."

"What were these benefits you mentioned?"

"Right, the benefits," continued Bill. "First, we operate a national network. We have been following your travels around the country. Hampshire, Oxford, London, you've really been covering the miles, haven't you?"

"You have to go where the work is."

"Look, when you are fully committed to ERASED, the work will come to you. You will get all the jobs in your area. Say within a forty miles radius of Faldwell. In return, if you get a job outside your own area, you forward it to us. That way you save all that driving and hotels. Just do jobs in your own area."

"And no advertising?"

"No advertising."

"So how do people find out about us?"

"Like I told you. There's a grapevine. You'll see. Mostly it's the police passing work on to us."

"Can I ask you a question?" said Ken, "How long has this grapevine been around?"

"As far as I know, it's always been there. It's just that no-one talks about it. For obvious reasons."

"Do we have to pay you?" asked Sonia.

"No, no, we're not in the protection business. But we do ask for subscriptions from time to time."

"Subscriptions? What for?" asked Ken.

"Nothing too much. Don't worry. Sometimes one of our members might get into trouble with some cop who doesn't know the ropes. We might have some legal expenses from time to time. Not often though. Our biggest expense is the Christmas party."

"The Christmas party?" asked Sonia with a look of incredulity.

"Yes, every year we have a get-together. Take over a big hotel in London, the Savoy or the Dorchester. One of those. Black tie. Very nice. Tickets a bit pricey but we have a really good time. Last year we had a retired Metropolitan Assistant Commissioner to make the after-dinner speech. We'll let you know nearer the time. Start booking about September."

"How many guests are there usually?"

"Oh last year must have been two, three hundred. This is a big organisation. We like to think of ourselves as the gold standard of rubbing out. Every chapel sends at least two, usually a couple who work together but sometimes a single member will bring a guest. It's very civilised."

"You said 'chapel'?"

"Oh yes. I forgot. That's what we call our branches—chapels. Sounds more respectful. More befitting a professional society. We did think of calling them covens or gangs but the General Assembly rejected that as too common. Likely to give the wrong impression. So we settled on 'chapel'. You two are now the Faldwell Upton Chapel.

"General Assembly?"

"Oh, yes, our summer meeting. Members get to vote on how we should be running things. Like those trade unions or political parties do. Really, though, just between you and me, it's just an opportunity for an annual piss-up."

"Can't wait," said Sonia.

"Any more questions because I've got a job on in Liverpool later today and I've got to get back?"

"I can't think of anything," said Ken. "You've just about covered everything, I think."

"Right then. Remember. Cancel your advertising. You will be getting jobs coming in—just post off any outside this area to the email address I am going to send you. Oh, by the way, you don't use this address for your emails do you?"

"No."

"Good, at least you're doing something right. And never, never, have any mail delivered here. The Post Office always opens it. Got to be off. I'll be in touch. Goodbye."

"I'll see you out," said Ken.

At the front door, Bill paused.

"You've got a diamond there, son. She looks like she understands what this business is all about. A lot of women get a bit squeamish at what we do. Understandably, I suppose. But your Sonia is on the ball. A real diamond."

"She is that," agreed Ken.

"Well, congratulations, Ken, you're now in ERASED. You passed the test."

"And if we hadn't passed the test?"

"Like I said before, Ken, my son, that's a silly question."

Bill was as good as his word. Even after Ken and Sonia had cancelled all their advertising, they still got a steady stream of electronic messages from anguished souls and now that they were no longer exposed publicly, the number of crank emails fell away. They were careful to sort the applications into two groups, those within an hour's drive from Faldwell Upton and the rest, which they duly forwarded to Bill, their contact with ERASED.

Business was quite brisk. There were some well-deserved eliminations to keep them busy out of college hours and although they mostly kept their charges down to a nice professional maximum of £50 an hour plus expenses, there was so much work and so little tax to pay that they pretty soon found themselves with the old money-laundering problem. A new car, small but efficient and not too flashy, was purchased for cash. They kept the old car with its collection of false number plates as a working vehicle. A dirty old Toyota was, they guessed, about as anonymous as one could get, automotively speaking.

Then there was the new apartment to go with their new house, a smart luxury pad not too far from the college. But even after these outlays, they still had a surplus which they periodically converted into jewellery or precious metals. Then there were the Premium bonds and lottery tickets. Just laundering their wealth was becoming a major problem.

And still the jobs rolled in. They sometimes felt overwhelmed at the sheer number of unpleasant people who really needed rubbing out for the good of humanity within forty or fifty miles of their little college.

People like Albert the Loanshark, no-one knew his real name, who charged rates of interest expressed in thousands of percent per week. Albert's particular way of working was to visit his old-age pensioners or single mothers on the day they got their benefits. Ken and Sonia were quite unanimous that when Albert the Loanshark fell from the balcony of one of the town's poorer apartment blocks after emptying the purse of a disabled single mother of three children, that justice had quite rightly been done.

Or there was the drug dealer who hung around the school gates handing out free samples of crack cocaine to twelve-year-olds. This was a particularly nice score for Ken and Sonia because the schools' parents got together a very nice collection indeed. After the dealer had been quickly stabbed with a hypodermic full of potassium cyanide, Ken and Sonia were kindly presented with three hundred pounds which had been gratefully donated by the relieved parents of Form 2.

One nice little earner they also enjoyed was the removal of Benny Boscombe, the manager of Aorta Estate Agents, who claimed a goodly share of the county property trade. Benny had grown rich by the favourite estate agent scam based on undervaluing the houses of people who wanted to sell. What he did then was to sit back and not to send any interested buyers to view the house. This had the effect of panicking a desperate seller under time pressure into selling their property at a heavy discount. Benny would then do a private deal from which he would receive a nice little backhander from a grateful buyer who got himself a bargain house at well under its market valuation. Benny's usual undervaluation would be a modest 10 per cent so that when he went to tell the seller that he had got them a cash sale at their asking price, the seller was usually overjoyed. The buyer would then split the 10% with Benny and the bent 'independent' valuer. Benny's usual victims were, naturally, the old, the single mothers, the infirm, the deeply stupid, the terminally naive, the heavily indebted and all those other vulnerable people who came within Benny's despised category of 'one born every minute'.

One such seller came to Ken and Sonia with a tale of being pressured by Aorta to offer his house at a heavy discount.

"Look," he said, "I know this racket. I did it myself when I was an estate agent."

"Poacher turned gamekeeper?"

"You could say that."

"If you know the score, why do you want revenge on Aorta?"

"Don't like them. Never did. A bunch of thieves. We go back."

So for ten thousand cash, eliminating Mr Benny Boscombe was almost a pleasure. Well, actually it was a complete pleasure. The plan was simple. Ken and Sonia noted that the Aorta office staff went home at the end of office hours but Boscombe himself stayed on and did the occasional property viewing himself in the evening. So they arranged an evening viewing of an empty house using, as usual, false names. Then there was a push down the stairs and the job was done. Easiest ten grand we ever made, agreed Ken and Sonia.

There were so many similar cases that sometimes Ken and Sonia found themselves with so much work that they had to call a halt and take a break just to recharge.

"I never realised philanthropy could be so exhausting." said Sonia.

"All those other benefactors—Mother Teresa, Albert Schweitzer, Saint Francis of Assisi—they must have been permanently knackered."

But now they had ERASED to answer to as well. Every day there was a continuous stream of supplicatory pleas from the wronged and the victimised.

"Makes you fear for the human race, Ken." said Sonia.

"Did no-one ever teach these bastards right from wrong?"

"Obviously not, or the world wouldn't need us."

So it continued. There was Marvin the amateur rapist. (Clothes stolen while he was molesting one of his victims in mid-winter. Died of exposure.) There was the fellow who cut off phone lines and sold the metal for scrap. (Car accident.) There was a reporter on local television who had a reputation for stealing stories from his colleagues. (Alcohol poisoning from spiked drink.) There was the bullying man-hating nurse who would always withhold pain killers from elderly male patients. (Weed-killer injection.) And one must not forget the traffic wardress known as Susie the Sociopath, who made it a point of honour always to double her daily ticket quota and who carried a six-inch nail with her everywhere so that she could add a complimentary paint scratch to every car she ticketed. (Fell in front of a train at rush hour.)

So they came, these victims, with their stories of mistreatment at the hands of bullies, lunatics, petty criminals, thieves, child molesters. They displayed a regular parade of the cruel, the dishonest, the liars and the cheats. There was, it seems, a never-ending train of people who were cruel to animals, who committed petty crimes below the police radar, who made lives unbearable because they didn't know how not to. The list was endless and sometimes Ken and Sonia despaired of ever getting to the end of it.

"And that's before we start on the politicians, the bankers or the lawyers." said Ken.

"Not to mention the crooked tradesmen, the bent council officials, the short-changers or even the real criminals."

"I never realised the problem was so big."

"It would be a lot bigger if we didn't stick to the ERASED code of conduct. Just think how many cases we would have if we included marital and domestic."

NINE

Ken and Sonia were sitting in the college computer laboratory when Ken got a call on his mobile phone.

"Mr Grassmann? Mr Kenneth Grassmann?"

"Yes."

"Where are you now?"

"I'm at work. Who is this?"

"i would like to talk to you about conflict deletion, Mr. Grassmann."

"I'm sorry. Later, perhaps?"

"I'll be at your house at 6.00pm."

And with that, the caller rang off.

Promptly at six, there was a heavy knock on the door. Ken opened it to find two men standing there. They were obviously police, so it was no surprise when the older, less scruffy one, produced his warrant card.

"Mr. Grassmann? I'm Inspector Buzzard and this is Sergeant Layton. We like to ask you some questions."

"Oh, Layton Buzzard! Very good!"

The inspector looked puzzled.

"Oh yes, sir, very good. Leighton Buzzard!! Oh yes, got it! Never heard one that before. Must remember it."

"Come in. This is my partner, Sonia."

"That would be Miss Lyttel, would it not?"

"How do you know?"

"Madam, it's our job to know."

"Right."

"Mr Grassmann. Did you know a man called . . ." and here Buzzard consulted his notes, "one Morton Alamein Scregg? I believe he was the principal of the college where you work?"

"Yes, of course. He died last year. Fell down the steps after getting pissed at lunch."

"And you sir, were, I understand, the last to speak to him."

"Yes, of course. It all came out in the inquest. I went through all of this with your Inspector Fordham."

"Chief Inspector Fordham he is now, sir. Promoted and moved to Glasgow."

"But you will have all his notes, all the case records."

"Indeed we have sir. Mr Fordham was very meticulous. Good case notes. Very good."

"I thought the case was closed," said Ken. "I did get questioned by Inspector Fordham. Twice as it happens."

"Yes, sir, that is one thing we need your help with. It appears from the case notes that Fordham thought you might have, er, 'pushed' the late gentleman down the stairs."

"That's not what the coroner thought."

"Quite, sir. But coroners have been known to make mistakes."

"You are not suggesting that I really did kill old Scregg, are you?"

"No need to worry, sir, just tidying up loose ends. Going over Inspector Fordham's caseload to make sure everything is in order. Part of my job, me being new to the area."

"Well, I can assure you that I had no part of Scregg's accident."

"But you did have a motive, did you not? Isn't it true that Mr. Scregg was having an affair with your wife at the time of his death?"

"Scregg would screw anything that wasn't nailed down. Anyway, she's an ex-wife now."

"Exactly, sir."

"Now, sir, I understand that you run a small private business called, er, 'Conflict Deletion Services'. Is that true?"

"Yes, we do a little counselling for people having relationship difficulties. Sometimes it helps to talk things over with a sympathetic outsider."

"Very laudable, sir. May I ask, what do you charge for this service?"

"It depends on what the client can afford. Could be nothing. Could be ten, twenty pounds an hour."

"Well, sir. That's very interesting. Tell me, do you know a man called Boris Tranley?"

"I don't think so. Should I?"

"I think you might, sir. Try to refresh your memory. Let me help. Mr Tranley was a senior planning officer with Borley cum Neston District Council."

"So?"

"Well, sir. Mr Tranley was found dead. We think he was murdered. A car like yours was seen in the area just about the time of his death."

"There must be a million cars like mine! Why do you think it was my car?"

"So you were never in," Buzzard looked at his notes again, "the *Frog and Bucket* pub in Blackbird Neston shortly before he was killed?"

"I've never heard of what, the *Frog and Bucket* pub? Or Blackthorn Neston for that matter."

"Well, sir. We do have some CCTV footage of a couple looking uncannily like you and Miss Lyttel from that very public house. You appear to be in conversation with an elderly gentleman we can't identify. Maybe you can help us. Do you know his name?"

"Can't help you, I'm sorry. I've never been there."

"Quite, sir. Now, can I ask you, do you know of a gentleman, also deceased, called Sir James Bruce-Bubbson?"

"Wasn't he that government minister? The one that fell off the roof at Heathrow? It was in all the papers."

"But you didn't know him personally, Mr Grassmann?"

"Sorry, Inspector, I'm a college lecturer. I don't move in government circles."

"Maybe you know his wife, sorry, widow? The beautiful Lady Arabella Bruce-Bubbson?"

"Seen her photograph in the paper. Attractive woman."

"What about you, Miss Lyttel, have you ever met Arabella Bruce-Bubbson?"

"Like Ken says, we don't move in those circles."

Buzzard went back to his notes.

"Now, Mr Grassmann, are you a member of the Conservative Party?"

"What kind of a question is that? Mind your own business."

"It's important, sir. Just bear with me if you would, please. Can I ask you whether you went to a Conservative Party Association branch meeting in Oxfordshire earlier this year?"

"No, I'm not a bloody Tory and I don't go to their meetings. What's all this about?"

"Well, sir. Can I ask you then if you have ever done any business with Birdas Car Rentals?"

"No. I haven't rented a car for years. Why?"

"So you don't know Mr. Birdas, the late owner of said Birdas Car Rentals Limited, after whom the company is named?"

"No!" exploded Ken. "I don't know Mr. Fucking Birdas, or whatever he's called. What's all this about?"

"All in good time, sir." said Buzzard, unfazed by Ken's outburst.

Buzzard went on.

"Did you know that all of them, Scregg, Bruce-Bubbson, Tranley and Birdas died unexpectedly. All except Scregg were open verdicts. We think that they were murdered."

"Really? Murdered?" said Ken with mock disbelief.

"Yes, sir, murdered," replied Buzzard.

"Who by? Me? Do you think I'm the murderer?"

"Could be, sir. Takes all sorts. Just making enquiries for the present."

"Well, you're wasting your time with me. I didn't do it. Any of them."

"If you say so, sir."

"I do say so. Most emphatically!" said Ken.

"Well, sir, just before we go. Do you know a man known just as 'Bill'".

"A common name. I know a few Bill's as it happens."

"No, sir. This is a special Bill. He runs an organisation called ERASED. Do you know anything about it?"

"I've no idea what you are talking about. What is this ERASED?"

"If you don't know, sir, then you have nothing to hide. And that means you have nothing to fear."

"That's about it, then," said Ken.

"Well, sir, no, it's not. I am afraid we don't believe you. We have reason to believe that you, Kenneth Grassmannn, are a member of the ERASED organisation and that you knowingly conspired with them and other persons unknown to commit the murders of Sir James Bruce-Bubbson, Boris Tranley and Oliver Birdas between April last year and today. We further believe that you, Sonia Lyttel, did aid and abet Kenneth Grassmann in the execution of said crimes."

"Are you sure you have got this right, Inspector?"

"I think we have. We will be asking you, in due course, to make a formal statement and submit to arrest at Faldwell Upton Police Station."

But Ken's mind was working overtime. What if, he thought, they did not have cast iron proof and they were playing with him, just waiting for him to give himself away? Why hadn't they been charged already? Why no formal caution? Why weren't they just thrown into the cells? Why hadn't they been told to get themselves a solicitor?

Only two reasons could explain why Buzzard was being so careful. One, he didn't have a case which would stand up in court. And the second? Well, wasn't it Buzzard who had brought up ERASED? Wasn't it Bill from ERASED who had told him ' . . . some of our best operatives are in the force.'? Was this an approach from the local bobbies for a little help? He had his answer ready.

"Inspector Buzzard. Your charges are ridiculous and you know it. In fact I strongly resent your insinuations that I would commit such serious crimes. You'd better go before I call a lawyer and we set up a formal complaint against you."

"Ha! Ha! Ha!" Buzzard broke out into a broad smile.

"Perfect!" he said. "Just the answer we were looking for! Pour us a drink and we'll put some decent business your way."

Sonia poured large whiskies for the four of them and Buzzard explained his plan.

"First, sorry about all that formal questioning. Just routine. Had to be sure you're on the level. We need to know that you won't break down under questioning. And we had to make it look right. Now, we know all about you and the great work you have been doing for the local community. We were very pleased to see how you took out the Faldwell Flasher in the woods as well as that little drug dealer who was giving free samples of crack cocaine to the school kids. All of us down the station loved that. Just loved it."

"Why couldn't you do it yourself?"

"Not so easy," said Buzzard. "Got to get evidence. Then there are social workers to square up, reports, probation officers, et cetera, et bloody cetera. You wouldn't believe how difficult it is do our job properly because of all the do-gooders and regulations. If we'd arrested that little toe rag outside the school he'd only get three months, which we pay for, before he's out doing it all again. Much easier to have a co-operative relationship with the right sort of privateer like your good selves. Saves us a lot of trouble—a whole lot of trouble."

"How did you find out about us? The grapevine, perhaps?"

"Exactly, the grapevine."

"So, what do you want from us now? I assume you are not going to arrest us."

"No, of course not. We, and I am quite sure I speak for the majority of the police, are very happy with the ERASED code of good practice. In fact, we approve of it. As well as it being a nice little post-retirement occupation for any poor copper who didn't get a decent posting on the Fraud Squad. Or the Vice Squad, of course. But if you spent your career with no opportunities to put away a little bit of money for your old age, then working for ERASED is a godsend. So we look after ERASED and they do those necessary dirty jobs we can't do ourselves because our hands are tied by the bleeding hearts."

"You have a job in mind for us then?" asked Sonia.

"Yes, a bit tricky but we will help you. Discreetly, of course. It's this. We have this new Chief Inspector. He's a bit of a hard case but worst of all, he is always making us fill up forms, account for every little thing we do, keep strict accounts. Everything by the book. You know what I mean. He's a lay preacher, for Christ's sake! Seems to think policing is a branch of the Salvation Army. Always sees the good side of every slimy little sod we arrest for pushing drugs or housebreaking. It's getting us down. Nobody can work in that atmosphere. Anyway, his latest trick is to threaten disciplinary action against anyone who cuts any corners. He's right, in one way, I suppose, but I'm sure you know—can I call you Ken?—I'm sure you know, Ken, that real good honest police work can't be done like that. We have to have a bit of well, latitude, to use our own initiative, as the occasion demands. Sometimes some of those little bastards need a little slap their mothers' should have given them. Teach them right from wrong."

"Is this Chief Inspector . .?"

"Melladew. Chief Inspector Melladew."

"Is he the target then? And you would not be too unhappy if he were to go to that great police station in the sky where his religious talents would be properly appreciated?"

"Couldn't have put it better myself."

"So," said Ken. "It would be normal to charge a fee for my professional services."

"Quite right, too," replied Buzzard. "The labourer is worthy of his hire. That's why we at the station have a little fund set aside for this sort of contingency. Never had to use it before. All our previous chiefs had been real coppers, come up through the ranks. Not like this little shit—public school, university degree, two weeks at Hendon and then sergeant in three months. So there's a bob or two in the bank for the job. Shall we say five grand now and five when we get a new chief?"

"I haven't said I'll take the job yet. I'll need your word there'll be no investigation."

"Don't worry about that, Ken. I'll take the case myself. I promise I'll really make a really crap job of it."

"And I'll need details—where he lives, his habits, that sort of thing."

"Tomorrow too soon to get started?"

"I think we can say that we're in business already, Inspector."

"Call me Tom. I'll be here tomorrow with the down payment and some information about our Chief Inspector Melladew."

With the deal sealed, all four shook hands and the representatives of the forces of law made their departures.

"I think we can turn the tape recorder off now," said Ken, "and store the tape in our safe."

Sonia and Ken began their research into the lifestyle of Chief Inspector Melladew using the information thoughtfully provided by Inspector Buzzard and Sergeant Layton. It turned out that Melladew was a very strict man indeed. He was one of those paragons of civic virtue who would probably flatter himself that he is one of the pillars of society. For example, he was a stalwart of the Faldwell Methodist Chapel where he preached regular sermons of powerful sententiousness. His excessively pampered car was carefully garaged and immaculately cleaned, inside and out, every Saturday, rain or shine. His garden apotheosized the very highest qualities of English tidiness while his house was no less than a shining declaration of all those things that were dearest to the heart of the middle-aged, middle-class, middle-brow, middle-of-the-road suburban Englishman by being no less than an archetype of smug comfort, modest restraint and respectability. It was a respectable house in a respectable street in a respectable suburb because the Englishman of Melladew's class has no higher aspiration than to be both tidy and respectable.

"So, we've got a real anal retentive wanker, here," said Sonia.

"Looks like it. More *Guardian* than *Daily Mail*, I suspect."

"Heavy on the good works and light on the dry sherry?"

"There was even an Oxfam poster in his front window."

"Just visible, but not too ostentatious. Let us not parade our virtue too obviously. That would be bad taste."

"So, how do we kill this fine specimen?"

"Let's go to church."

Ken and Sonia spent the next Sunday morning at the Faldwell Methodist Chapel whose existence they had not previously been aware of. It was, in fact, the only time they had ever been to a church except for the odd funeral, such as James Bruce-Bubbson's. They had both skived off Scregg's final public appearance, like most of the other teachers at the college.

The chapel was not full. In fact, there was only a small, almost token, congregation made up almost entirely of lonely elderly women plus a couple of adolescent male social misfits. In twenty years time, thought Ken, I will still be too young to be coming here. But Ken and Sonia were not there for spiritual guidance or for moral uplift or to pass an hour breaking up a lonely week in a pensioner's maisonette. No, they were there to observe their quarry in his natural habitat. For this morning, no less than Harold J. Melladew M.A.(Oxon.) himself, would be giving the sermon. They spotted him immediately given that he was one of the younger attendees and certainly the best turned-out in his expensive suit, a look which was quite out of keeping with that of faded genteel poverty favoured by the lady parishioners or the look of dishevelled scruffiness of the two young boys. During the hymns, Melladew could be heard singing lustily about fighting the good fight and onward Christian soldiers, his discordant voice easily overwhelming the timid singing of all the other people present.

When it came to his sermon, Melladew strode manfully up to the rostrum and began his declamation.

"You are sinners!" he bellowed at the three of four rows of little old ladies and the two harmless boys. Plus of course Ken and Sonia, who felt uncomfortable to be so addressed.

Soon though, after ritual denunciations of man's basic evil, Melladew warmed to his theme.

"Work! Work! Work! God's work! That is what all of you must devote your life to!! All of you, for if you do not, God will find you out and will punish you!!!!"

Pretty soon he was at screaming pitch, with threats of eternal damnation for "fornicators, drunkards, the godless, thieves, liars and people who break the law."

A little old lady leant over to Sonia and whispered to her, "He's a very wonderful man, isn't he? A saint. Do you know he's also a police inspector? A wonderful man."

No, he's not, thought Sonia, he's a fucking lunatic.

Such was the force of Melladew's impassioned fortissimo oratory that both Ken and Sonia found it difficult even to let their minds wander and shut out this preacher harangue. That was not possible because Melladew's rabid exhortations were just too loud. About the only thing you could say in his favour was that he could never be accused of understating his case.

"The sins of the flesh!!" he was shouting, "The sins of the flesh are an abomination. An ABOMINATION!!! . . . ."

I wonder, thought Ken, if these old dears, mostly long widowed, really need this lecture in avoiding sins, especially sins of the flesh? It would be difficult to imagine a less sinful congregation. Their problems were more likely lack of opportunities for sinning rather than sin itself. A bit of sin now and again might have been a lot better for them than this kind of verbal cruelty.

Ken and Sonia reached a point when they could stand it no more, and, almost by mental telepathy, they stood up at the same time and quietly, discreetly they made their way to the exit and a much-needed drink at the pub across the road. But Melladew had seen them.

"Do not fear the truth, friends. Do not turn your back on the word of the Lord!" he shouted at their backs as a parting benediction.

Outside, the couple stood for a minute to catch their breath.

"He's raving mad!"

"Completely round the twist!"

"He's got to go. He's definitely got to go."

"We need a plan."

"No, my dear, first we need a drink."

"Beware the demon drink!! It's against God's will!!" laughed Sonia.

While there could no longer, after his chapel performance, be any doubt about the desirability of helping Melladew go to his well-deserved celestial reward, there was still the tricky problem of exactly how one could terminate a chief inspector, even with inside help from his underlings. It was a strange feeling for Ken to begin to even feel some sympathy for Melladew's constables and sergeants, even for Buzzard. Not only did they have to put up with what would, no doubt, be a bullying management style, but they have to suffer his holier-than-thou religiosity as well. Ken made a mental note to ask Buzzard if Melladew had installed a swear box in the police general office. Both of them now fully understood why Buzzard had been in such a hurry to get the job over and done with. A monster like Melladew was an offence to all decent people and the sooner he went on to a better place, the happier the world would be.

"Chief inspector. Probably has a driver."

"So a road accident is out."

"Can we get near enough for the weed killer, do you think?"

"Difficult. Put it down as a possible. Remember, we don't want to get into a pattern. What I believe they call a *modus operandi*. We've used weed killer a couple of times."

"What about the old 'high building' routine?"

"Where? As far as we can tell, he doesn't go near any high buildings. Pushing him might be hard. He's obviously fit. Probably quite strong. Oxford rugby blue."

"Yes. He looks like a typical marathon-running squash-playing fitness freak."

"Letter bomb?"

"Could be messy. People could get hurt."

"The Scregg Descent, perhaps?"

"Falling down a staircase? Possibility. Bear it in mind."

"Let's watch his movements for a week or so. That might give us an idea."

So Sonia and Ken did a little gentle monitoring of what the Chief Inspector got up to. Buzzard had said he was a creature of habit. He always got into the office at eight o'clock on the dot. Most days it was meetings and police business until 12.15 then lunch in the police canteen. He ate alone, said Buzzard. If there was a big case on or a TV interview he would leave the office for those but usually he was doing meetings and working in his office until 6.00pm.

"Any social life?" Ken asked Buzzard.

"Not what I'd call social," said Buzzard. "He goes to a gym Tuesday and Thursday after work and some prayer meeting on Wednesday, as far as we can tell."

"But never any socialising with the other officers?"

"Hardly," replied Buzzard. "I can't see Holy Joe going to the sort of places where real coppers relax."

"Such as?"

"Come on, you're a man of the world. We're only human. A few drinks, maybe a club with some nice girls. You understand. He wouldn't exactly fit in. We don't even tell him when there's a coppers' night out."

"I am getting some ideas here. Gym and prayer meeting, is that all?" asked Ken.

"As far as we know. Look, the lads are getting a bit, like impatient. How long is this going to take?"

"Can't hurry a job like this, I'm sorry. Ask them to hang on a little longer, can you?"

"Right," said Buzzard, "but let's have some action soon."

"I promise. No more than two weeks. I think I know how we are going to do it."

"Oh," added Ken, "one question has been intriguing me. Has Melladew introduced a swear box in your office? I only wondered."

"You bloody psychic, or something? How did you guess?"

"Well, it figures."

"He's a Jesus freak. It's like being back at school. He even times how long we take in the bog."

"He's got to go," agreed Ken. "Won't be long now."

The next day Sonia made a trip into the town library to read the *Methodist Recorder*, where she was able to get a timetable of the preacher rota for the Faldwell area Methodist chapel circuit. Sure enough, Harold Melladew's name featured as a regular. And the Sunday after next, he was due to be guest preacher at Upton-by-Wallwell Methodist Chapel, a mere fifteen miles from Faldwell Upton itself.

"I think that's our window." said Sonia.

"I think so. Just need the stuff."

Neither Ken nor Sonia had ever done anything technical before, but Sergeant Layton was very helpful with his advice. Ken was very surprised at how light and small it was. But Layton had assured them that it was enough for what was needed and warned them to be sure to use the stickers and to be careful to stick it firmly well below the ledge of the lectern where it wouldn't be seen. They tested the activation mechanism a few times and even had a full dress rehearsal on a lonely field way out in the country, on a quiet rainy afternoon. They had to be careful here but Ken remembered hearing a story from a man who would test fire his illegal pistols by driving ten miles into the countryside, firing one round and then driving away quickly.

The following Sunday, Ken and Sonia arrived early at the chapel where Melladew was scheduled to give his weekly fire-and-brimstone performance. The doors were opened at 8.30 by a caretaker who immediately after opening up went home for his breakfast. Ken and Sonia went inside, deftly stuck the device to the underside of the lectern and then went back to their car which had ben parked in a car park across the street, to await the start of the morning service. As before, there was hymn singing and some announcements before the star turn took his place. Ken and Sonia had no trouble hearing Melladew's stentorian peroration from across the street and once he was well under way, they drove away from the village to the limit of their mobile phone range before tapping in the magic key.

The tiny electronic signal then made its near-instantaneous journey from Sonia's cellphone via innumerable satellites and exchanges to arrive microseconds later at the detonator of the bomb which had been superglued beneath the lectern where Melladew was, at that moment, bellowing at his placid audience.

"And if you are steeped in sin!! If you are steeped in sin!! God will seek you out and strike you DOWN!!!"

He was on the point of thumping the lectern at the very moment when the final invisible connexion between cellphone and detonator was completed. The subsequent explosion, limited, by virtue of police ingenuity, to a small area around the reader at the lectern, swiftly presented Chief Inspector Melladew with an opportunity to verify for himself whether those impassioned threats about the afterlife, which he had so often inflicted on his God-fearing congregations, were actually based on fact or not.

Already driving away from the scene, Ken and Sonia heard the noise of the explosion, and, like the good citizens they were, immediately informed the police. When they got home, the story of the explosion which had killed a senior policeman at church was already headlines on TV. A scrum of reporters was interviewing the officer in charge, Inspector Buzzard, who played his part beautifully.

"Tell us please, Inspector Buzzard, who do you think committed this crime?"

"Now, now, gentlemen, and ladies of course, it is far too early to be sure of what exactly took place here this terrible morning but we have already set up an incident room and we are making inquiries."

"Did you know Chief Inspector well? He was new here, wasn't he?"

"Yes, he was. He was a fine officer. A first-class police officer who will be very sadly missed. The prayers and feelings of all our force go out to his friends and family."

"Who do you think could have done it?"

"Well, as you can see, we have only just begun our inquiries and we will leave no stone unturned to find the person who would commit this outrage. This is an act of terrorism and unfortunately terrorism is all too common in this world in these times. Unfortunately, the police have to confront terrorist threats every single day of their working lives."

"So you think this is a terrorist crime, then, Inspector?"

"It's too early to say. Far too early. But it is a distinct possibility. We can think of no other motive for this terrible crime. Chief Inspector Melladew was a committed Christian and church-goer. We can't think that he had any enemies who would want to harm him."

Which was just about all it took to cast subtle suspicions upon Faldwell Upton's small, law-abiding and peace-loving Muslim community who would subsequently find themselves unfairly and repeatedly visited by Buzzard's officers during the next few weeks until the incident was overlaid in the public memory by newer crimes and consigned to the 'unsolved' filing cabinet.

A few days later Ken got a call from Buzzard to arrange a meeting.

"Well, Tom, job done?"

"Job done, Ken. Nice one."

"You'll be needing a new chief. Will you get it?"

"Possible. They may have had enough of over-promoted nancy boys."

"And maybe a leg up for Sergeant Layton as well?"

"Hope so. The lad's deserved it."

"So, you're here to pay me?" asked Ken.

"Not so fast," answered Buzzard. "We still don't have a suspect yet."

"The deal was that you'd pay me when the job was finished. And it's finished. Do you have the money with you now?"

"The deal was that I would pay you when there was a new Chief Inspector."

"So then, Tom, baby, let's hope that your promotion comes through soon."

And come through it did. Buzzard was made Acting Chief Inspector pending confirmation which would follow after the current investigation into the death of Chief Inspector Melladew. Ken set up another meeting with the newly-promoted Acting Chief Inspector.

"Congratulations," said Ken. "That just about completes our business."

"Not quite. I still have to wrap up the Melladew inquiry. Quicker if I could deliver a suspect. And that, Ken, means you. Sorry. Nothing personal. You understand how things work. It's your freedom or my job. No contest really."

"I can see your point," conceded Ken. "But let's look at this from my point of view, shall we? I would definitely prefer my freedom over your job. Plus, of course, the five thousand you owe me, 'for services rendered', as it were."

Buzzard chortled, "No chance! You must be off your trolley if you think I'm going to pay you and let you go free. Why should I? And don't tell me that you'll say I was in on it. I'll just deny it and fix the evidence. Your word against mine. You won't stand a chance in court. So, Mr. Grassmann, you are now under arrest."

"Well then, why not take this?" replied Ken, handing over a small package. "It's a tape recording of our first meeting when you asked me to do the job for you. I have twenty copies ready to go to all the papers and TV if I ever come to any harm or get arrested. Did you know that in this country, conspiracy to murder carries a bigger penalty than murder itself? So if I go down, Tom, baby, you and Layton are coming with me. So that would mean there would be no chief inspector's pension for you. I am told that judges are particularly heavy on bent coppers. I don't imagine the other prisoners will be too gentle on you either."

"I don't believe you," riposted Buzzard. "You're making it up. There is no recording."

"Go ahead, try me. It's not worth calling my bluff, though, is it? Your safest bet would be to pay up with a smile and stick to our deal."

"There's nothing on this tape. I'd have seen the recorder when I was at your place."

"That's a complimentary," said Ken. "The other twenty are in a safe place ready to be posted. Listen to it in your own time. Shall we say five thousand, used notes, next Monday?"

"Where?"

"What about the car park of Faldwell Methodist Chapel, Monday at eleven o'clock in the morning? A nice gesture of respect to the departed, don't you think?"

"That's the day of the funeral."

"Right," said Ken. "So it should be safe. Nice comforting police presence."

Ken went to Melladew's funeral not out of a sense of duty nor out of respect for a fallen warrior in the never-ending struggle against crime and disorder. No, Ken went to the service for the far, far loftier motive of getting his money. He waited outside to watch the procession of guests including the great and the good of the county, many of them adorned in uniforms resplendent with substantial gold braid and rows of medals. Buzzard sidled up to Ken and slipped a package into Ken's pocket.

"That's it," Buzzard whispered out of the side of his mouth.

"Finito," replied Ken. "Is that the widow?" he asked, indicating a thirty-something woman with a forced smile.

"Poor Mrs. Melladew," said Buzzard.

"She looks well enough to me," said Ken.

"She's a good catch now," said Buzzard. "Pity she's spoken for."

"What do you mean?" asked Ken.

"Every Wednesday. When Melladew was hard at prayer. Young chap from Wallwell."

"You tracked them?"

"Of course. Standard police procedure. Got to know what everyone is up to. Poor woman, she used to be very nervous, highly-strung. Must have been quite a strain for her, living with Melladew and having a secret like she had. Melladew was especially hot on the sixth commandment, as he called it. Madame Melladew has been very much better since the elimination. Better than I've ever seen her before. You did her a real favour."

"You must know her pretty well. She hadn't been here long."

"Well, you know how it is. Got keep in with the boss's wife. Get on the wrong side of her and it's curtains for your career."

"And you 'kept in with her'?"

"From time to time. Very nice woman. Very generous. Never knew what she saw in Melladew. Isn't a bit like him. She's much more outgoing. By the way, I might have another little job for you up in Wallwell. Now that we understand each other."

"Sorry," said Ken, "ERASED rules. We never do marital or domestic."

"Actually, Ken," said Buzzard, "you just did. Don't spend it all at once."

TEN

So, Buzzard had used him to eliminate the husband of his mistress, thought Ken. He was genuinely shocked at the man's duplicity. Did he not understand the code of honour of ERASED and its tireless acolytes who were decent, honest members of a noble priesthood dedicated to peace and goodwill? Ken found himself growing quite indignant at having his professionalism corrupted in this way. And by a policeman!

After a few days, his righteous anger subsided a little and he turned his mind to the next job on the list, the quite necessary removal of a megalomaniac office manager at a textile company in a large town some twenty miles from home. After she had been disposed of, Ken reflected, his daily email count would be significantly smaller, since he regularly received up to a dozen pleas each morning from victims of her uncontrollable rages. The descriptions of the woman contained in these plaintive supplications left Ken and Sonia in no doubt of the sheer desirability of sending Tamsin Fortuna Chasuble to a much warmer place where she would have the opportunity to spend the rest of recorded time with other similar troubled souls against whom she could vent her incessant rage. For that indeed was her primary *modus vivendi*—her instant recourse to anger as the standard response to any problem involving human interaction. It was clear, from the consistent tone of complaints about her, that anger was just about her entire emotional range. Ken and Sonia wondered just how such a monstrous parody of humanity had ever ascended to a position of management, especially management of a team of young and mostly emotionally immature clerical workers who could not but be intimidated by her and be psychically damaged as a result.

The answer to this last question was simple. The name of the company for which Tamsin Chasuble performed the duties of office manager was Chasuble 'Kings of the Tubular Bandage' Hospital Supplies Limited, the family firm, and the only company which would ever employ such a monster, for whom, after an erratic career at school and college, a job had to be found. Naturally, the rate of staff turnover at the family business was record-breaking. Sometimes a new employee would last as little as two hours before they overturned their desks and stormed out following one of her tantrums. Those who remained were usually the excessively timid, the economically desperate or the sullenly resentful, the last nursing grudges and awaiting opportunities for revenge. It was this final group which was mostly responsible for the high level of complaints which ERASED received about her.

Strangely Tamsin herself did not notice staff discontent, nor did she possess sufficient self-awareness to consider that her manner was anything other than normal, even admirable. The sudden departures, the screams of frustration or the regular public arguments as some staff member left because they had reached breaking point, none of these, she believed, ever had any connection with her intemperate management style. No, every turbulent confrontation could only be because of some failing by the employee him—or herself. Each meeting with a colleague was, to her, an opportunity for a display of childish temper, which she perceived to be 'strength of character'. Her staff, whom she quite inexplicably considered to be 'her team' or even more ludicrously, 'her family', would, for the most part, avoid her as much as possible, something which was difficult to do when she would suddenly fling open the door of the general office and shout

"STOP WORK! STOP RIGHT NOW! I HAVE AN ANNOUNCEMENT!!"

She would then launch into some tirade which would continue in a stream of consciousness until she ran out of breath. Then she would ask, aggressively,

"ANY QUESTIONS?"

If anyone was naive or stupid enough to ask a question, she would respond with

"I AM NOW GETTING VERY ANGRY!!"

Then she would stamp her foot, turn on her heel and sweep out of the room, slamming the door in her wake. This would happen at least once a week.

Naturally, she was also an ardent feminist, believing that the male of the human species had had it far too easy for far too long and that it was her duty to redress the imbalance by hitting them as hard as she could, as often as she could. She was confirmed in this extreme view by the fact that every man she had ever employed had, at least once, screamed back at her, sometimes even threatening her with violence, especially if the effects of the previous night's relief drinking had not yet worn off. Nobody had actually hit her, although a few had come close. But the effect of all these near-violent confrontations was merely to confirm in her mind her unshakeable prejudices about the strength of her character, her forgiving nature, the poor quality of humanity in general and, above all, the ineffable inferiority of the entire male sex.

"A bit like Vice-Principal Melys Morgan-Pugh, only worse," observed Sonia.

"Thank goodness they appointed her to that college in Newcastle."

"Amen to that. Although I do feel some sympathy for our poor Geordie colleagues."

"Don't worry, love, ERASED have a very active Tyneside branch."

"So, how do we do the business for Tamsin Chasuble?"

"Well, why don't you take a look at her? Get an interview. They take on new office staff all the time. For obvious reasons."

So Sonia wrote a letter of application for a job, and was, unsurprisingly, called for interview. When she arrived at Chasuble Hospital Supplies Ltd., she was conducted to an interview room where Nicky, the current office temporary, asked her to fill up an application form, which Sonia turned into a fun exercise in creative fiction. Having been landed with teaching the graduate basic literacy course by her college head of department, she was in need of ideas about how to keep them quiet for two hours every Tuesday, so filling up of an application form in a false name served the additional purpose of class preparation. A nice change from teaching sociology graduates how to read.

The interview was with Tamsin F. Chasuble herself. Since, Sonia reasoned, she would not want to be offered this job and realising that she almost certainly would be offered it, given the Chasuble staff turnover rate, Sonia reckoned that she might as well enjoy the afternoon out. So she made a little game with herself that she would try to use all the standard interview clichés in as short a time as possible. She would make sure that she would say 'challenge', 'passionate' and 'rewarding' within the first three sentences.

"Tell me why you want the job, Mrs. Patel."

"I have always loved hospital supplies. I have always been very passionate about them."

"I'm afraid it's not very glamorous, Mrs Patel," said Tamsin Chasuble.

"I think it will be a challenge for someone with my background. I want a job which will be rewarding," said Sonia.

As the interview churned on, through the traditional ping-pong script of empty phrases and meaningless platitudes, Sonia had an opportunity to observe Tamsin Chasuble on her home turf. She did not like what she saw. The office manager was a fat, florid woman with hyperthyroidic popping eyes. What is more, she also had a distinct body odour which, Sonia wondered, might actually be the smell of authentic infernal sulphur. It was time, Sonia decided, after about fifteen minutes into the interview, to stir things up a bit.

"Do you operate equal opportunities here?" she said.

"Of course!" thundered Ms. Chasuble. "Women always get first choice over men when it comes to promotions."

"That's not what I meant," said Sonia. "What I meant was whether men are discriminated against? I notice there are not many men working here. I actually like working with men."

Sonia carefully noted that Tamsin Chasuble's face colour was becoming a little more purple.

"Here," said Chasuble, "we find that men can be a distraction. They upset the harmony of the team."

"Oh I hate that, 'we're a team' attitude. I go to work to earn money, not to play football."

"Well," said Ms Chasuble, "I can tell you that we really are a team here!!"

"Well, I am not sure I like the sound of that. I don't like working in a team. I prefer to work on my own. And

I do like to have men around. As many as possible," Sonia replied, adding a theatrical, lascivious wink.

Sonia could see that Tamsin Chasuble was now becoming very angry indeed. So, thought Sonia, one more question should be enough to push the bitch over the edge. She asked it.

"If I were to take this job, it would have to be on the condition that I have a share of management decision-making. I assume that there is some sort of staff committee where important decisions are talked out? I hope this is not the sort of place where you are just given orders without any chance for you to put your own point of view."

Chasuble was now wriggling and squirming in her seat in a desperate effort to control her rage.

"Are you OK?" asked Sonia solicitously.

"I'm fine! I'm fine! I'm afraid this interview is over! I don't think we will be offering you a job, Mrs Patel. I don't think you are the sort of person we are looking for! We will pay you your travelling expenses if you speak to Nicky."

"So, Mrs Patel," said Nicky. "Return ticket from Aberdeen, one night's overnight stay. Hundred and fifty pounds sixteen pence. Sign here. How did it go?"

"Well," said Sonia. "I didn't get the job. I don't think I impressed her at all."

"Lucky you. You don't know how fortunate that makes you."

Back home, Ken and Sonia were enjoying a bottle of champagne, bought with the Chasuble interview expenses.

"Is it on, do you think?" asked Ken.

"Oh, I think so, she thinks everyone loves her. Everybody else is out of step. So she's not likely to be on the lookout for any enemies. What's amazing is that she never thinks anyone who falls out with her would ever hold any grudge. It's pathetic. I did hear one funny story from a girl called Nicky, a temp I met when I was there."

"Go on."

"Well, there was this young guy was taken on. Apparently she had a go at him with all the office present and made him look bad in front of everybody. To get his own back, what he did was wipe every single computer file he could find and then shredded every office document over lunch when the office was empty."

"Yes?"

"So, when she came back after lunch, he went to her office. She thought he was going there to apologise to her because she had screamed at him that morning. Before she could say a word, he unzipped his pants, pulled out his penis and pissed all over her desk! Apparently she was so shocked, she couldn't even say anything until he'd already gone."

"Ha, ha, ha!!"

"The story goes that she called the police but the two cops who came just fell about laughing. She was on Valium for a month."

"Well, I'm going to enjoy rubbing this one out. Any ideas how?" asked Ken.

"Road accident is possible."

"Did you notice anything about her habits when you were there?"

"Well, yes, I did," said Sonia, "I noticed that she eats a lot of chocolate. Could be diabetic. She's certainly fat."

"Poisoned chocolate?"

"Good idea."

So Ken and Sonia bought a very expensive box of chocolates and carefully injected a chocolate from the centre of the box with the same tasteless lethal weed killer they had used on Birdas. Then they carefully resealed the box in a cellophane transparent wrapper using the special wrapping device in the college mail room. Next Sonia wrote a short note under her pseudonym of 'Mrs Patel', apologising for not doing very well at the interview and would Ms Chasuble please show her well-known kindness and reconsider her decision because she really wanted the job. It was dropped off at the Chasuble offices by Ken dressed as a special delivery courier.

Tamsin Fortuna Chasuble's funeral took place ten days later. It was a very, very happy occasion for most of the bandage suppliers' employees and just about anyone else who had met her over the years, many of whom turned up to confirm for themselves that she really had gone on to that great bandage factory beyond the end of the rainbow.

The pressure of demand for conflict deletion services was relentless. What had started out as a charitable vocation was gradually being transformed into a serious business.

"Any more work and we will have to give up teaching."

"Buzzard reckoned that college lecturer is just about the best cover we could have."

Their next planned project was a small time thug whose preferred entertainment was picking fights with total strangers and beating them up. In fact, to judge from their correspondence, Ken and Sonia could easily have chosen any one of a dozen similar young men with the same antisocial tendencies. This particular specimen just liked hitting people. Well not only hitting them, but also kicking them, breaking their arms, gouging their eyes—he was quite versatile. Just as long as he could hurt someone unknown to him or do a bit of damage, he was happy. He could get very sentimental about 'the kiddies' or his old Mum—'pure gold, a diamond'—but apart from those, his only interest in people was how much pleasure he could get from knocking them about. But he did have his principles. For example, he never stole from anyone or hit kiddies or old ladies, so in his own mind he was perfectly innocent. But good honest fighting never hurt anyone, did it? Serves them right if they can't defend themselves, he reasoned.

"All too many like him," said Sonia.

"We'd better remove him before he becomes Home Secretary."

"This should be fairly easy. Nobody's going to miss him."

"No, and Buzzard will give us no trouble."

They were making plans to remove this odious lout by dropping bricks on his head, or some such. (The details were still to be worked out.) when events took a sudden life-changing turn.

Ken was sitting in the college staff room when a nondescript but well-dressed man was suddenly and silently sitting beside him. Ken had not heard him enter, so discreet and self-effacing was his manner.

"Mr Grassmann? Kenneth Grassmann?"

Ken nodded.

"My name is Smith. We would like to talk to you and Miss Lyttel."

"Go ahead."

"Not here. I have a car outside."

There was something about this man's manner which did not permit disobedience and Ken found himself being escorted to a smart black BMW car which was simultaneously opulent and commonplace. To his surprise, Sonia was already sitting in it. There was a smartly suited young woman in the driving seat.

"What is this?" asked Ken. "You don't look like the police."

"No, Mr Grassmann, we are not the police. We would like you to come to a meeting with our senior officer."

"Senior officer?"

"Yes, senior officer. He'll explain everything."

The rest of the half-hour journey was passed in near-silence save for a little mindless 'nice-weather-for-the-time-of-year' chitchat. The car ride went out of Faldwell

Upton into the countryside for what seemed like tens of miles before turning off on to a B-road and then into a series of unmarked minor roads of decreasing width until they were proceeding down a single lane, little more than a track, which was enclosed on both sides by high trees. Eventually they came to a gate. Ken and Sonia could then see that the high trees along that side of the road were, in fact, hiding a heavy steel fence.

The driver stopped the car and tapped some of the keys on her mobile phone whereupon the gate swung open. The car then drove a few hundred metres to an old office block camouflaged in a hollow at the side of a disused second world war airfield. Apart from this office, there was no sign of any human habitation anywhere around. They had not even passed a village or any houses for the last fifteen minutes. Ken and Sonia had no idea where they were or why they had been brought here.

They looked at their surroundings and saw that this was a place which had not been used for its original purpose for decades. The concrete of the airstrip, where it was just visible through the undergrowth was criss-crossed with cracks and potholes in which the birch and the willowherb had already staked their claims. The whole place had an air, on that grey afternoon, of incomparable bleakness. The two-storey office block itself, though, was obviously still in use. There were a couple of cars outside, one a grey Ford with military number plates, the other a black BMW similar to the one they had been delivered in.

"Ministry of Defence," said Sonia. "I wonder what they want from us?"

Smith heard her.

"No problem, Miss, we'll soon have you back home after the meeting."

At the entrance to the building, Ken and Sonia were surprised to see an armed sentry. They were conducted to a reception desk where Smith ran his ID card over a scanner and then signed in. Ken and Sonia were frisked and ordered to put their possessions—handbag, wallet, pocket contents etc. into a basket which was then locked inside a steel frame. There were several other baskets containing personal paraphernalia inside the frame also. After their possessions had been locked away, Ken was given the key. Finally, they were photographed and prints of their right index fingers were taken. After that, they were let through to meet the promised senior officer.

He turned out to be an urbane civil service type who was waiting for them in large office with two other men and one woman. These four sat themselves across the table from Ken and Sonia, who were, by this time, very frightened.

"Good afternoon, Mr Grassmann, Miss Lyttel," the senior man began. "First let me introduce my colleagues. This is Major Tate."

'Tate' nodded.

"And then Mr. Lyle. The lady on my left is Major Marks. Spencer's my name."

All Ken and Sonia could manage in return was a rather dull, 'hullo'.

'Tate and Lyle', 'Marks and Spencer', thought Ken. Now, wasn't that original?

"So," began 'Spencer', "you must be wondering why we've brought you here?"

The two captives nodded.

"Quite understandable in the circumstances. Sorry about all this James Bond stuff. A bit of a bind this security. But quite essential, unfortunately. National security, you know. You understand, I'm sure. You must be wondering what the devil this is all about. Don't worry. Would you like some tea? Coffee? I'll get some sent up before we get down to business."

'Spencer' pressed a button at his side and a young man in RAF uniform opened the door.

"Williams, could you get coffee, tea, for six please? There's a good chap."

Spencer was all smiles.

"So, Mr Grassmann and Miss Lyttel, it's very nice to meet you finally. We already know quite a bit about you. We know, for example, your address in Faldwell Upton and we know about your jobs at the Upton Faldwell Community College. Your Principal, Ms Cloughe, speaks very highly of both of you."

"Yes?" asked a puzzled Sonia.

"Oh yes, indeed," replied Spencer. "So highly in fact, that she was most disappointed when we told her that you will need to take a year's leave of absence."

"A year's leave of absence? Why and starting when?"

"Well, starting next week, actually. As for why, well we'll be coming to that," and here Spencer motioned to his three colleagues.

"Next week!" said Ken. "You can't do that! It's the middle of term. We have classes to cover."

"Don't worry," said Spencer, calmly. "It's all been taken care of. Principal Cloughe has been most helpful."

"We never found her so."

"We rarely have any trouble. We're very grateful to her. It'll be 'Dame' Kathleen Cloughe in the next honours list, if this goes through. 'For services to further education' the citation will read. Keep that to yourselves, of course. We have always found that more or less anybody can be made to see our point of view with the right inducement—some bauble or other. I sometimes despair of the weakness of the human race when I consider how cheaply so many of them can be bought. But I digress. Back to business. Next week you cease to be college lecturers and you start working for us."

"Suppose we don't want to?" asked Sonia with as much defiance as she could muster.

"I am sorry, my dear, but I'm afraid you don't have a lot of choice," said Spencer.

"I thought this was a democracy. Free speech, free to come and go. That's what I tell my students, anyway."

All four of the interviewers smiled broadly at this little outburst. Spencer was laughing.

"Of course it's a democracy, my dear," he said patronisingly, "and that is why we want you to help us keep it that way. Unfortunately, it is going to be necessary for you and Mr. Grassmann to suspend some of your traditional British liberties for a little while. In the national interest, of course."

"We could just get up and go," retorted Ken.

"Don't be silly," snapped Spencer. "You can't go anywhere."

"Yes, we can. You haven't kidnapped us, have you?"

"Well yes," replied Spencer. "In a way you could say that we have kidnapped you. But don't worry, you will be taken back home safe and sound after this meeting."

Here Major 'Marks' cut in.

"Actually, we don't like to use terms like 'kidnap'," she said. "It sounds so very criminal. And we are not criminals. Far from it. We feel we are offering you the opportunity to do something useful for your country."

"And if we refuse?"

"As Colonel Spencer has already said," replied Major Marks, "you have no choice. You will be seconded to us for the next twelve months."

"If we refuse?"

"The reason you are not in a position to refuse," said Spencer, "is this file."

He tapped a thick manila file lying on the table in front of him.

"This file," he went on, "contains some very interesting data about you two and what you have been getting up to. You've both been rather naughty, haven't you?"

Here 'Tate' joined in.

"Even in these enlightened times, people can still get upset by murder. It's still illegal. Add in to that, say, conspiracy with various policemen and with that bunch of amateurs from that organisation, what do you call it?"

"ERASED," said Ken.

"Yes, ERASED," continued Tate. "I would guess you've probably run up several hundred years of prison with your little escapades. Even with concurrent sentences, I can't see either of you getting out in less than forty years. You, Kenneth Grassmann, will be a very old man by then. And prison does tend to break people."

"That's enough, Tate," interposed Colonel Spencer. "Mr Grassmann and Miss Lyttel are our guests."

"So," began Ken, "you know all about what we have been doing and if we don't throw up our careers and work for you, then we will be spending a lot of time at Her Majesty's pleasure."

"That's more or less it," said Spencer suavely, while Tate glowered from the sidelines. "Except, of course, that we could never allow your sort of case come to a public trial."

He let those last words hang in the air for a moment while Ken and Sonia digested their real meaning.

"So it's all down to you people, then? Who are you?" asked Ken.

"Who we are, Mr Grassmann," said the one called 'Lyle', speaking for the first time, "is not something you need to know. Suffice it to say that we are a very important branch of the official business of Her Majesty's Government. We exist entirely to keep the country safe and we work only in the national interest. You two, on the other hand, seem to be more of a score-settling private company entirely outside the law. Settling personal vendettas for money. And that is highly irregular."

"What my colleague is saying," came in Spencer, "is that private businesses like yours make it very difficult for us, the legitimate upholders of the law. We do, after all, have a legal mandate for what we do and you do not. Which means that we really only have two options when your sort of operation tries to 'go it alone', so to speak. One of those is to enrol the freebooter into our legitimate branch of the British law enforcement system. If, of course, they have the right profile."

"And the other?" asked Sonia.

She was rewarded for this mild impertinence by Spencer's most condescending smile.

"So, let's get on with it," said Spencer.

"First," he said, "your present activities will have to stop immediately, for reasons I hope you now appreciate. You seem to have done quite well out of it—nice new house, a pleasant apartment, second car, some gold coins, a few decent antiques and, let me see, a total of, what is it, two hundred and fourteen thousand, five hundred and twenty pounds and sixty-eight pence in twelve bank accounts. Those figures, by the way, are correct up until midnight last night, including interest. There's the list if you want to check it. You are going to have to be satisfied with that, I'm afraid. No more freelance work."

He handed over a sheet of A4 which was a fully detailed and itemised list of all Ken and Sonia's assets down to the last penny.

"Right," continued Spencer, "let's talk about the, how shall we say, 'human' cost of your operations so far. First there was Mr Scregg, then the Honourable Sir James Bruce-Bubbson MP, followed by, let me see, Messrs Tranley, Birdas and Boyden. Then there was Chief Inspector Harold Melladew, a local estate agent called Mr Benny Boscombe, a Miss Tamsin Chasuble and someone called Miss Suzanne Bottomworth. And several others. Shall I go on?"

"I don't think I recognise all those names. What was the last one? Susan somebody?", said Ken.

"Miss Suzanne Bottomworth. Traffic warden. Known colloquially as Susie the Sociopath."

"Oh," said Ken. "Yes, very tragic. She fell under a train, you know."

"Yes, we know. You pushed her."

"No we didn't," said Ken. "And we didn't push Scregg either."

"Don't waste our time. We have photographs. Possibly Scregg was an accident because there was an inquest. But the other twenty three? We have plenty of evidence." said Spencer. "If we wanted to put you on trial, we could do so without any problems. And we could get a conviction on every case. Courts tend to believe us. And we always have very good evidence, even if we have to manufacture it ourselves."

"I see," said Ken.

"Good," said Spencer. "I'm so glad that you do see. It makes it much easier for us to negotiate. Let me tell you what you will be doing this next year. What we have planned for you."

Then Spencer outlined how the next year of the couple's lives would be arranged.

"First, you are going to move from Faldwell Upton to somewhere nice and anonymous in south London. London is where most of the work is, after all. You will rent out your house for the year. One of our people will arrange all that. You don't need to do anything. When you go into your college tomorrow, you will tell everyone that the college has organised a lecturer exchange with a community college in Utah in the States. Naturally it will be a real college and you will be on their staff list as visiting Brits. All emails and mail to and from there will be sent back to you in London and you will be shown how to redirect it back via the US. Our American cousins are being very helpful. Meanwhile, the Principal of Upton Faldwell College, Miss Cloughe, will arrange for your work to be taken over by other teachers. In return for her DBE, she has been required to sign the Official Secrets Act, as you two will be doing before you leave this evening. I don't have to spell out to you, as we had to explain to Dame Katheleen, as she shortly will become, the, shall we say, 'terminal' consequences of not signing it or of breaking its provisions."

"So," asked Sonia, "what do you want from us."

"I'm coming to that," said Spencer. "But consider first that without your complete commitment to us, we could easily turn you over to the regular police for prosecution. Or, if we thought it best, we could even go further than that. On the other hand, I don't think you will find that what we expect in return for your freedom will prove too onerous. In fact, it is quite well within those talents which you have been demonstrating so effectively ever since you first entered the 'conflict deletion' business."

"We have no choice. That's the deal?" asked Sonia.

"Quite right Miss Lyttel. As we told you before, you have no choice. Can I go on now, please?"

"Please do."

"You will move house over next weekend and from Monday you will be full-time members of our organisation. All the arrangements have been made. We have chosen you specially from many possible recruits because you will be doing work pretty much the same as your conflict deletion work. The main difference being that we will choose the targets, not you. You will be given various tasks from time to time. But with another big difference—you will be trained to carry out this work professionally. So next week you will begin proper training. We don't like our operatives to be amateurs. Some of your work so far has been very amateurish. I see you have a question, Mr. Grassmann."

"Yes, why us? Don't you have your own professionals?"

"Good question, if I might say so," answered Spencer. "Yes, we do have our own people, of course. You will be operating mainly in the UK and Europe where we have to keep rotating our staff as they become known to other agencies or . . ."

"Or?"

"Or they meet with occupational hazards. I'm sure you understand what those might be. You two will be new faces. Unknowns. Our country's enemies, and there are plenty of those, will not know you and therefore they will not be expecting you."

"So, why us in particular?" Ken persisted. "You must know about ERASED."

"Yes, we are quite familiar with ERASED. We did note that you had a meeting with Mr William Hamish McWiggin on May seventeenth at five thirty pm."

"Who?"

"Oh, so sorry. You probably just know him as 'Bill'. Or 'Scouse Bill' as he is sometimes calls himself."

"Yes, Bill. Of ERASED. Couldn't you have used one of his people?"

"Good point. He has at least a hundred and fifty people in his network. We have all their names."

"So why us and not one of them?"

"There was a lot of competition but we decided you two matched the best psychological profile for new operatives in this field. We may use someone else in the future but we already have some work lined up for you. We calculated that you have an aptitude for this line of work as well as being immediately available. I am sure your students at the community college can manage without you. We also liked your idealism, for one thing. And you haven't been squeamish when it comes to the fatal moment. We like that too. No place for emotion in this business. A lot of people enter this profession because they think it is well-paid and glamorous. They are usually hooked on James Bond films, all girls, cars and drinking, with a bit of violence thrown in. Attracts entirely the wrong sort. It's not like that at all. We also liked the fact that always you went for exactly the right targets—riff-raff like bent planning officers and estate agents. No one will cry over them or write letters to the MP complaining that the police haven't solved the problem of what happened to them."

"OK," continued Spencer, "any more questions before I go on?"

"Yes." asked Sonia. "How do you work with the ordinary police? Do you co-operate, share information?"

"Well, naturally, I can't tell you everything that goes on. But, in most cases our relations are cordial. They usually do what we tell them. Your local man, Chief Inspector Buzzard. A fine man, first rate. Absolutely one hundred percent reliable. Anything else?"

"What about the practicalities?"

"Oh yes, the terms. First the job description. After two weeks training, you will wait for our call with details of what we want you to do for us. One of our operatives, a man called Smith, will get in touch."

"We met Smith coming down."

"Yes, very likely. Actually, we employ a lot of Smith's."

"Now, payment, the nitty-gritty," said Spencer. "You will continue to get your regular teachers' salaries for the year. In addition, we will add what we call a 'professional adjustment' to your current pay. I don't know how you manage to live on what the community college pays you. We expect our officers to maintain decent living standards. So this adjustment is about twice what you are getting at the moment. In addition there as a non-contributory pension scheme and medical benefits in the event you encounter any injuries in the course of your duties."

"Is that likely?"

"Regrettably, yes," said Spencer. "Although we are more likely to lose our personnel permanently. Probably won't happen to you. But best to be on the lookout. So, this is the itinerary for the next few days. You will be packing up tomorrow and on Saturday, precisely at fourteen hundred hours, one of our vehicles will collect you from your home in Faldwell Upton and bring you to our safe house in London. You will then be provided with all the necessary documentation for the move. Your own house and apartment will be let by Aorta Estate Agents and the rent will be paid into your account. For the rest of this week you must pretend that you are being transferred on a lecturer exchange with the college in the United States. Try to look excited. From next Monday you will be, officially at least, civil servants grade 4B2 attached to our organisation. It is likely that you may, from time to time, be asked what you do or where you work. You are to answer that you work for the Department of Rural Affairs Records and Archiving Office cataloguing European Union farm data. That is dull enough to stop any further questions."

"Is there anything I've missed, do you think? Gentlemen? Major Marks?"

"No, nothing from us, Colonel. You seem to have covered it all."

"I have a question," said Ken,. "How did you find out all those details about us?"

"Ha, ha!! Clever question." said Spencer. "Not really too difficult. I think you could say that we can just about get any information about anybody within minutes. It's this new-fangled information technology those boffin johnnies keep coming up with. Actually, this is essential because we are vital to the national interest. So it is absolutely of paramount importance to national security that we are able to get a complete run-down about anyone more or less on demand. In the olden days, we had to go around the houses, get permissions and all that business. Do you remember that chap, what was his name? Yes, 'Spycatcher'. Wrote a book. Those days, thirty years ago, it was so primitive. Now, press a button, type in a name and you've got the lot—bank accounts, phone calls, emails—everything. Then bung it in a computer program to do a profile and bingo! It's all there."

"So no privacy anymore?"

The four interviewers chortled.

"Not as far as we're concerned, none at all. The man in the street can't do it, of course. Even the computer geeks out there can't do it, although they're always trying. But as far as we are concerned, privacy of the individual went out of the window, what, oh, ten years ago. Better this way. Safer. All in the national interest. A country that doesn't keep tabs on its people is letting its citizens down. But if you've nothing to hide, you've nothing to fear."

Spencer stood up and the meeting was over. He shook the hands of Ken and Sonia.

"So nice to meet you both. Thank you for coming. Just the formality of signing the Official Secrets Act and then you can be on your way. Smith will take you back home."

A few minutes later, Ken and Sonia were back in the car with the same 'Smith' and the same driver, feeling just a little shell-shocked. It was already dark and the lighting outside the office block was so minimal that, from the outside, the building appeared completely blacked out, as if totally unoccupied. Ken wondered where Spencer and his cronies lived, where they parked their cars. How they came and went.

"Well, it's not like we have any choice, is it, love? We're working for 'them' now." said Ken to Sonia.

ELEVEN

After a long silent drive in the dark, the car was suddenly under the street lights of Faldwell Upton. The driver indicated right towards Ken and Sonia's house.

"No," said Ken. "Can you please drop us in the centre of the town? About here will be fine."

They were outside the college.

Smith passed over a large envelope.

"Your brief, sir. Goodnight."

And with that they were standing outside the college.

"Stranglers Arms?" asked Ken. "A lot to talk about."

"We could do that at home."

"No, better here. If the house wasn't bugged before, it certainly is now. They're sure to have been in and planted something. We won't be overheard over the noise in here."

So they pushed their way through the crush of thirsty students in the bar of *The Ford Zodiac*.

"Do you really think they will be listening to us?"

"I would think the likelihood is somewhere round about one hundred percent. Difficult to hear us over this row."

The landlord greeted them like old friends.

"Hello strangers! Long time no see. What brings you back here?"

"Hello Mike," said Ken. "How are you?"

"Can't complain, no one would listen." Mike made his regular joke.

Ken and Sonia got their drinks and found a couple of seats near the door.

"So, we're working for the goon show, now."

"Not a lot of choice, as Spencer kept telling us."

"So we'll just have to go with the flow. Get ready for a move to London."

"It might be a good idea to clean all computer files, burn correspondence *et cetera*."

"I think that's a bit late by now," said Ken. "They already know more about us than we do. Destroying the evidence is just bolting the stable door."

"You know," said Sonia, "I always thought that this sort of KGB stuff, you know, collecting all this personal data, I thought that went out with the Soviet Union."

"No, my darling," said Ken, "I am sure all governments do it. These spy types are all so paranoid, they just do it as a matter of course. We used to criticise the old Russian or East German communists for monitoring everybody's every waking moment because we were the good guys and they were the bad guys. In fact, all spooks are the same. It's just that our spooks are on our side and theirs aren't. Computers just make data collection easier."

"Makes you wonder why they bother?" said Sonia. "People are the same everywhere."

"Not if you're in the intelligence trade, they're not. There are pure white good ones, like us and those on our side. And then there are deeply evil ones on the other side. It's a very simple philosophy."

"Doesn't the enemy change, from time to time?"

"Yes, that's what makes the game so fascinating to the Spencer's of this world. Last year's enemies are this year's friends and *vice versa*. The Russians were our friends, then they became our enemies, now they're our friends again. Same with the Germans. The easiest way is just to keep tabs on everybody, friend and enemy alike."

"A bit like religion really, isn't it? People are either evil or good but they can be converted from evil to good with a bit of confession. Conversely, they can break one of the rules and suddenly become evil. Spooks are not exactly famous for their fine subtle judgements. Black or white is good enough, I suppose. I wonder why anyone should want to bother to collect all this information about everybody and who reads it for God's sake?"

"I think that's easy to explain," said Ken. "First, the world has always had its fair share of control freaks who want everyone else to see the world in exactly the same way as they do. They make laws to make sure no one steps out of line and then they have to check up on everyone to make sure they are obeying those laws. Now that they have computer networks, it's a lot easier to do the checking up."

"At least they don't burn people at the stake anymore."

"Well, they probably would if they could. But a revolver does the same job more quickly."

"Or ERASED."

"Yes, or us."

Back home, they opened the envelope which Smith had given them. It was a list of instructions for the move from their comfortable suburban villa to an anonymous Victorian terraced house in Croydon. No one could accuse the security services of not being completely thorough. There was a list of everything they would need to take and instructions on how it would be packed up. Two men in overalls arrived on the dot of 2.00pm on Saturday afternoon and loaded everything into a white unmarked Ford Transit. At exactly 2.30pm, the standard black BMW arrived with a driver and a man dressed in a grey suit. Ken and Sonia had seen neither of them before.

"Good morning, Mr Grassmann, Miss Lyttel. My name is Smith. We're here to take you to your new abode in south London. Leave your house keys please. The driver will take you."

Ken handed over the keys to their house which the national security organisation was now going to rent out on their behalf. Actually, their house would not actually be rented. It was earmarked to become a safe house for security operatives working in the Faldwell area.

"I hope you told everyone that you are taking a year off in the States?"

"Yes, we did. Everyone was very jealous."

"Good. Your house and your new apartment will be safe in our hands. We will look after them, don't worry. And you will be receiving rent for both of them. All personal papers *et cetera* removed, as we asked you?"

"We shredded what we could and put the rest into sealed boxes in the loft."

"Utilities OK?"

"Paid up. Standing orders all taken care of."

"Good. Our chaps will go through it all again. Just to be sure," said Smith. "Goodbye and have a safe trip."

Ken and Sonia got into the back of the BMW and it was driven away. They just caught sight of Smith opening their front door.

"Have you thought," Ken asked Sonia, "that we are just about non-existent by now?"

"What do you mean?"

"Well," Ken continued, "think about it. All signs of our ever living there have been taken away. You can be sure Smith will go through the place with a fine toothed comb to make sure all traces of us are removed."

"What about the college?" asked Sonia. "Our friends will still remember us."

"Unlikely, I would have thought. In two weeks all our colleagues will have forgotten everything about us, including our names. There may be the odd postcard from the US. But if I were one of the Smiths, I would make sure those tailed off after a couple of months or so."

"Aren't we still on the college records?" asked Sonia, "We'll still be on salary, according to our new masters. How will they manage that?"

"Shouldn't be too difficult," replied Ken. "Cloughie has been well-bribed. She should be able to keep the pretence going for a year. She would have sold her mother for vivisection to get a damehood."

"Are you saying," asked Sonia, "that we have become unpersons? Completely off the radar?"

"I think so," said Ken. "I don't suppose they've actually deleted our medical and national health records or torn up our birth certificates. They've no need to. But I imagine they've taken out things like our phone records, electricity accounts, council tax, electoral roll, things like that where people can be traced. Yes, we have become non-people. We can be sure Spencer's boys will make a proper job of it."

"Which means . . . ." began Sonia.

Ken completed the sentence for her.

"Which means that we have become totally disposable."

"Shush," said Sonia, "better not to say too much in the car."

Which was a very wise precaution as it turned out. Another 'Smith' was waiting at the safe house in Croydon where they were deposited.

"Good afternoon, sir, miss," he began. "Welcome to your new home. I hear that you are fully aware of your new position. We have indeed removed all those records which you will no longer, while in our employ, need to spend time keeping up to date. We do prefer our employees not to try to keep up with their previous way of life. You will be working in a business where it is not possible to serve two masters. So we rely on your hundred percent commitment. Now, please, if you don't mind, I am going to have to search your personal luggage to make sure you didn't bring anything not on our permitted list."

"What, no body search?" asked Sonia.

"Good gracious no!" replied Smith. "All that groping? No, no, that's just for those perverts at the airport. We're a bit more professional than that."

"How do you know I don't have a machine gun in my underwear?"

"Very funny, miss. Very amusing. Actually, you were X-rayed in the car without you knowing it."

"Tell, me," asked Ken. "What if, just on the off-chance, we bump into someone we know?"

"Then you tell them that you are still at the college but you are on temporary secondment in the United States. Then you can tell them that you are just in London on a short visit."

"Are we still going to use our real names?" asked Sonia.

"Here are some more instructions," said Smith. "Sorry about all this paperwork. Part of the job, I'm afraid. We are part of the Civil Service, after all. Everything in triplicate, unfortunately. Your new names are Jones and Robinson. Not very original, I grant you. But I do see from your file that this is not the first time you have resorted to false names. Anyway, look around. You will find that this is not too uncomfortable a place to live in for a year or two."

"Or two? I thought the deal was one year only?" asked Ken.

"Just a slip, sir. You may actually take to the work. It has a lot of advantages. Good pay, foreign travel, no nine-to-five. You can get to enjoy it. Anyway, read the file. Work starts on Monday. Meanwhile I will leave you to explore your new house. You will find the larder is fully stocked. Decent, if limited, wine cellar, drinks cabinet, all mod cons., as they say. So goodbye Mr Jones, Miss Robinson. Be ready eight am. Monday morning. Dress casual, jeans and T-shirt. Oh, and pack overnight bags for a three-day stay. Just the basics."

"One last question. Can we go out, like down to the shops?"

"Of course you can. What do you think we are? You're not prisoners here. Just be careful. Don't advertise your presence."

Ken went over to the table and took some writing materials out of his suitcase.

'Nothing important by speech. Place bugged. Writing only. Then destroy paper', he wrote.

'Laptops?' wrote Sonia.

'Hidden spyware on laptops', wrote Ken. 'Sends back every key stroke'

Punctual at eight o'clock on Monday morning, the car arrived to collect Ken and Sonia from their new home. They drove slowly through the south London suburbs heading towards rural Kent. Eventually, after a two-hour tedious trip against the heavy traffic they arrived at another nondescript and well-hidden group of Ministry of Defence buildings on a disused airfield. A young man, wearing an RAF sweater with epaulettes, opened the car door.

"Mr. Jones? Miss Robinson? Here for the training course for civilians? Follow me. The driver will bring your bags. You will be staying here until Thursday. It's only basic accommodation, I'm afraid. Just like a hotel room. Not much in the way of room service. But it's only for a couple of days."

He conducted the couple to an office where a middle-aged man was waiting.

"Good morning Mr Jones and Miss Robinson. You can call me Smith."

He explained why they were there.

"I understand that you have had quite a lot of changes these last few days," 'Smith' began. "Always a lot of fuss and details, getting new people ensconced. Should be easier from now on. Let me explain what we do here."

"We are," he said, "the training unit. Our job is to make sure that all our operatives are as well-trained as possible in the short time we have at our disposal. We may not be able to turn you into fully-fledged James Bond's in three days but hopefully we are going to be able to give you enough basic skills for whatever the chappies upstairs have in mind for you. Don't ask me what that is, we are just trainers. They don't tell us what they use you for. Our job is to make sure you know what you are doing and don't bugger things up in the process."

Ken and Sonia said nothing, waiting for him to elaborate.

"So," he went on, "you will stay here until Thursday and take the basic training. At the end of the course you will have some idea how to stay safe in the field and not eliminate the wrong people. It's a full schedule, nine to nine. Here are ID's for food and laundry. The canteen is open twenty four seven. Just ask the duty officer in the general office if you need any help. Classes start at one pm. Straight after lunch."

They ate lunch in the canteen. A few other people were eating separately. At one o'clock they presented themselves at the classroom. They were the only students.

First they were given a pep talk about security and how important it was in the modern world. The teacher identified a long list of the enemies of the British way of life, not to say the whole edifice of western civilisation which, they were informed, is under constant threat from innumerable evil forces out to undermine our cherished ideals of peace and motherhood. Then there was another lecture about the various ways which our side, the decent guys, uses to take out, erase, delete, terminate, eliminate or otherwise remove members of the other side, the not-so-decent guys.

It appears that the preferred disposal methods were not those quick and efficient methods considered most suitable for the task by film-maker, such as the gun, the bomb or physical violence. No, the presenter of the class told them, such methods upset the general public and lead to questions in parliamentary committees. There might even be a few newspaper column inches of indignation which could be safely ignored but would still cause the director of the department a little embarrassment. The department preferred always to maintain a low profile. Far better, policy decreed, to rub out the unwanted by more ambiguous, indirect and less overtly criminal methods. The car crash, poisoning, falling off high buildings or in front of fast-moving trains—methods which could be more readily covered up as innocent as far as the readers of the tabloids were concerned. They were much preferred to those cruder elimination techniques which are more obviously and undeniably illegal. It was undoubtedly their experience and efficiency in using such oblique and less-violent methods of despatch which had led to the couple's selection in the first place.

The three days passed surprisingly quickly for Ken and Sonia. There was constant brain-washing about the correctness of the noble calling of rubbing out those dangerous enemies of society and there were classes about exactly how to do it. Ken and Sonia learned which poisons to use and how to load them into a short-fire hypodermic syringe which could be loaded into the end of an umbrella. Then there were the contact poisons which could be smeared on the surface of an object which would be then handled by the victim. They learnt the best way to build a bomb with the unmistakeable signature of whatever terrorist group was currently in number one position on the public hate list.

They also learnt the ancient and venerable craft of the letter bomb and the many ways in which a car ignition can be re-wired to make it a total death trap. Their lecturer, Smith, assured them that the technology has been much refined. They learned, for example, how to use a new development which the demonstrator was very proud of, a centrifugal device which could be quickly added to the inside of the wheel of a car to puncture its tyre at high speeds. One class, given by a young lecturer with intense popping eyes, was on how to burn down a building without anyone suspecting arson. He was clearly a pyromaniac—his voice rose several slavering decibels as he described the course of a fire through a building.

They also had classes in disguises and how to plant listening devices into remote personal computers and mobile phones. There was even an interesting lecture on money-laundering and fraud which Ken thought might be quite useful should they survive long enough to escape their new career.

By Thursday morning the training was complete. They were taken back to the first office. The man they had been introduced to the previous Monday had been replaced by a new, but Identikit-similar, middle-aged man in a dark-grey suit.

"What's happened to the man who was here on Monday?" asked Ken.

"Oh, Smith? Not here, I'm afraid. You can call me Smith. You did well. Ready for action?"

"It's been very interesting."

"Glad you enjoyed it. Your driver will take you back to London."

"What happens next?"

"Can't tell you that," said Smith. "Need to know. The field department will be in touch. Those operative wallahs will contact you. Most likely next week. Nothing much happens over the weekend. Don't worry. There's certainly plenty for you to do. You didn't get all this expensive training for nothing. Then it will be down to you. Remember your training and stay fit."

Smith shook their hands.

"Goodbye Mr. Jones. Goodbye Miss Robinson. It's been a pleasure. Here's your driver."

"Smith, please make sure our colleagues get back to Croydon in one piece, be a good chap."

TWELVE

The first job of Ken and Sonia's new career as civil servants Grade 4B2 was not long in presenting itself. A few days after their training course, they got a phone call.

"Hello," the voice said. "My name is Smith. I am calling from DEFRA. I will be at your house in one hour. Please be there."

He then rang off.

"This must be it." said Sonia. "I only hope the job is not someone I like."

"Well, we'll see. We have no choice, after all."

'Smith' was a nondescript middle-aged man in a dark-grey suit.

"Are you sure we haven't met before, Mr Smith?" asked Ken.

"I don't think so, Mr Jones. I'm quite new. You must be thinking of someone else."

"Well, come in. Please sit down. Would you like some coffee?"

"That's very kind of you," said Smith, taking a file out of his briefcase.

"This is the job we want you to do for us. Quite straightforward. You are beginners, I understand?"

"Yes, but we took the training course last week."

"Good." said Smith. "We don't see any problems with this job. Actually we would appreciate a quick result. Powers on high, you know. Getting a bit restive to see this one taken care of ASAP."

Smith opened the file and took out a photograph.

"That's the one. His name is Finbarr Duckworth. Have you heard of him?"

Ken and Sonia both shook their heads.

"Well, our Mr Duckworth has been a bit of a bad lad. He's got one or two things on his charge sheet that are, strictly speaking, against the law of the land."

"Why not just charge him then?"

"Well, that's just the problem, you see. A trial in court would be embarrassing. Various people, whose names you certainly would know, would have to testify. It could be very unpleasant. That's where you come in."

"So, you want us to delete Mr. Duckworth, to save some bigwig being embarrassed."

"Precisely!"

"Why can't you use one of your regular people?" asked Sonia.

"But, Miss Robinson, you are one of our regular people. Ever since you signed the Official Secrets Act and took the Queen's shilling. You are now subject to our orders."

"OK," conceded Sonia. "Tell us more about Mr Finbarr Duckworth. What has the fellow been up to?"

"Well," said Smith. "I can't tell you too much, given the people involved. Suffice it to say that you will probably be able to put two and two together once you read the stuff in this envelope."

"Do we get a copy?"

"'Fraid not." said Smith, "You can only read it in my presence. Then I must take it away with me. Security."

He handed over a large envelope full of A4 photocopies of press cuttings. Puzzlingly, none of them mentioned

Duckworth. They were, all of them, about a very well-known face indeed, and one which featured regularly in the glossy magazines and society gossip columns. Princess Amelie, as well as being umpteenth in line to the throne was a regular on the party circuit. 'Princess A. Canned!!' shouted one tabloid over a paparazzi snap of a dishevelled young woman at a party during the Cannes film festival. 'Amelie Piles on the Pounds' was the headline over another unflattering photograph from one of the lower end red-tops. Then there was a snatched snap of the Princess in Harley Street with 'Princess Am Goes to the Docs'.

"So, Her Royal Highness is pregnant?"

"Not any more," replied Smith.

"We thought we hadn't seen much of her lately."

"Yes, she's been kept out of the public eye for a while," said Smith.

"I thought you were able to stop this sort of story about the royals getting out?" asked Sonia.

"Well, yes, that is what we would normally do. A little word here or there. A little threat to the journalist responsible. Maybe a knighthood to the owner of the rag. There are several things we could do."

"But," said Ken, "are you saying this one leaked out in spite of all that?"

"Yes," said Smith. "Unfortunately, there was a bit of a leak."

"So, who's this Finbarr Duckworth? How does he come into it."

"Let me give you a little background," Smith replied. "First of all, as you guessed and probably the whole of the population guessed, the royal lady was indeed pregnant. And, when she goes back into circulation, she will no longer be pregnant, courtesy of a very discreet clinic in Harley Street. Naturally, it is very difficult to keep this sort of story completely quiet but we can manufacture a fairly plausible cover story which the papers will print if we tell them to. After a while, the story will go away except maybe for a few nutters running conspiracy theory websites. Fortunately no one takes them seriously and so the whole thing is containable."

"But this time it's different?" asked Ken.

"Yes," Smith went on. "This time it's different. This time the story is worth a million. And not just in this country. You see, the Princess's paramour is not just your average English chap who can be relied on to do the decent thing and marry the girl and keep quiet. No, the father of Her Royal Highness's aborted child is said to be none other than one Marlon Q. Hoemaster. Have you heard of him?"

"Marlon Q. Hoemaster? You mean the American rapper?"

"The very same," confirmed Smith.

"My God!" said Ken. "The most famous, most foul-mouthed, drug-soaked entertainer in the world put HRH The Princess Amelie in the pudding club!"

"Quite. Mr Hoemaster is not exactly the kind of son-in-law her parents, the Duke and Duchess, had been hoping for. Like I say, we've been able to keep most of this out of the press but there is still one problem. The Princess's parents were at their wits' end over it all. They were on the point of kicking her out until they were persuaded that the scandal would not be appreciated at all down at Buck House. And now that the government is on one of its periodic morality drives about teenage pregnancies, HMG don't want to look like idiots either. So they paid off the American and they've taken poor Amelie out of circulation until they can find her a husband. Silly little bitch, she doesn't know how much trouble she's caused."

"Surely this is not the first time there's been some family trouble. It's a big family after all. Bound to be some black sheep."

"Well, of course," said Smith. "In the old days this sort of thing was all very hush-hush. People guessed what they were up to but no one dared say anything. Have you ever wondered why royal men have so many 'godchildren' and why they are always going to christenings?"

"But not now, eh?"

"No, not now," agreed Smith. "Far more difficult these days."

"So how do we come in? You mentioned this other fellow. Duckworth? What's he got to do with it?"

Smith explained about Finbarr Duckworth and how he had come to be part of the plot.

"Finbarr Duckworth is a nasty little shit who has managed to get hold of records from the abortion clinic and he's pieced together the whole story. He's asked the Duke for money to keep quiet. Naturally, the police have warned him off but he is still threatening to go public. Obviously we could have him arrested and charged for attempted blackmail but it's all very delicate."

"So, what's the position at the moment," asked Sonia.

"The position at the moment is that we have told him that we will consider a deal but it will take a week. We have until next Friday, so there's not much time. Meanwhile he's been stopped from doing anything right away. Some of the heavy mob from his local police station have put the frighteners on. Naturally we have the press all covered and we are monitoring his phone, mail, computer, that sort of thing."

"What is he likely to do, if we don't stop him?"

"Well, he's threatening that if we don't pay him a hundred thousand, he will publish abroad. There are, it appears, plenty of foreign publications with even fewer principles than our own rags."

"Why not just pay him and get rid of him?"

"Paying him is out of the question. He will just come back for more. But getting rid of him? That's a different matter. And that is where you come in."

"By Friday?"

"By Friday."

"Can we take the photograph? What about an address?" Ken asked Smith.

"No problem, take the photo. This is the address where the little bastard lives."

Smith handed over a ready-printed address. Finbarr Duckworth lived about twenty miles away in north London. Smith shook hands and got up to leave.

"Let's hope for some good news before Friday," were his parting words.

Ken and Sonia went out into the garden where there were no hidden microphones.

"This is our big test."

"Let's not screw it up or we're next."

"Car accident?"

"Probably the best plan. I'm sure our new masters will be able to square things with the local cops. So, it should be reasonably safe. Or we could try one of those clever poisons from the course."

"Why not try poison first and if we don't get a chance then hit him with a car."

"You are forgetting, my dear. The cars are back in Faldwell Upton."

"We could buy an old banger tomorrow."

So, the following day, solely for the purpose of transferring Mr Finbarr Duckworth to the afterlife, Ken and Sonia bought a ten-year-old Ford Mondeo for six hundred pounds. Unfortunately, it had nearly two-hundred thousand miles on the clock so they crossed their fingers that it would actually make the twenty mile journey to north London. They then had a pair of false number plates made up and looked up the location of the car-crusher nearest to Duckworth's apartment. Then it was just a matter of driving to N17 to observe the comings and goings of Mr. Finbarr Duckworth.

Next morning at daybreak, they were waiting discreetly outside the block of flats where Duckworth lived. It was to be a long wait. Duckworth did not appear until early evening, when Ken and Sonia were on the point of giving up and going home to devise a Plan B. But no, just after six o'clock, a man who was obviously Duckworth came out of the ground floor flat of the block and made his way down the street to the local pub. He was a thin, bitter-looking man with the prematurely lined face of the heavy smoker. He walked too slowly for a man in his forties, stooping and dragging his feet.

"Ideal," said Ken. "Fancy a drink?"

Ken and Sonia parked in the pub car park and went into the bar of *The Withered Scorpion*. Duckworth was sitting at a table with two other men. Ken and Sonia took their drinks to the other end of the room where they could observe him from a distance. It promised to be another long wait. But after about half an hour one of Duckworth's ugly companions got up and left. That left just Duckworth and the other ugly. It was time for a distraction.

Sonia undid the top two buttons of her blouse and went over to the bar.

"An orange juice, please," she asked the barman, meanwhile turning to look at the two seated men. She smiled at them and they couldn't help but respond to such a brazen invitation.

"Let me buy that," said Duckworth.

"Ooh! That's very kind. Whatever would my husband say?"

"Your husband doesn't need to know," Duckworth answered lasciviously.

"Is that your husband over there?" the other man put in.

"Oh no, my hubby's at work. That's just a friend."

"A boyfriend, then? Who's a naughty girl then?"

"Stop it, you're making me blush!" Sonia said flirtatiously.

"I bet it would take a lot to make you blush."

"Ooh! Don't be so rude. I'm not like that. He's just a work colleague."

"Is that what you call it? I wouldn't mind working with you."

"Hey, Brian, come over here," Sonia shouted to Ken.

"What is it, Geraldine?" Ken played the simpleton boyfriend.

"Well, Brian," Sonia replied, "these two gentlemen were wondering if you are my boyfriend. I told them we just work together."

"We're just good friends, aren't we Geraldine, love?"

"That's right, Brian!" Sonia gave a big wink at Duckworth.

"Why don't you come and sit by me," said Duckworth.

"All right," agreed Sonia. "But no funny business. Not with my work colleague here."

"Oh he can come and sit here as well. One woman and three men. A lot of women like that."

Sonia tapped Duckworth's arm playfully.

"Now that's enough," she said. "I'm a respectable married woman just out for a quiet drink with my friend."

"I believe you, thousands wouldn't!"

"Ooh! Now you're being naughty!"

At this point the ugly got up to go to the gents. This was Ken's moment. He glanced at Sonia.

"What's your name?" Sonia asked Duckworth.

"You can call me Finbarr," said Duckworth. "It's Gaelic for virile."

"Ooh!" said Sonia. "Now who's bragging?"

And then, in one quick movement Duckworth lunged at Sonia. At the same moment the contents of the phial of slow-acting poison which Ken had been carefully nursing under the table were transferred to Duckworth's half-empty pint of Guinness.

"Ooh! Down boy!" said Sonia. "Not so fast!"

"So, do you have a phone number, Geraldine?"

Sonia rummaged around in her bag and brought out a pen. She pulled over a beer mat and wrote 'Geraldine Smith' on it plus the first number that came into her head.

"Sorry," she said to Duckworth, kissing her hand and placing it on his forehead. "Got to go. Duty calls. Work is the curse of the drinking classes, as they say. Goodbye Finbarr. Cheers. Drink up. Nice to meet you. Say goodbye to your friend for me."

And with that they were out of the pub, into the old car and back on the road.

"Do you think you gave him enough?" asked Sonia when they were back on the M25.

"Well, that chemist fellow on the course said two millilitres will kill a 100 kilogram man. Duckworth was about 75 kilo, so I put twenty mils in his beer. That's about fifteen times the lethal dose. Should do the trick."

"Let's hope. What a scumbag that man is. I'll need a bath the minute we get in. He stank, did you notice? Couldn't miss it."

"What about this car? We didn't need to buy it after all."

"Let's keep it. It might come in useful. Save buying another. We'll keep it parked out of sight."

"Quite right. Wouldn't like anyone to think we are the sort of couple who will drive a clapped out Mondeo."

"I thought you were worried about it being traced."

"Well, that too, of course. Good job we bought in under false name and address. I'm sure Spencer or Smith or whatever his name is will have removed our records from the vehicle database. So we're safe."

They got a phone call late the following day.

"Excellent work, both of you. Great job. By the way, my name's . ."

"Yes, we know, Smith," said Ken.

"How did you guess? No matter. A very professional operation if I might say so. Beautifully done. 'Brian', 'Geraldine'. Excellent choice of names. First class operation. Just a few ends to tie up at our end. We got the doctor to write 'heart attack' on Duckworth's death certificate. Quite believable. The man smoked like a chimney. Serves the bugger right."

"Wait a minute," Ken asked. "How did you know what names we used? How did you know we were using Brian and Geraldine?"

"Well, it was your first job. We like to keep an eye on our recruits. See how they measure up in action. See if they pass muster. You passed with flying colours."

"You were watching us?"

"Not so much watching, almost taking part," said Smith. "Just about holding your hands all the way through. Just in case. But no need to on this occasion. You excelled yourselves."

"What? You mean the ugly fellow with Duckworth was one of yours?"

"Absolutely! When he got up to go to the gents, you didn't miss a trick. We admire quick thinking like that. Miss Robinson was superb. She will make quite the femme fatale. Great actress. Once again, congratulations. A job very well done. Just one thing though, that 'ugly fellow' as you call him will not take kindly to being called ugly. He fancies himself as a bit of a ladies man. Quite the charmer is our Mr . . ."

"Smith?" asked Ken.

"Yes, as it happens, Smith. Anyway, take it easy for a day or two. We'll be back in touch next week."

"One thing before you go," said Ken, "Before we got the idea of the way we actually did it, we were thinking more along the lines of using a car. So we laid out six hundred pounds for an old disposable Ford Mondeo which we were going to have crushed afterwards. It turned out we didn't need it after all. Can we claim on expenses?"

"No problem. No problem at all. We pay all the expenses for our people. And I can confidently say you are now one of our people. We'll send over some DEFRA expenses forms. Special code on them. Go straight through to our cashier and the money is paid directly into your account. Once again, brilliant stuff. Have a nice weekend."

"Hello", said Smith on the phone, "I've got another little job for you. Can we meet? Your place. Now?"

"OK."

When he arrived, Ken and Sonia recognised him immediately.

"It's Bill, isn't it?"

"No, it's Smith, actually."

"No, go on, You remember us. Faldwell Upton? ERASED?"

"Hello again, Mr Grassmann, Ms. Lyttel. Or should I say Mr Jones and Miss Robinson? Nice to meet you again."

"What's with the name change, then?"

"Oh, Smith's my real working name, of course."

"So why were you called Bill? Scouse Bill, if I recall?"

"That was just my field name. For ERASED. Let's stick to Smith."

"So you're not Bill and I notice the Liverpool accent has gone as well. Are you saying that ERASED and your lot, from wherever, are the same?"

"Not exactly. What I can tell you is that we use a lot of agents and there is a fairly heavy turnover. For obvious reasons."

"So," put in Sonia, "are you saying that ERASED is where you get your recruits? I thought ERASED was all freelance."

"Yes, it is. Mostly." said Smith. "We like to think of it as a semi-professional feeder into our main organisational structure."

"Like non-league football feeding into the professional league?" asked Ken.

"Precisely. We get a lot of new talent from there. Which is where we found you two, of course. Then they are offered a career at the professional level. It also means that when they leave us, there will be guaranteed employment in the lower levels of the game. Not that that happens too often, of course, given the nature of our calling."

"So you have a new job for us?" asked Sonia.

"Yes, we were very impressed with your first outing. All that unfortunate business with Princess Amelie has now been cleared up. Time for you to move up a grade."

"More money?" asked Ken.

"Very funny. Don't be silly, Mr Jones. This is the Civil Service. No, what we have in mind is a little trip up north. I'm sure you are up for that."

"Where up north?"

"Well, Glasgow actually. Just a couple of days. Next week."

"OK. You said 'up a grade'?"

"Yes, I hope you will not find the next little task too distasteful. Not, of course, that you can refuse. A refusal now would certainly terminate your future careers with the service."

Smith put an almost imperceptible emphasis on the word 'terminate'.

"Tell us about it."

Smith slapped a file on to the table.

"Here he is. Larry Lollie. Actually Lord Lollie. Or to give him his full title, Lord Larry Lollie of Leeds. A man who enjoys his alliteration. Friend of prime ministers, film producers, various assorted millionaires and sundry international criminal riff-raff."

"Is he the next target?"

"Good heavens, no!" retorted Smith. "He's the reason but not the target. The target is one Melinda MacCoggin. This is what she looks like."

"Why her? I can understand rubbing out Larry Lollie. Who would miss him? Not even Lady Lollie, if what I read in the papers is true."

"Quite," agreed Smith. "Larry Lollie is indeed a world-class piece of work. But he is better connected than the Prime Minister. So he lives but poor Melinda must not."

"And why is that? What has she done to deserve our attention?"

"Nothing much really, but our friend Lord Lollie wants rid of her. And with the sort of friends he has, what Lord Lollie wants, Lord Lollie gets."

"Well, Bill, sorry, Smith, it sounds like you don't approve, yourself."

"It's not for me to have an opinion, Mr Jones," Smith answered. "In this job, as I'm sure you have already found out, it is best not to let your own feelings interfere with the business. What I think about Lollie or Miss MacCoggin is immaterial. We're professionals doing a job. Sometimes what we do is necessary, sometimes not."

"And we're thinking that this one is not. Are we right?" asked Sonia.

"It's up to you to decide. Just remember that Lollie is very, very powerful. Although no-one quite understands how he got there. But that's not our concern either. Now here are the newspaper clippings, addresses *et cetera*."

Smith handed over an envelope. The clippings went back ten years. They had forgotten the details about Sir Larry Lollie, as he then was, before a grateful monarch saw fit to ennoble him. Lollie had made his vast fortune as a property dealer and he was a generous donor to all the political parties. Like many a parvenu, he had sought respectability to go with his billions and he had invested in an Elizabethan mansion in the midst of the English countryside which he had refurbished to the very highest standards of opulence and vulgarity.

"You could even bring King of Saudi Arabia here and he'd be impressed," he would boast in his broad Yorkshire. "Not bad for a slum boy from Bradford." He pronounced it 'Brat'fud'.

Meanwhile, the scented Lady Lollie, the former Miss Reinforced Concrete 1988, who had twice been voted Top Topless Model, had decided, shortly after receiving her title and meeting the Queen, that enough of Lollie was enough and she subsequently spent her time on the French Riviera and in the Maldives, living on an allowance from Lollie which was payment in return for her silence about her husband. This estrangement was of no consequence to Lollie himself, who was able to use his independence and his money to lay on weekly house parties for his influential political and business friends where they could be guaranteed entertainment of memorable dissoluteness. For although Lollie was a northern working-class prude himself, he was well-aware of the profit and influence to be found by exploiting the decadent tastes of the English ruling classes.

Naturally, the house parties needed supplementary broad-minded guests who were well-versed in catering for louche patrician tastes, so a regular supply of party girls and other assorted ephemeral night creatures, ladyboys, catamites and so on, would be bussed in on Saturday morning and despatched back to London on Sunday evening, once the appetites of the rich and powerful had been fully sated.

"If you can't use yer money to enjoy yersel', what's point in making brass in first place?" Lollie would tell his guests. What he didn't tell them was that he had hidden cameras in every room.

All had gone well for Lollie as he had ascended the greasy pole of power and privilege. Discrete little blackmailings and bribes had secured him the traditional advancement through the ranks of the British social strata. He was, after all, only doing what numerous other self-serving chancers and social climbers had been doing for centuries as they had restocked the gene pool of the English aristocracy.

Ken and Sonia broke off their reading to ask Smith a question.

"Did Lollie ever use ERASED?"

"No, amazingly, he never actually had anyone rubbed out on his own orders as far as we can tell. Of course, he had a lot of important friends and they could have done it for him. There was always a bit of a bad smell that time when he bought up Galactic Film Studios after the previous owner, what's his name, Sir Charlie Zambucca, had been found dead of an overdose. But nothing was ever proved on that occasion. Still I wouldn't put it past him."

"So this . . . ?"

"Miss Melinda MacCoggin."

"Melinda MacCoggin. Wasn't she in some sort of trial? Wasn't Lollie involved?"

"Read on," said Smith.

The clippings featured Melinda with photographs and her life story which had been in such demand during her fifteen minutes of fame some eight years previously. Melinda had been a working girl, a lowly toiler in the sex industry, a whore, a prostitute, a brass, a hooker. Her choice of profession had been quite pragmatic. Other career choices open to a poor working-class girl without much formal education in an area of poverty and unemployment are somewhere between very limited and non-existent. If she is pretty and friendly, the horizontal life is one of the few professions open to her which pays decently and doesn't need a college diploma.

Melinda's workday schedule at the time had been to make use of the daily Glasgow to London Intercity Express. Three times a week she would board the 7.45 train out of Glasgow Central and work two or three tricks before the train pulled into London Euston at 11.10. Then she would spend an afternoon on her back in a nice co-operative hotel in South Kensington which catered for working girls, followed by the 20.38 train back to Glasgow on which she would meet one or two of her regular clients and drum up new business in the buffet car. She soon built up a regular clientele of sales managers, bankers and self-employed businessmen and it was only a matter of time before she was asked whether she also did weekend work. The weekend pay rate was pretty good and after she had arranged for her mother to do the weekend child care, she soon became one of Lord Lollie's regular hostesses. But Melinda, in spite of having little in the way of formal education, was a sharp cookie and she soon realised that she would not be spending long on the Lollie party gravy train before her star faded and she was replaced by younger talent. Better, she reasoned, to leverage her temporary role by a little insurance in the form of photographs, tape recordings and a diary.

Not every VIP and bigwig in British public life had been invited to share in Lollie's munificent hospitality. In spite of his generosity with his friends, Lollie also had many bitter enemies on whom he lavished not hospitality, but seething hatred. One such was Sir Monty Ambrose, Chairman and Chief Executive of NewsiVersal, and proprietor of one of the sleaziest and least literate of the down-market red-top tabloids. As the lowest possible journalistic common denominator, the paper had a vast circulation. Ambrose also owned a fair chunk of British TV so the reach of his influence was enormous. Leading members of the government, or at least those not owned by Lollie, had even been known to be made to endure dressings-down from

Ambrose in his Wapping office. It was rumoured that he had once reduced a Chancellor of the Exchequer to tears for not following his paper's line on European Monetary Union. So when Ambrose heard from one of his underlings that a girl the minion had met on the train was in possession of something which would both boost the circulation of his papers and, at the same time, exact some revenge against his long-time enemy, Ambrose devised a little sting.

For Melinda, this sting was both an opportunity and a bonus—a payoff from Ambrose and a little blackmail cash from Lollie. So she phoned Lollie with the news that she had a big dossier on his parties and the price of her silence was twenty thousand pounds. They set up a meeting at Victoria Coach Station and Lollie brought along with him a brown paper envelope containing the money. The deal was done and Melinda passed over the tapes and photographs. Meanwhile NewsiVersal's snappers had taken photographs of the meeting. So it was just a matter of publishing the story of the payoff next morning in all NewsiVersal's tabloids and on all the NewsiVersals TV stations.

Rather than be thought a laughing-stock, Lollie saw himself as having no option but to sue NewsiVersal for libel and with the help of a judge who had been a regular at one of Lollie's S&M nights, Lollie was given the decision and Melinda MacCoggin was publicly branded a liar. Ambrose was ordered to pay Lollie damages of two million pounds and to print a grovelling apology. But Newsiversal, instead of paying up and apologising, went on to appeal the verdict. The appeal judges, never having been guests or payees of Lord Lollie, were, therefore, much less sympathetic than the original trial judge had been and the appeal was upheld. Lollie was found to have perjured himself, for which crime he served a token modest sentence of six months, shortened to the minimum as befits someone with a lot of money.

"I remember it all now," said Sonia. "Didn't he write a book about prison?"

"Yes," said Smith, "It was called 'My Ordeal' by Lord Larry Lollie. Complete rubbish. A total waste of paper. Anyway, Lollie never forgave Melinda MacCoggin for, as he sees it, grassing him up."

"But she's the innocent in all this, surely? She can't have got much out of it."

"No she didn't. Once she'd been in court, she couldn't even work tricks on the train anymore. Her business went right down, in a manner of speaking, sorry about that. No more Kensington hotels. More like Saturday nights at the local pub. She still lives in Glasgow, as you can see. But she's on benefits now. She made a bob or two from Ambrose's papers and the odd photoshoot. She also did a couple of scenes in a porn movie, but once she'd faded from view, her income dried right up."

"It seems, well, er . . , wrong, to have to remove her. She's not doing any harm to anybody."

"I agree, Miss Jones, but orders are orders and Lollie has the ear of some very big people. If he wants her rubbed out, then we have to do it."

"We should really be eliminating Lollie himself, not this poor girl."

"Again, I agree. Maybe next time it will be Lollie we'll be taking out. We can only hope. This is the worst part of the job, hitting innocent people. Most countries do it all the time, often on a much bigger scale. But it doesn't seem quite British, somehow. My advice is just to do it and not to think about it."

It was a long quiet drive to Glasgow, and three days later, a long and painfully silent drive back. They had entered their new profession of assassin with hope and optimism. To date, all their victims had been deserving. There is no doubt that rubbing out the likes of Birdas or

Tranley or even Finnbarr Duckworth had been, who could doubt it, beneficial acts of kindness to humanity in general. Those three, and the others, had been removed as a form of corrective balance to be set against all those daily arbitrary pointless deaths of the good and innocent. But this was different. This was an act of spite by a rich and vindictive man who could have an ordinary person removed for no other reason than personal malice. They both decided that, should the opportunity ever present itself, Lollie himself would not be spared their crusading justice.

The deed itself, the termination of a blameless woman whose worst crime had been to get mixed up with the wrong sort of wealthy psychopath, was done quickly, by swift hit and run car accident. Ken and Sonia reckoned that they owed it to her to get it over quickly. She had been one of society's victims, seeking only enough to feed herself, her child and her mother. She had done nothing wrong except in the eyes of those puritans who see whoredom in moral terms which she did not. As far as she had been concerned, she had been a prostitute purely out of economic necessity and a lack of talent or opportunity to earn her living in any other way. She had little alternative but to pay her way by taking small amounts of money in return for brief sexual pleasure.

They reported back to Smith in London.

"We don't want to do any more of those." said Sonia, "We came into this business to help innocent people, not act as personal executioners for monsters like Lollie."

"I'm sorry." Smith replied. "That's the last one like that we're going to ask you to do."

"Why did you ask us to do it this time?"

"Ah," said Smith. "I thought you might ask that. One reason was to check whether you are the sort of people who can put emotion out of your mind on an important job. It was a sort of test."

"So, you let us murder an innocent woman in cold blood, just to test our commitment. To see how readily we would obey your orders?"

"Something like that," replied Smith.

"Well," said Sonia, her voice breaking, "that poor woman! We are not going to kill anyone else like that. Couldn't you tell Lollie and people like him who want to hire common murderers, just to fuck off!"

"Well, yes," Smith answered calmly and smoothly at her outburst. "We could indeed tell Lollie to 'fuck off' to use your unladylike phrase. But I'm afraid it doesn't quite work like that."

"So Lollie runs you, is that it?" asked Ken.

"Not quite. I'm afraid I haven't quite told you everything."

"What do you mean?" Sonia asked.

"What I haven't told you is that we are not a private execution squad so that people like Lollie can settle their old scores. In fact, Lollie had very little to do with the decision to rub out Melinda MacCoggin. I doubt if Lollie even knows about the existence of our department. The relationship between Lollie and Miss MacCoggan is purely coincidental."

"So then why did you ask us to terminate her?"

"Well, it seems our Melinda MacCoggin was not quite the hooker with a heart of gold that she first appeared. Shortly after her story appeared in the Ambrose press, she received a call from, shall we say, a government which is not counted amongst our very best friends. A very unpleasant little country they run. Melinda MacCoggin got into bed with them, in a manner of speaking. They offered her a free ride on their financial magic carpet in return for whatever she had on those party-goers at Chateau Lollie. After she'd been dropped by our side, she's been working as a recruiting sergeant for them. Honey trap they call it. Our side, their side, neutrals, all sorts. Usually compromising photographs. I'm sure you get the picture. She was very good at it."

"Them?"

"Rotten little feudal state in the middle east. Can't give you all the details. 'Nuff said. End of story. Something bigger coming along next week. More in your line. Have a good week. Be in touch. I'll let myself out. Bye!"

Ken lifted up the gin bottle.

"Drink?"

"Big one. Then another."

THIRTEEN

Langley Adams was a well-known figure. He had once been prime minister for several years, his term of office having ended a decade or so earlier. Since then he had roamed the world like a rock star, giving a lecture here or a speech there or cutting deals between big players on that elevated playing field where business meets government. His stopping points were usually those countries where he had been much involved during his term in office and with which he had done various profitable deals, sometimes even in the British national interest. Arab sheikhs, Kazakhstani tycoons, Russian oligarchs, Mexican drug billionaires, all these and more were eager to offer hospitality to Adams and his large entourage as he made his rounds to pay due homage to the very rich and to the very, very rich.

Having been in office for six years, there were many such friends and contacts, all of whom had prospered during Adams' short reign and his subsequent peregrinations to their courts had resulted, no one could be exactly sure of the precise mechanism by which it had happened, in Adams becoming very rich himself. His long contact with the extremely wealthy had, by some mysterious osmotic process, transferred money to Adams himself, who could now hold his head up high in the palaces of that small elite group of men who are, in reality, the real owners of the whole world.

As Adams had ascended to membership of this group himself, his entourage had grown. Wherever he went in his private jet, he was accompanied by his financial advisers, his bodyguards, his secretaries and other sundry hangers-on, including a small group of elegant, beautiful young women whose occupation was mainly confined to nail-filing and reading glossy magazines.

Not that Adams himself ever took advantage of these youthful fashionistas—they were for his lieutenants. As a committed Christian, Adams was well aware of that religion's obligations regarding compulsory uxoriousness. He did, after all, make a substantial part of his income from delivering tub-thumping sermons on the lucrative religious lecturing circuit where he proclaimed his 'faith' and where he denounced sinners and lovers of money as unfit for the Kingdom of Heaven. One of his best-selling money-spinners was an international network of multi-faith religious schools where decent, fee-paying, middle-class parents could send their children to what were, in effect, expensive, up-market Sunday schools. Boosted by his name-brand, the Adams MultiFaith Academies were making very big money indeed. Naturally, he was most concerned to protect this income source, which was one reason why he did not avail himself of the services on offer from the upper-class groupies aboard his personal airliner. He was not the sort to risk the income from his religious businesses by any hints of sexual impropriety.

On the other hand, though, Mrs Adams herself was no cynosure of sexual allure. It would have been a strange perversion for a man to find her in any way attractive. She was a fat, strident dragon who ruled Adams with a poisonous, sharp tongue. Not only was she completely immune from sexual advances by virtue of her overwhelming ugliness but it would have taken a very brave man indeed to risk her man-hating wrath by approaching her. But that did not mean that Adams lacked for sexual partners. Discretion being the uppermost consideration, there was a regular turnover of members of his secretarial staff who were well-paid for a few months aboard the Adams road show. There was also the occasional liaison with an obliging exotic *houri* as part of the traditional hospitality provided by Adams' former business partners, usually those who owed their nation's air force or power stations to a mutually profitable deal which had been struck while Adams had still been prime minister.

Adams himself would have preferred the sort of playboy lifestyle enjoyed by one of his oldest friends, former US President Al Higgs, who openly flaunted his mistresses on his travels between golf courses in various tropical tax havens. Unfortunately, Adams still retained some of his early puritanism and felt constrained to continue to preach the evils of anything to do with matters sexual. Added to which, Adams was constantly aware of just how much hard cash his faith schools and sermons were contributing to the growing stash of money he was assembling for his eventual retirement.

There were people, Adams incredulously, occasionally, conceded, who disliked him. They were, Adams frequently told himself, jealous of his success, his high moral standards, his achievements on behalf of the country and his undeniable superiority as one of the finest human beings who had ever drawn breath. Not, of course, that everyone concurred with Adams' self-assessment. In fact, he was not merely disliked but truly detested by a large proportion of the British population. He put this negativity down to the inherently British jealousy of others' success, and as a result, he spent increasingly long periods abroad, well away from the mean-spirited carping of the British media. These days, he much preferred the United States, where he was given his due deference as a near demigod in a country which sees no irony in holding that personal material wealth be a natural consequent of fundamental hair-shirt Christianity. Adams' American deification, however, did not extend to the European side of the pond, even though he did not involve himself in British political life anymore. Consequently, when in Britain, he found it wiser to maintain a low profile. So inconspicuous did he make himself, that many ordinary Britons, those who did not follow serious current affairs, would not have known, had they been asked, whether he was still alive or not.

On the other hand, his enemies did have some cause for genuine complaint. They did point out that many of his foreign dealings were with regimes where mass murder was a normal part of domestic statecraft And they certainly had a point that maybe he shouldn't have given all the UK's phone, social security and financial records to the CIA. There even remained a little residual resentment at the way he had sold the Bank of England to an American investment bank—the very same bank, coincidentally, which was now adding so generously to his personal offshore pension fund. Many thought indeed that selling all the British gold to an American hedge fund at the very bottom of the world precious metals price cycle might not have been entirely in the British national interest. And there were even some people who had still not forgiven him for appointing a Russian oil billionaire, no longer welcome in Mother Russia, to be Her Majesty's Secretary of State for Energy—'a brave and inspired appointment', his sycophants had said at the time.

But, on the whole, Langley Adams had received sympathetic media coverage from the media. His enemies, although numerous, were neither rich nor well-connected and so were of little significance. Indeed, most of the published criticism of the former prime minister was confined to the conspiracy theorists and the blog-nutters.

Ken and Sonia were therefore surprised when a new 'Smith' arrived at their house and put his photograph on the table. They stared at image of the ageing figure, at the popping eyes and the orange permatan, with justified distaste.

"Langley Adams!"

"Langley Adams," Smith confirmed. "He's your next target. Do this one OK and we can start thinking about a contract release."

"One last job?" asked Sonia.

"Indeed yes. It will be difficult to get work once word gets around that you were the ones who erased Langley Adams."

"Why is that?" Ken asked.

"Stands to reason," said Smith. "Once word gets out in the elimination community that you did the Adams job, no one is going to trust you within a mile. Plus, the bastard still has a lot of nasty friends out there. There may even be some revenge. Not a worthy thing of course. We're professionals and revenge is an unworthy emotion. But some of the people Adams has been doing business with, well, they don't have our high moral professional standards."

"Suppose we do this job and get away with it. What will happen to us then?"

"Don't worry, we won't throw you out. There will be new identities, false passports. All that sort of thing. We've done it before."

If there's one thing I've learnt in life, thought Ken, that is never to trust someone who starts a sentence with 'Don't worry'. Especially if they are called Smith.

But what he actually said was, "How are we supposed to get to him? He must have an army of goons looking after him."

"He does, indeed, have his 'goons'," Smith replied. "He cycles about ten of them. Mostly ex-police, a couple of freelance heavies. One firearms expert."

"And all those against just the two of us?" said Sonia.

"Well," Smith went on. "The odds are not as bad as they sound. First, there are never more than three of his bodyguards around him at any one time. And, more to the point, most of his heavies are also working for us."

"Don't tell me, if you can't," asked Sonia. "But how did you fix that?"

"Actually, it's a fair question. Easy to answer. We have told Adams that we will look after him and provide the bodyguards. Normal practice. Adams thinks we're looking after him out of respect for him as a former prime minister. It's our job to look after any foreign ruler who comes here. They always say they want to bring their own people and we always make it impossible for them to do that. So we finish up looking after all those guys. Adams thinks he chose them himself. No point in letting him in on the secret."

"So, if we can get close to him, his thugs will look away?"

"Of course. They'll be on orders."

"Why us, if you have your own boys right up close."

"Easier to hide you afterwards. If he's rubbed out by one of his bodyguards, all hell will break loose. Think about it. No important person we need to butter up will ever trust us again if they think our people are likely to turn on them. When Adams is killed, it will be headline news everywhere. We can hardly arrest a bodyguard now, can we? We have to think of our international reputation."

"So, you'll arrest us instead?"

"No, someone else is going to take the fall, not you. He's Iranian. We have the very man in mind. He will be bravely taken out by Adams' boys while you two escape in the confusion. There will then be a diplomatic incident. Much indignation. Closing of British and American embassies in Tehran *et cetera*. That's when our Israeli friends will step in with their high-level bombers. Which, incidentally, it was Adams who brokered the deal for. You'll be using a Russian gun. As issued to the Iranian secret police."

"Let me try to get my head around this," said Sonia. "You want us to eliminate Langley Adams so that you have an excuse for starting World War Three?"

"No need to be quite so melodramatic. It won't be as bad as all that." replied Smith. "In fact, the Israelis will be removing the Iranian nuclear plants so there will be no nuclear war. The Iranians don't have any friends, so there will be no one to come to their aid. There might be a few Arab hotheads who'll get worked up about it but most of them hate the Iranians even more than they hate us. So it will soon die down."

"Why rub out Adams? Why not just send in the planes anyway?"

"Good question." smiled Smith, "A couple of reasons. First Adams is thinking of making a comeback. Going back into what he calls 'frontline politics'. We don't want that. He would disturb the way we run things now. We like our clapped-out politicos to just go away and quietly make their money. We have no problems with them making a million or two from shady deals from their old contacts and then off to the golf course. Maybe, if they like, they can do the odd bit of charity work where they can do no real harm. Something like the Arts Council. But once they've had their chance to make their packet, they should have the good grace to get lost. Problem with Adams is that he doesn't know when to stop. He already has all the money he needs so he should just retire quietly. Trouble is, the bastard has no style. It's all that god-bothering. Probably thinks he should be the next pope as well."

"You said two reasons."

"Oh, yes. A bit tricky this one. It appears that a couple of Adams's friends have changed sides since he was in office. If he comes back, it could be embarrassing. Can't go into details, of course, but you know how he always used to bang on about loyalty and honesty? Well, our new enemies, who used to be our friends, one of them is now threatening to release all the papers about how Adams arranged for them to buy a shipload of that foul stuff we make at our chemical weapons place down near Salisbury. Trouble is, they used it on one of our old friends. One of our old friends with a lot of oil, that is. Naturally our old friends are, not unreasonably in my view, a little bit pissed off with Adams. And now that they've found out what he did, they want Adams put on trial. Obviously we can't allow that. So the word is out that Adams is due for permanent retirement. From the very top."

"Any ideas about how we are going to do it?"

"Well, yes, we do. We see that you both had small arms training when you were on the introductory course."

"But we've never used guns."

"We thought about that, so we will be setting up a little refresher course next weekend. A shooting range near Basingstoke. You'll enjoy it. The deed itself is scheduled for a week on Sunday, when Adams does the reading at his posh church."

"What about this poor Iranian hitman? The one who's going to take the blame for the hit? How do we get him to church on a Sunday?"

"Why do you think we chose this particular time and place? The Iranian lives across the street from the church. He won't be working that day. We will give you a sign and then you shoot Adams with the Russian pistol we will supply you with. It's standard issue for the Iranian Embassy security people. We have changed the serial number to one from a consignment from Uzbekistan to Iran last year, just in case there's any sort of official report to be written. Further details at the next briefing, but what we are thinking about right now is that you wait for Adams to come out of the church. You will be in a car on the other side of the road. At our signal, you shoot him. Make a good job of it. Hit him several times. As soon as our chaps in Adams's bodyguard hear the shots, they will break into the Iranian man's apartment and take the fellow out."

Smith leant back and smiled, obviously pleased with his plan.

"I can see a number of problems," said Ken. "First off, what if we don't get a clear view of Adams when he comes out of church? What if the poor fall guy is not home that day? And how do we know we won't get caught up in the crossfire? We might even get shot ourselves. There will be plenty of witnesses."

Smith was making written notes. Finally, after a pause, he answered Ken.

"Oh, yes, things can go wrong. They do. Quite often. What we have to do is to have a decent plan and then try to minimise the risks of something not working out. But first, getting a clear view of Adams. I think we can rely on his bodyguards to move out of the way for a couple of seconds. That's when you have to go in for the hit. He will not have any body armour, we'll make sure of that. Remember, he thinks he's immortal. He actually thinks he doesn't have an enemy in the world. Then question two. What if the Iranian dupe is not home that day? He will be, I promise you. One of our female agents will get invited home on Saturday night. He's a creature of habit. Always goes out looking for women on Saturday night. Always the same, *Bollocks* night club every week. Without fail. And don't worry about witnesses. It's not as if it's ever going to get to court. This will be a political assassination, bravely resolved by Mr Adams's quick-thinking personal bodyguard."

"You haven't answered our main question?" Sonia said. "What is going to happen to us? Wouldn't it be safer for you to eliminate us as well, once the job was done? A couple of stray bullets from your people?"

"No, no, no, Miss Robinson!" said Smith emphatically. "You will just have to trust us. You will just be bystanders. If there are too many bodies to take away, we have to involve the local police, ambulances, reporters. No, a quick kill at a single target like this is best. It'll work, I promise you."

"So we are, in theory at least, expendable, are we not? Even if it is inconvenient to rub us out this time?"

"That is true, Miss Robinson. In this service, we are all expendable. But we are not just some bunch of trigger-happy cowboys. We are a very necessary public service and we have to behave responsibly. We always regret it when we are left with no other option for the national good. And we are always very concerned to look after all our people. We don't like casualties. We hope all our operatives live long enough to enjoy the magnificent civil service pension and a happy old age."

"Is that very likely?"

"Very likely indeed. I am hoping to retire myself very soon."

"What about temporary operatives like us? Are we any safer than your regular people?"

"In your particular case, Miss Robinson, yes, both of you will be fine. Don't worry. We have great plans for you. If the Adams job works out, we have something special in mind. Can't say more than that until nearer the time."

"I thought this was going to be our last job?" Ken said indignantly.

"If this job goes OK, we can think about a re-negotiation of your contract. Then you can go back to ERASED or your technical college or whatever you like. We'll see. First things first. One job at a time."

Smith made to leave.

"Here are the details of the small-arms training course. Saturday morning, one night's stay. Car will be here at seven. I hope you enjoy it. It's not many people learn how to shoot properly. It's a useful skill. Oh, and take this emergency phone number, just in case."

After Smith had left, Ken turned to Sonia.

"This might be the right time to make our wills."

Sonia sat down to write her reply.

"What's to stop them rubbing us out next Sunday, while they're about it? Leave things tidy."

"Maybe we should write everything down. As insurance." wrote Ken.

Then they carefully burnt the paper they had been writing on and crushed the ashes to a powder.

"We're getting paranoid, my darling."

"I wonder why."

FOURTEEN

The two day break at the shooting range was surprisingly enjoyable for Ken and Sonia. They were picked up early on Saturday morning and transported by the usual black BMW for an hour or so down the M3 to somewhere near Basingstoke. Well, it could have been near Basingstoke, but after they had left the motorway and progressed through the country lanes to the usual disused airfield it could have been anywhere. They were met by a sergeant wearing military fatigues and after putting their bags inside their room, it was off to a classroom for a a morning of classes on ballistics, firearms laws, firearms handling, safety and the different types of small arms. After a lecture about human anatomy and how to destroy it most efficiently using fire power, it was time for lunch. On the Saturday afternoon, they took their first trip to the range. They had had some elementary training in using small arms on their first training course but this was now the real deal and they were required actually to handle a weapon for extended periods of time and to fire it repeatedly at man-shaped distant targets until they had achieved a satisfactory level of speed and accuracy. This practice continued, exhaustingly, into Sunday. The trainer, a be-turbanned Sikh called Sergeant Smith, explained why such long practical training was so important.

"People watch too many films. They get the wrong idea about small arms," Sergeant Smith told them.

"First," he said, "most people think it's just like the movies where one shot is fatal and the target just falls over. It's not like that. Sometimes you have to hit a target several times before he is neutralised. Especially if he's wearing body armour. So, if you want to get in and out quickly, you have to fire off several rounds in quick succession, or there's a good chance you'll not get a fatal hit."

"Why not use a machine gun?" asked Sonia.

"You could do, but they are not very accurate. They tend to spray bullets all over the shop. A lot of innocent bystanders could get killed. That's the other thing civilians don't understand. When you see it in the films, the operative and his target are on top of each other. Never more than thirty or forty yards apart. Only an idiot could miss at that distance. That's the movies for you."

"I thought the practice targets were a long way away." said Ken.

"Yes," Smith went on. "For good reason. We were told to set targets for you two at about a hundred and fifty metres for your training here. I don't know what you are going to be aiming at and I don't expect you to tell me, but it looks like your hit will be at about that distance. You should be OK with this little Russian job they want you to use. We've tested it and it is accurate enough to hit a human target most times, in good weather that is, at up to seven hundred metres. That's half a mile."

"Should be enough," Sonia said in reply.

"Let's hope so," replied the Sergeant. "Speed and accuracy. That's the watchword in this game. Quick in, quick out. Nice and clean. And no second chances. As long as you concentrate on the things we are telling you, you should be OK."

Ken and Sonia enjoyed their two days on the shooting range just as their contact back in Croydon had said they would. But it was non-stop, with barely any time for a break to gather breath right up until they came to say goodbye to Sergeant Smith at teatime on Sunday, at which point they were quite tired out.

"Do we get to take the weapon home with us?" Sonia asked at the end of the final shooting practice.

"'Fraid not." said Smith. "You will be issued an identical gun just before your job. It will be well-checked by our people. You will need to sign for it and for the rounds of ammo. Then it will need checking back in afterwards. Government property. All has to be accounted for."

"Just remember what we told you. Stay calm. Take it easy. Line up your target. Give it four or five shots and then get the hell out," was Smith's parting benediction.

"Thanks for everything, Sergeant" said Sonia, and gave him a peck on the cheek.

"Stay safe, you two."

The car to take them back home was already waiting. Sitting at the wheel was a young woman in a dark blue naval uniform with a single chevron on the sleeve.

As they got in, she consulted a clipboard and then turned around to them to confirm the address. That done, they drove through the security gate, out along the country lanes and then back on to the M3 motorway towards London. After about twenty minutes, they turned south on to the M25 London outer ring road where the traffic was suddenly much heavier. The driver's voice came through the intercom.

"Please make sure your seat belts are fastened," she said, in a voice betraying her Yorkshire origins.

Ken opened the sliding window.

"Is there a problem?" he asked.

"Dunno. Could be. We may have company."

"Someone tailing us?"

"Grey BMW. Might be one of ours."

With that, the driver suddenly hit the accelerator and the car shot forward. Soon she was weaving through the outer lanes of the Surrey M25 between the Sunday afternoon suburban traffic. Ken looked back to see, to his horror, that the pursuing BMW was still right behind.

"So it's not one of ours."

"No, sir," said the driver. "It's not one of ours."

A game of cat and mouse soon developed as the two vehicles sped along the motorway. Both cars were soon doing well in excess of a hundred miles an hour. All pretence of sticking lawfully to the outer overtaking lanes was abandoned as the driver fought to avoid the traffic by dodging from lane to lane and on and off the hard shoulder. They quickly passed the exits for Reigate and Leatherhead and headed down the hill in the direction of Gatwick Airport with headlights blazing. The air was filled with noise from motor horns and the scream of police cars. The young naval driver was giving long blasts of the horn to warn the cars in front of them to move over and move over quickly. But still the grey BMW stuck with them.

As they approached the M23 Croydon slip road, the driver tried a feint by pulling out into the right-most lane. The pursuing BMW obligingly followed suit and moved out as well. Then, just at the last possible second, the driver wrenched the steering wheel to the left and swerved violently on to the M23. It was done so quickly that the grey car behind could not turn left in time. The sudden change of direction, and the stamp on the brakes, meant that the BMW which had been behind was suddenly in front but going too far fast past the slip-road exit to follow them. But that second was just long enough for the black-suited passenger in the BMW to fire a single shot at the young woman driver.

Her training and her youthful quick reactions were the saviour of all three of them. She stamped on the brakes and the car skidded to the side of the M23 slip road where it smashed through the energy-absorbing crash barrier. It finally came to a stop when it hit a tree and the front end crumpled like a squashed drinks can. The brave driver was seriously hurt. Luckily, she had not been killed, but she had taken the bullet in her shoulder, its fire power having been reduced by the protective glass window which it had penetrated.

She was slumped in her seat belt, crying with the pain. Sonia was unconscious but Ken, who had been sitting on the side of the car away from the smash, still had his wits about him. The last thing he did before passing out himself was to press the speed dial for Smith's emergency number on his mobile phone.

What none of the three occupants of the car saw was the immediate arrival of lots of onlookers and rubber-neckers plus several brightly-coloured police cars. The first police vehicle to arrive called up the paramedic emergency service and a helicopter was summoned to take the three injured to hospital. Meanwhile the police cleared the area and sealed off the slip-road.

The normal police procedure would have been to close the area down for several hours while they carried out a full investigation. But, on getting the phone signal from Ken's mobile phone, Smith knew instantly that they had a problem and a couple of high-level phone calls soon told him what had happened. The Surrey Police were then ordered to stop their inquiries and destroy all their notes about it. A Ministry of Defence low-loader quickly arrived to take the crippled vehicle away.

One radio broadcast warning drivers that the M23 slip road from the M25 was closed for a major accident did leak out, but all subsequent references to the story on radio and TV and in the press were blocked. Within half an hour, all trace of the incident had completely disappeared from the record. One or two of the drivers who had been out that afternoon, plus the various policemen who had been following the chase from a safe distance, did search the news media and the Internet for details of what had actually happened but they found nothing. The news blackout was almost one hundred percent.

Ken and Sonia were kept in hospital overnight, but apart from a few cuts and bruises, they were declared fit and well, medically at least, and they were discharged the following morning. A nondescript well-spoken and expensively suited man who introduced himself as 'Smith' was already waiting outside the ward with a couple of bodyguard types.

"Sorry about all this security. Hope you don't mind. Had to put a couple of chaps outside your room overnight. Just routine. You're both OK now, the docs tell me."

"We're fine. What happened to the driver?"

"Brave girl," said Smith. "Saved your lives. Luckily she's not too bad. She'll be out of commission for a while. Took a bullet in the shoulder. Operating this morning. Quick thinking, the way she gave that BMW the slip."

"We'd like to see her to thank her. We owe her so much."

"Sorry," said Smith. "We can't allow that. Security. Need to know and all that. Her parents are with her now."

"What do you think happened?" Ken asked.

"Let's talk about it in the car."

In the car, Smith described what they thought had been the sequence of events."

"Obviously you were followed from the shooting range. They were going for a quick kill. Taking you out. Seems like they use the same methods we do. Fortunately your driver was fully trained for this sort of eventuality. But so, it seems, was theirs."

"Theirs?"

"Difficult to say who," Smith told them. "It's not as though you have been involved in any sort of national security work. All your targets have been domestic so far. Most ungentlemanly if it were one of the foreign buggers. We don't get involved with other internal security services as a rule and they don't bother us in return. It's an understanding we all have. Wouldn't do for anyone to break it."

"Unless it was Iran. They don't seem very gentlemanly. And if they had got wind of your little plan for next Sunday, they might be a little annoyed," said Ken.

"That is true," Smith replied, "but how would they have found out?"

"An informer?" asked Sonia.

"I hope not," replied Smith. "Most dishonest. Only you two plus my colleague, Smith, and two others knew what was going to happen. And don't worry, we don't suspect you."

"That's good to know," answered Sonia. "But tell me, just for the record. How do you know it's not one of us?"

Smith laughed.

"Well, it couldn't possibly be you. For a start, we are monitoring everything you do twenty four hours a day. Good idea, by the way, communicating by writing so we won't overhear you. I think we have a complete record of all you've ever written like that since you first went to Croydon from Faldwell. Cameras under the paint, in the walls, three-sixty degree coverage. The works. Then we have psychological profiles of you both. You are both borderline terrified. Our mind doctors reckon you'd be too shit-scared to go to the opposition even if you knew who the opposition is. No, you two are not the leak. We'll find him, don't worry."

"Then what?"

"Then he'll just disappear. This is our business, don't you know? And we are damned good at it."

"By the way," said Ken. "You're going in the wrong direction. Croydon's the other way."

"New safe house. Brighton. Now whoever it is knows who you are, they'll certainly come looking for you. All your things have been transferred. Part of the service. Just to be on the safe side, there will be a couple of our strong lads within calling distance. Number's in this envelope. Just speed dial and they'll know what it's for."

"What about the Adams job? Is that still on?"

"Sorry, no. Not for you at any rate." Smith told them firmly. "We still need to get rid of him, but I think we'll probably have to go for Plan B now. A pity about all that small arms training. A bit wasted now."

"What do you mean, 'wasted'?"

"Well," Smith replied, "the shooting range thingy was just for this one job. Now that someone or somebody seems to know about it, we can't risk you. It could easily go wrong. When they see you it could become a right old shooting match. Doesn't look good outside the poshest church in London. Entirely the wrong image. No. I'm afraid someone else will be eliminating our Mr Adams."

"So whoever it was who shot at us, if they're not foreign, then are you saying they are working for Adams himself?" Sonia asked incredulously. "Are you saying that people like Adams can have their own private armies?"

"Well, actually, yes," Smith replied. "That's exactly what I am saying. Look, supposing you want someone removed permanently, then there are not too many options. Naturally, we do it all the time but then we are professionals working for Her Maj. Or we could use semi-professionals like ERASED but ERASED is really more or less the same thing as us since we control them. Or then there are amateurs like you were, before we brought you on board.

But, frankly, using amateurs is a bit hit or miss. The quality isn't always there. Sorry, no offence."

"None taken. So how come Adams has his own protection squad?"

"Well, it stands to reason doesn't it? He used to be in overall control of the whole HMG show and, to be fair, he did turn a decent profit on behalf of all us taxpayers. So naturally, when he went freelance, he knew that any nice smooth-running business operation needs to remove the odd obstacle from time to time. And he was in a perfect position to persuade one or two of his ex-employees to move from the public sector to the private sector as well. He knew that any half-competent billionaire would need his own private security, so he might as well buy the best. Which is us."

"So why remove him now, if he is just doing what they all do."

"Well, for one thing he's getting a bit too big for his boots. Starting to get in the way of our legitimate operations. For example, eliminating people we need and leaving people we would rather get rid of. As long as he's around, the whole thing is going to be out of control. He's becoming a bit of an embarrassment. At least with the regular criminals like the Russian Mafia or the South American druggies, they may have their own private executioners but we know that they will always stick to rubbing out their own kind. They know that if they get in our way, we are better at it than they are. But with Adams, he seems to think he's still running the show."

"So, what's next for us? Sonia asked Smith.

"Oh, just lie low for a bit. Enjoy the sunshine in Brighton for a week or two. We have something in mind. No hurry. We'll keep you fully informed. You've had a hard time lately. Put your feet up and wait."

"Will the next one be the last job, then?"

"Can't say it will be the last. Not my decision. But once we have it all planned out, it will certainly be important."

"So, what will happen to Adams?" Ken asked.

"Watch the telly. It'll be headline news for a couple of days. Most likely next week."

Ken and Sonia entered their new home, which was laid out and newly decorated in exactly the same way as their Croydon residence had been. Even the colour scheme was the same—what Sonia had christened 'ministry sick'.

"No point in writing notes anymore."

"Everything is recorded.

FIFTEEN

Over the next week, as their routine gradually re-asserted itself, Ken and Sonia got one message from Smith telling them to watch the TV news. On it there was a short item about a brave young female naval petty officer who was shown receiving a medal at Buckingham Palace for bravery in one of the UK's foreign wars. She was shown with arm in a sling, standing bravely between her Mom and Dad in front of the Palace.

"I'm so glad she made it," said Sonia. "Let's send her a card. The least we can do."

A week later came the dreadful, earth-shattering news that Langley Adams, former Prime Minister, had been treacherously blown up by a suicide car bomber while on a private visit to the Middle East. At least that was what was reported to have happened. For several days TV and radio coverage would be given over to little else. All the time-honoured clichés were trotted out by everyone who had known him, from the American President right down to the Downing Street duty policeman—'. . one of the world's greatest statesmen . . .', '. . a major player in the world of international diplomacy . . .', ' . . . immense contribution to world peace . . .' etc. etc. etc.

The present prime minister, who had been, in reality, ultimately responsible for the ordering of Adams' deletion and for authorising the placing of the blame for it on to some out-of-favour middle eastern fundamentalist group, was magnificent in his tribute. Phrases like 'immeasurable loss' and 'terrible tragedy' preceded an announcement that the late Langley Adams would be the subject of a unanimous recommendation from the entire Cabinet to the Nobel Prize Committee that their rules be amended so that the next Nobel Peace Prize, could, in these exceptional circumstances, be awarded posthumously to the greatest peacemaker of his generation.

The current PM did consider some emotional display to accompany this speech, as is customary these days. Some tears perhaps or a little breaking of the voice as he struggled to contain his grief? But no, his publicity staff advised him, that really would be going over the top. Far too emetically cringe-worthy. Much better, he was told, just to keep it dignified. Even great actors, and the PM was a good actor but not great one, find deep emotion difficult to carry off convincingly, he was sensibly advised.

There was, naturally enough, national rejoicing when the news came through about the death of Langley Adams. Even one or two of the TV reporters and newscasters were having trouble keeping a straight face as they intoned the sombre facts. In the streets there was an almost tangible feeling of relief that some humanitarian terrorist had finally disposed of the old fraud. If it had been a terrorist, of course. Ken and Sonia doubted that very much.

After a day or two, all the excitement was directed towards the celebrations of the great man's state funeral. All the schools were shut and work was to come to a standstill for the happy event. But it was not for Ken and Sonia to be able to join in the fun. On the day itself, they were summoned to a meeting. The car arrived at 8.00am as usual and they were taken to an office in Uxbridge, to the west of London. There, just near the train station where the Metropolitan Line terminates, stood a four-storey nondescript red brick Victorian office block. From the outside, it was completely anonymous. The windows were permanently shuttered but behind them lights burned night and day. Here and there, at street level, one could see gaps in the shutters but there was nothing to be seen behind. The ground floor appeared to be a void, an empty hall surrounded only by shuttered windows. The car park for the denizens of this building was beneath that and was approached from some distance away, through the main town car park across the street. People working in the building would park below ground and then would take the single secure elevator to the first floor. Entrance to the block from the street was by a single door, which was made of steel camouflaged with wood cladding, behind which was a single security guard inside a bullet-proof glass cage. Leading off from this one entrance was a single flight of stairs. No-one was ever seen coming or going through this single point of entry. Outside, the anonymity of the building was emphasised by a single brass nameplate, whose wording had been rubbed almost to invisibility. It would have taken very close scrutiny to have discerned the faint ghostly impression 'CO-OP' on it. So thoroughly had the designers of this secret building worked on its anonymity that thousands of Uxbridge citizens must have passed it countless times without ever giving it a second glance.

The car dropped them off in the car park and they were met by yet another faceless young mandarin.

"Good morning. Hope the traffic wasn't too bad. My name is Smith. We will be going to a meeting this morning but before then, there are just a few formalities. Sorry about all this. Security. Better safe than sorry. Only take a moment."

They were then fingerprinted, photographed and their retinas scanned. Then they each had to yield a small sample of DNA via a swab inside their cheeks.

"Used to have to do blood tests." Smith told them. "Could be a bit messy. One or two branches still insist on it. A couple even still demand anal scrapes. Glad to say we've moved on from there. Pride ourselves on being more up to date."

They were then issued with visitor's ID's and escorted to the first floor where they were greeted by two more men.

"Good morning, Mr Jones, Miss Robinson. Has Mr Smith been looking after you all right?"

"Splendid! My name's Harrod and this is Mr Selfridge. We just want a few words. Get your view, that sort of thing. Let's go into my office."

"Right," said Harrod, "first things first. I take it you know this young lady?"

He handed over a photograph of a glamorous well-dressed woman in her early thirties.

"Well, not personally," said Ken, "but you would have to be living on another planet not to know who she is."

The young woman in question was, at that moment in time, the best-known, most photographed, most famous woman in the world. No one who had ever walked past a newsagent or station bookstall would have failed to see a thousand versions of her image. Charitable, sainted, yet fashion-plate elegant, would have summed her up for three-quarters of the entire world's population.

"Quite," replied Selfridge, "well, she is your next target."

"What!! Rub out the Countess!!"

"Yes," confirmed Harrod, "she is your next target. She must be eliminated. You have some familiarity with the aristocracy, I understand. Did you not remove that man who was pestering our beloved Princess Amelie?"

"Well, yes," Ken said, "but he was not exactly top drawer. He was just a little crook. We never actually got anywhere near the princess herself."

"Of course, this would need to be a much bigger operation. But you did quite well with the late Sir James Bruce-Bubbson MP, did you not? He has some royal connections. And you did that job while you were still amateurs. I hope you are not worried that this job will be too big for you. We have been following both your careers and we have been very impressed. You've come a long way very quickly. We think you are ready for your moment in history," Harrod suavely assured them.

"I am not sure," said Sonia. "It's much bigger than anything we've ever done before. Just getting near the target would be difficult. And how are we going to do the research? She's bound to be guarded by an army of bodyguards."

"Yes," said Selfridge, "but then it's not as if you have any choice in the matter. Take this job or nothing."

"Nothing?"

"Yes, nothing," Selfridge replied. "Literally."

"And afterwards?" Ken asked.

"Afterwards retirement, if you do the job to our satisfaction. Anyone who does this one will be poison in the termination business afterwards. So it will need to be new identities, a modest pension, somewhere nice and warm to live. A new life."

"So, this will be our final operation? After that no more?" Sonia asked.

"Precisely."

"You may wish to consider why we have especially chosen you for this particular task?" Harrod asked them.

"Well," he went on, "in a way this has been what your careers have been all about. We had you down for this some time ago. You ought to feel flattered. We are entrusting you with the efficient execution of the elimination event of the century because you have already proved to us that we can rely on you and you won't let us down."

"But her! Why her?" asked Sonia.

Selfridge explained.

"All that public image, the charities, the good works. Well, it's not for real. She has to be kept busy. She has to be given a lot of things to do or she would be completely unmanageable. As it is, we have to spend all our time keeping her off television and out of the papers."

"She's never out of the papers."

"Quite," said Selfridge. "Even with all our efforts, we still can't keep things completely quiet. Fortunately, most of the editors will do what we tell them. So most of the lurid stuff never sees the light of day. The public gets what we want them to get."

"But, rubbing her out. Isn't that a bit, well, er, medieval? Sounds like a Shakespeare play where the royal family go around bumping each other off," Sonia said.

"Ah, yes," replied Harrod to Sonia's outburst. "How much easier it must have been in those days."

He was almost nostalgic in his tone.

"The Plantagenets never realised how easy they'd got it. No newspapers, no telly, no health and safety, no courts, nothing like that. The king's word was the only law. If he wanted someone bumped off, all he had to do was click his fingers and they were gone. Our Countess would have been off to a nunnery in no time flat, given the sort of things she's been allowed to get up to. It all started going wrong in the seventeenth century. That Oliver Cromwell has a lot to answer for."

"So, you're asking us to put the clock back six hundred years?" said Ken.

"Ha, ha! No, nothing like that. It's just that these days, it is still necessary to remove the occasional impediment which may arise from time to time. In these more enlightened times it has to be done more carefully. Any essential removal has to be made to look like a plausible accident or the MPs and the press tend to get upset. But the principle's exactly the same as when Henry the Eighth was chopping off the heads of those queens who had suddenly become an embarrassment."

"And the Countess is an embarrassment? I thought she'd had just been voted Most Beautiful Woman of the Twenty-first Century."

"So she has. We wrote that. Fictitious poll in some paper. Had to keep her quiet after she signed up to pose nude for some American men's magazine."

"Didn't she get some medal from the Pope for her work with children in West Africa?"

"She did indeed," said Selfridge. "The Grand Cross of the Order of Santa Maria Immaculata, if I remember correctly. The West African children she was working with were not those poor raggedy orphans we imported for the photoshoot. Her interest in West African children tended to the more adolescent, male variety."

"My, God!" said Sonia. "What else is there?"

"An awful lot, I'm afraid, my dear, and none of it very pleasant," the urbane Harrod told her.

"So, I have a question," said Ken. "Why now, if you have the situation under control?"

"That's a good question," Selfridge replied.

"You see," Harrod took up the point. "Normally we wouldn't care. But her husband, the Earl, is getting a bit fed up with her. A lot of things really. I know, he used to be a bit of a playboy himself so it's a matter of people in glass houses not throwing stones and all that. Pot and kettle, you could say. But he's getting on a bit now and he can't quite cut the mustard like he used to. He's starting to look a bit silly, what our transatlantic cousins call a 'schmuck', having a much younger wife who still likes to 'put it about', to use another

American expression. He's more or less *hors de combat* these days. On the other hand, she seems to have reached that age when she has stopped caring about what people think. We always used to be able to rely on her being discreet, but that seems to have gone out of the window these days. Could be that stuff she smokes, of course."

"What Mr Harrod hasn't mentioned," broke in Selfridge smoothly, "is that the Earl also wants to settle down with his own current *inamorata*. Plus, of course, there is the little matter of the couple's four children. Now that they are getting a bit older, people are starting to ask why they all look different and why none of them looks like His Lordship. You might have noticed that the middle two are a slightly warmer shade of brown than the oldest and youngest?"

"Why does this matter?" asked Ken.

"Why it matters is that the Earl is very well-connected indeed."

"How come?"

"Well, apart from being inside the royal family. Not likely to inherit himself, of course, he's a long way back. But his current squeeze is . . , well, have you guessed?"

"Not Princess Maria?"

"The very same. Heiress to the throne. Just as the gossip columnists have been hinting."

"So, he wants to marry HRH Maria and he wants rid of the Countess?"

"Precisely! If he marries Princess Maria, he could one day find himself very important indeed. And if he divorces the Countess, that will not go down very well at all. First of all, the world's press will have a field day if he divorces the most saintly woman since the Virgin Mary. Even worse, all the restraints will be off and the Countess herself will, well, who knows what the stupid bitch could do? Posing for Playboy magazine could be the least of it."

Selfridge had put the case for the extinction of the errant Countess with exemplary clarity. And given that Ken and Sonia had been given a do-or-die ultimatum themselves, they found themselves being charged with murdering the world's sweetheart. Not a position they had foreseen for themselves on the day when Principal Scregg had got himself too drunk to walk downstairs safely.

"So, you will do it," said Harrod. It was not a question.

"You've got us," said Ken, reluctantly.

"Good man. Now down to the details. Mr Selfridge has a plan. Would you show them? Please, there's a good chap."

"Well," began Selfridge, "there are a few constraints on how this thing needs to be done. First, it can't be done in this country. We don't want any problems with the British police. Foreign police can always be criticised for something. If necessary we usually make sure they get a reputation for incompetence. Any problem involving one of our nationals that doesn't get solved can always be put down to the laziness of the foreign *gendarmes*."

"The second main thing is that it must look natural. Landslide, avalanche, washed away in a typhoon are all good. Unfortunately we can't arrange that sort of thing ourselves. So we are down to man-made accidents. I don't have to tell you two, of course. In your short but illustrious careers you have employed most of them. But I'm sure you know that it usually comes down to falling out of a high window or an automobile accident. Falling a long distance will be tricky to set up although we can usually rely on the Countess to be full of some mind-numbing substance or other. Which means that, at the very least, we can be sure she won't know what's hit her."

"So, a car accident, then?" Sonia asked.

"We think so," agreed Selfridge. "Preferably abroad and with a collision of sufficient violence. Hopefully one that makes the car burst into flames and destroys whatever evidence you might inadvertently leave behind. Any ideas where you would like to do it?"

"No, we haven't spent much time abroad. It rather depends on where the Countess will be."

"Yes, of course," agreed Harrod. "But Her Ladyship does like to trip the light fantastic in all sorts of places. Best time will be overnight, one weekend when she is coming home from a party. She tends to party most nights—French Riviera, Estoril, Costa Smeralda, more or less anywhere where she can get drunk, get high and get laid with her rich friends. You don't have to decide now. We will work on it over the next week or so and get hold of her schedule, so we can choose the right time and place. And hopefully one where the local *gendarmerie* are not too bright."

A silly question, I know, but how will you find her schedule?" asked Sonia.

"Yes, it is a bit silly. For one thing, every rag in Fleet Street knows weeks in advance where she is going to be so they can make sure their *paparazzi* are in place. And for another thing, we always like to keep track of where important people are going and what they are doing. It's usually us who tell the papers. But only if we think that telling them is likely to be useful to us, of course."

"So you have her phone hacked?"

Harrod gave her a patronising smile.

"So, once we have a schedule, we can make plans for the job." Ken asked.

"Yes," said Harrod. "We'll get a list of cities where she is going to be and we will start some preparatory work. False identities for you two, the right vehicle, maps, that sort of thing. More nearer the time."

"I'm sorry to keep on with my stupid questions," said Ken, "but I can see a lot of fallout from this job afterwards.

There is going to be blanket media coverage. All sorts of people are going to be suspected. Not least us."

"That's not a stupid question at all." replied Selfridge. "In fact, I am glad you are thinking ahead. You are right, this is going to be the biggest news story since the Second World War. Which means that we, that is, you two, can't afford to cock it up. So it's important that we go over the plan very, very carefully. As you know, in this business we can't eliminate all risk, but we can minimise it to as safe a level as possible."

"And what do we do about the publicity afterwards?"

"You can leave that to us. We will tell the rags what they can say and what they can't say about it. They already have the obituaries ready and waiting. That's normal practice. All that's missing will be the date and place of death. Then they will fill the rest of their editions that week with pictures of the late Countess as . . . well, you know how they will play it."

"And the conspiracy theories? Don't you worry about them?"

Harrod laughed. "You mean Elvis Presley Found Alive and Well and Living on Mars? That sort of thing?"

"No, not so silly," said Ken, annoyed at being laughed at., "more like the Who Killed JFK sort of thing."

Harrod resorted to his patronising tone.

"Actually conspiracy theories are very useful. We like to have a good few conspiracy theorists writing Internet blogs after we do an important job."

"Whatever for?"

"Well," explained Harrod. "If we get nutters writing about how the British Secret Service rubbed someone out, we feel safer because we know that no one will ever believe them. When you delete the Countess, there will be a million pock-marked overgrown schoolboys sitting with their laptops in their bedrooms telling the world that it was the British State what killed her. The fact that these loonies are saying it means that most people will think it was a genuine accident. Sometimes we even start these rumours against us ourselves. Stands to reason doesn't it? Who would you rather believe, some unwashed anonymous blogger with a silly pseudonym, like Grax Warrior or Bogbrush, or something equally stupid, or the Editor of *The Times*?"

"So, that's it for today. We will have another meeting next week when we can let you have more info. Smith will see you out and the driver will take you back to Brighton. Goodbye Mr Jones, Miss Robinson."

SIXTEEN

The driver took Ken and Sonia back to Brighton and their safe house.

"Walk on the beach?" suggested Ken.

"In this weather?"

"All the better. Place to ourselves. Wrap up warm."

Once they reached the beach, Ken thought aloud.

"If this is to be our last job and it's going to be a biggie, we are not going to be any further use to the Smiths at the MoD."

"So where does that leave us?" Sonia asked.

"Where it leaves us, my darling, is in very serious trouble. Very serious indeed."

"What do you mean?"

"Well, look at it from their point of view," said Ken. "We will have outlived our usefulness. More than that, we will be accessories with inside knowledge of the conspiracy to terminate the Blessed Countess. I can't see Selfridge and Harrod letting us live. Far safer to arrange for an accident for us as well, shortly after we rub out the Countess."

"Is there anything we can do?" asked Sonia.

"Let us examine the possibilities. We need an escape plan of our own. Meanwhile we need to play dumb. Go along with the plan. Then look for an escape opportunity."

They made two more visits to Uxbridge for further briefings while the fine details of the plan to terminate the Countess were worked out. It was to be carried out when the Countess would be visiting Frankfurt shortly to receive the prestigious award of European Humanitarian of the Year.

"Later on," Selfridge informed them, "she will be travelling south along Autobahn A5 towards Baden-Baden where there will be a celebratory party. Her car will be a heavily-armoured grey Audi which will be departing from central Frankfurt around 6.00 pm. You will be given a signal informing you that she has left the *Kongresshaus*."

"The first three kilometres from the *Kongresshaus* will be through the city traffic where a hit will be impossible. But then there is a kilometre or so of normal road before it joins the autobahn. It's in this last section where there's a window of opportunity. The traffic will still be travelling in both directions without a central crash barrier but it's where the cars began to pick up speed as they approach the A5."

"It's in this short stretch, which is no more than a thousand metres, where the deed needs to be done. By that time of the evening, the daylight will be poor but most drivers will already have their headlights on, so driving will be difficult. The eyes of the drivers won't have adjusted to the darkness and most of them will be tired at the end of the week. The headlights are a good cover. In that sort of half-light, it's impossible to identify the shapes of other road vehicles properly. It is when a lot of accidents happen. If you do it right, it should just look like another unfortunate hit and run in bad light. Next you need some driving practice."

Sonia and Ken then spent a day at the advanced driving centre where they were required to unlearn all they had ever been told about driving safely and slowly.

The instructor was a blunt-speaking northerner. "Call me Smith, Sergeant Smith."

"Look," he told the pair, "when you first learn to drive they tell you that you have to drive defensively. Keep inside the speed limit. Look out for other drivers. Use your mirrors. Try to anticipate what the other driver will do. Always wear seat belts."

"But here," he went on, "it's entirely the opposite. When they tell you at the British School of Motoring that what you are driving is a lethal weapon they got it dead right. Never forget that. The car is probably the most efficient killing machine ever invented. So forget all that safety first stuff you learnt at the BSM. What we are here to teach you is how to use this weapon to maximum effect."

And he taught them. He taught them how to cut in on another vehicle so that the driver instinctively pulled away into even more danger. He taught them how to mount the sidewalk and take out an unsuspecting pedestrian. He showed them how to manage a head-on smash and survive themselves while leaving the other vehicle a tangled heap of metal. He taught them all the tricks of the car-borne stunt man, the wheelies, the handbrake turns, the leaps over holes in the road. Most importantly, he taught them how to get out of a collision unharmed in a car which was still running.

At the next meeting with Selfridge and Harrod, Ken took the opportunity to ask a question which he had been wondering about.

"Why are we doing this in Frankfurt?"

"Several reasons," Harrod informed him, "first, there will be less media coverage. No interviews of eyewitnesses, no CCTV and that sort of thing. That's why we selected a particularly obscure stretch of road for the event. A good place to do an accident because there are no houses nearby. Second, to the German police it will be just another road crash. There will be the usual routine investigation and our politicians will make a token bit of fuss. But that will soon die down when all they find are dead ends. If we did it here, there would be all sorts of people sticking their oars in for years to come. We'd never hear the end of it"

"Aren't there local people who could be used for this job? German termination experts? Home territory? Local knowledge could be an advantage,"

"Well, that is certainly true in a way. There are quite a few German people who would be very well-qualified for this sort of work. The Germans even have their own version of ERASED. In fact, and this is completely classified, there is even a European level ERASED, called EuRASED, if you will. Mind you, they can't even agree what language to use, so they're a bit useless."

"Why not use one of those?"

"Well, Jones, you will certainly know the old expression that if you want a job doing well, do it yourself. This is a big job and we need to be sure it's going to be done cleanly. Plus the fact that it is only good manners that we don't ask some other outfit to do our work for us. It's a matter of honour that each country is responsible for its own terminations."

"But don't you have some sort of two-way relationship with the Germans? I'm sure they are very efficient at it."

"Oh, yes, they are very efficient. The best that money can buy. Too efficient sometimes. But think about the fallout if it got out that Her Holiness the Countess had been dispatched by a German hit squad. We don't want to start another world war."

"Do the Germans know about the job?" asked Ken.

"Well, sort of," Harrod replied. "We've told them that we are planning something big on their turf. No details. Better if they don't know."

"How do they feel about that?"

"Well, they've promised to stay out of our way, so you should have no trouble there. Don't worry, a time will come when we'll have to do the same for them. A bit like the freemasons, this business."

"When do we go into action?" Sonia asked Selfridge.

"D-day is a week Friday. She picks up her gong about four PM and then leaves for Baden-Baden at about six. Should take about twenty minutes to get to the A5. So be in position to move in behind her car at about six-twenty. Here's where you wait."

He got out a large scale street map of south Frankfurt and laid it out on the desk. There was also a recent aerial photograph.

"You will wait in this lane, it's called '*Heinegasse*', in the car, which will be a nice anonymous VW Polo, from five fifty onwards. Expect the signal on the phone we will give you at about six and be ready to move into the traffic stream as soon as you hear this second signal, also on your phone. You won't hear it until her car is within two hundred metres from you. It will come from a transmitter which we attach to her car while she is in the *Kongresshaus* receiving her medal. This means that you will have approximately eight to ten seconds to move out of the lane into the traffic stream behind her. Then you will have no more than two minutes to overtake and destroy her vehicle before the chance is missed. Sergeant Smith tells me that you are fully trained in all the methods of doing that. We've put a lot of thought and time and trouble into this operation. Make sure it goes through properly."

"We haven't talked about afterwards. How do we get out of Frankfurt?"

"Don't worry," said Harrod. "We've thought about that as well."

"Yes," Selfridge took over, "the escape plan. You will drive the Polo on to the autobahn and merge with the traffic. It will be rush hour so the traffic will be heavy. Who will notice another VW Polo? Then you take the first exit towards the little suburb of *Zeppelinheim*. It's a narrow country road with lots of trees and at this point "—he indicated on the map—" you park the Polo. Another car, an old brown Mercedes 200E, will be waiting there. We will give you the keys. Take the plates off the Polo and put them in the Merc. There will be a can of petrol in the Mercedes. Make sure the Polo is well doused in petrol. Then open the petrol cap of the Polo and jam the tank safety flap open. We need the petrol tank to explode immediately. When you are two hundred metres away from the Polo, send a signal by the mobile phone and it will fire a radio-controlled detonator. You will be given the phone and the detonator when you get to Frankfurt."

"Your escape route will be in the Mercedes down the autobahn," he continued. "Drive to Mannheim and check into the Mannheim Novotel. A reservation has been made there in the names of Mr and Mrs Grant. Check out early next morning and settle your bill in cash. Leave the Merc. in the hotel car park and get a taxi to the train station. Here are the tickets for the train to Paris. One of our people will meet you next day at the Gare de l'Est."

"And our new identities, as promised?"

"There will be a full set of documents, cash etc. in the Mercedes. Plus further instructions about what to do when you get to Paris."

Then they went over the plan several more times until Ken and Sonia were word perfect in every detail. Harrod gave them final instructions.

"You will be on the 5.00 PM BA flight from Heathrow Wednesday, day after tomorrow. You are checked into the Ibis Hotel in central Frankfurt for two nights under your regular names of Jones and Robinson. Use the same passports we gave you last year. No point in having too many false names, it can get confusing. One of our consulate staff will meet you at Frankfurt."

"Name of Smith?" Ken asked Selfridge.

"You know, I think it is. Anyway, Smith will hand over the Polo you will be using on the job. He will also be your guide while you look over the field of battle so that you are completely clear on exactly where you are going. Wouldn't do for you to get lost. Pack bags for three nights."

"Well, that's just about it," Harrod told them. "One more final briefing tomorrow to confirm the final arrangements for Wednesday. Our Mr. Smith will come to Brighton to do that. Have a good trip. Let's hope we are celebrating success by Saturday."

The following day Ken and Sonia went for a walk on the beach. They were sure they were being observed from the promenade and, who knows, whoever was watching them may have been lip-reading what they were saying. More likely, if they were being monitored, Selfridge and Harrod would have had some minute microphones stitched indetectably into the linings of their clothes. But they were now approaching the end game in their relationship with that part of the British state apparatus responsible for the disposal of those human beings who had become 'impediments'. Whether they were being efficiently eavesdropped or not, the final stage of the whole business was upon them. If they were to come out safely the other side of this planned sensational assassination, they would need more than carefulness. They would need to summon up all their reserves of cunning and duplicity.

For whatever the issues of patriotism and service to one's country might be pertaining, there was no doubt that Ken and Sonia were not in some sort of co-operative joint enterprise with Harrod and Selfridge and all the Smiths. Rather, they were helpless prey at the mercy of cruel and ruthless predators. What Selfridge and Harrod and the rest of the Smiths were playing with them was a deadly game which would inevitably end with their own deaths. There could be no doubt that their smooth controllers had no intention of letting Ken and Sonia live for a minute longer than the end of their usefulness once the Countess had been safely disposed of. Even more, Ken pondered as they walked along the Brighton promenade, Harrod *et al* would also know that Ken and Sonia would have worked all this out for themselves and would be looking for a personal escape plan. So, even if their lips were being read by some spook with a telescope and even if there were tiny microphones secreted somewhere about their persons, it would not matter if they were overheard discussing their own escape. They could discuss it as if they were not aware that they were being overheard because that is what Harrod and Selfridge would have expected them to do. Not to have let on that they knew what was being planned and that they knew that Harrod and Selfridge knew that they knew, meant that they could relax their vigilance when it came to their own private conversations. To have dropped all pretence, though, would also have been suspicious. So they still went through the routines of limiting their discussions to noisy crowded pubs or the seafront or by writing.

"What can we do?" said Sonia, her voice breaking with desperation.

"I think we should go through with their plan as far as driving down the autobahn to Mannheim and then, instead of checking into a hotel we should get the ICE train to Stuttgart. There's an airport there with regular BA flights back to London."

"Do you think that's our best chance, Ken?"

"I think so. If we are in Mannheim in a hotel we will be sitting ducks. If we take the train to Paris, we will be spending five hours on a slow train with plenty of opportunities for them to dump us somewhere in the middle of the French countryside."

"So that's our new plan, then. Cut and run at Stuttgart? What about passports and so on. All we'll have will be the false passports they are going to give us when we change cars after the big job."

"Yes," Ken reassured her. "I've thought of that. So I made a call to an old girlfriend. She took a quick trip to Stuttgart with some new ID's. Specially forged. Not perfect but hopefully should do the trick. We can pick them up at Stuttgart Airport."

"A phone call? Isn't that dangerous? The goons will be listening in."

"A risk, yes," said Ken, "so I bought a new SIM card. A one-time number just for that one call."

"Won't they be bugging your phone?"

"Yes, they will. But I just used it the once. They can have the phone itself if they can put all the pieces back together again."

"You smashed it!"

"Not yet. But now's as good a time as any."

And with that, Ken took out his mobile phone, extracted the SIM card and threw it into the sea, placed the mobile phone on the ground and brought his heel down on it. Then he scooped up all the bits and put them in a several rubbish bins. He was sure he was being watched.

"Good idea to look thorough. Fancy a drink?"

"Let's enjoy it. It could be our last," Sonia agreed.

They stepped into the early evening bar of *The Queen Victoria*, known locally as 'The Old Queen', this being Brighton.

"I can't see Selfridge's men following us in here," Ken said.

"Don't be too sure about that," Sonia replied. "Most of his boys look like they went to public school."

It was quiet inside. Sonia sat down and Ken went to the bar where the barman, dressed in frilly pink shirt and waiting beneath a large portrait of the Countess herself, was in attendance to serve his small early evening clientele. Ken spent a few minutes in conversation with him.

"What was that all about?" asked Sonia when Ken came back with the drinks.

"Oh, nothing. Appears they're thinking of changing the name of the pub. Apparently 'The Old Queen' sounds a bit common. Gives entirely the wrong impression. The landlord wants something a bit more upmarket as befits a gastropub."

"He could always call it '*The Gay Hussar*', said Sonia. They both laughed uproariously, breaking the tension.

"He could, but it appears that this place is the epicentre of the Brighton branch of the Countess's vast fan club. He's thinking of applying for permission to change the name from '*The Queen Victoria*' to '*The Countess*'."

"He will have no problem getting permission after next week," said Sonia, "once our little plan becomes world news. But back to business. This plan of yours. Is it going to work?"

"Trust me, we'll beat those bastards."

They looked around at the few customers, mostly young single men with faces redolent of inner misery and turmoil. None of them resembled the type of smart brisk hard-faced spook they had met at Uxbridge or the various Ministry of Defence training camps they had been to. But you never can tell, so Ken brought a piece of paper and a ball-point pen out of his pocket and started writing.

'Will need to make fast chnges to plan. Do as I say' he wrote.

'?' wrote Sonia.

'Trust me. Self. & Harr. prob. know abt Stuttgart already' Ken wrote next.

To which Sonia replied "Shit. Now we're in rl troubl'.

"You could say that," said Ken out loud.

The waiter came round lighting a candle on each table, an innovation which the landlord had introduced as part of his long term plan to upgrade this nineteenth century boozer into a sophisticated modern eaterie for the discerning young man about town.

"Can I borrow your lighter for a minute? Ken asked the waiter.

"Of course you can, dear, be my guest."

Ken took the lighter and set fire to the piece of paper he had been writing on, crumpled the ashes to dust in the candle-holder and handed the lighter back to the waiter.

"Much obliged," said Ken.

"My pleasure, I'm sure."

On Tuesday morning they had a visitor from the Uxbridge office to their house in Brighton. He was a smartly dressed man in a grey suit, white shirt and club tie. He had the look of someone who was instantly forgettable.

"Good morning," he said, "I'm Smith. From Uxbridge."

"Mr. Smith, we were told to expect you."

"Yes, just a few last minute details. Bit of a bore but there you are. Security. Can't be too careful. I'm here to help you pack. Show me what you are carrying."

Sonia and Ken were then directed as to what to take for three nights stay and which items were not permitted. Smith carefully went through everything to make sure that there would be nothing about them or their luggage to identify them and their connexion with the UK assassination department, if the worst came to the worst.

"Just a precaution," Smith assured them, "don't want to make it too easy for Jerry if this thing all goes tits up. Sorry, miss, pardon my French."

"That's all right," said Sonia sarcastically. "I've heard worse."

"Well, that's about it," concluded Smith. "I'll be off now. Enjoy your flight."

"Do you believe him? That he was doing last minute security checks in case we don't make it?" Sonia asked Ken, after he had gone and they were walking along the Brighton promenade.

"Not for one minute." Ken replied. "He wants to be sure we haven't got any papers of our own we're not telling him about. So that we think we have no choice but to go along with their plan for the escape."

"But we could have false passports in the house."

"He knows we haven't. They probably search the place every time we go to Uxbridge."

"So we're stuck. We haven't any way of escaping the Smiths. We will be stuck in the middle of the German countryside with the papers the Smiths have given us and a vehicle which has been provided by the Smiths. And the area will be swarming with police. According to Selfridge and Harrod, it's our best chance of getting away. So we have to go along with it."

"Looks like it," said Ken. "One last glass before our lives change? Say goodbye to The Old Queen?"

"Why not? Eat, drink and be merry, for tomorrow . . ." Sonia left the sentence unfinished.

"Let's hope it doesn't come to that."

"You have a plan?"

"No, no plan."

Sonia wondered if Ken were telling her the truth, but fear of the hidden microphones made her bite her lip so she didn't ask.

At *The Queen Victoria* Ken got the drinks and, as before, spent a few minutes chatting to the barman, who had changed his frilly pink shirt for an opalescent lilac number.

"You chatting him up?" asked Sonia. "Not turning gay on me are you?"

"Right now, my darling, I have other things on my mind."

The car arrived on the dot at noon for the two hour trip up the A23 and along the M25 to Heathrow Airport. After the long tedium of waiting around they boarded the British Airways flight for the short hop to Frankfurt.

Another Smith was waiting for Ken and Sonia at the arrivals gate in Frankfurt Airport Terminal 1 when they landed at 7.00pm on Wednesday evening. He was a man of few words who steered them towards the courtesy bus for the Ibis Hotel. The three of them travelled together out to the hotel on the edges of the airport. When they alighted from the bus, Smith spoke for the first time.

"That's the car you will be using." He pointed out a dirty grey VW Polo in the car park. "I will give you the other stuff tomorrow. Early start. There's a lot to do. Be ready at nine. Make sure your watches are on German time."

With that, he left Ken and Sonia standing there, turned around and marched over to a black BMW in which a black-suited driver was already waiting. Ken and Sonia were left to check in, put their minimal luggage in their room, take dinner and get an early night.

The next morning, Smith was punctual, as the Smiths always were. At 9 AM precisely he was waiting in the hotel lobby to conduct them to the car for their sightseeing ride around Frankfurt.

"This is the *Kongresshaus* where the Countess will get her medal. She then comes down this road, over the bridge on to this main road here."

He read out the street names and road numbers as he went. He also checked the timings and made notes on a clipboard.

"Need to be doubly sure about the time factor. We need to be absolutely sure we are as near as we can get it. Traffic volumes and the daylight change quickly in the evening.

You're seeing everything in broad daylight. We will be doing the same trip this evening during rush hour. Then we have to factor in the fact that traffic on Friday is about fifteen percent heavier than Thursday and that adds at least another ten percent to the time for the same journey during the day. We have been measuring traffic volumes and times for the last few weeks."

"So, you've been planning for a long time?"

Smith did not reply. Just the merest sneer escaped his lips.

They then took in the road up to the autobahn and the turnoff to *Zeppelinheim.*

"This is where the Mercedes will be waiting." Smith showed them a space under the trees.

"It will have your escape clothes, some cash and new passports in the names of Grant, Mr and Mrs Grant. There will also be two tickets for the Mannheim to Paris train tomorrow morning. Be on it. Every policeman in Germany, from Hamburg to Stuttgart,"—and here Smith paused for emphasis—"is going to be looking for an English couple called Jones and Robinson. This is a very efficient country, so they will already have your descriptions from the hotel and British Airways. A quick change of identities is important if you want to make it back to England in one piece."

So they picked up that we are going to high-tail it to Stuttgart, thought Ken. He knew they had been overheard.

Smith then conducted them through the whole routine twice more, once in the afternoon .sun and then early evening when the light was fading. Finally he handed over a mobile phone.

"Take this *handi*," he said, using the German word for a cellphone.

"It's fully charged. Switch it on at five fifty tomorrow when you are in place in the *Heinegasse*. It's programmed to receive a signal like this." He demonstrated the noise.

"That means the Countess has left the *Kongresshaus*. Then again, another beep, when she gets within two hundred metres. That's when you move out. And here."

Smith handed over a sealed grey rectangular metal box about the size of a matchbox.

"It's a detonator. Put it on the back seat. Just to repeat what you've already been told, take the can of gasoline from the boot of the Mercedes and torch this VW. Use the *handi* to send number 4116 and it will fire the detonator and ignite the petrol."

"Right," said Ken.

"Well, good luck," said Smith with the resigned air of a man reluctant to trust a professional job to what he considered to be mere amateurs.

Ken and Sonia drove the Polo back to the Ibis Hotel and parked it carefully. Before finally closing the driver's side door for the night, Ken put a tiny postage-stamp sized piece of newspaper between the door seal and the bottom of the door. Anyone opening the door would dislodge the scrap of paper, hopefully without the intruder knowing.

Ken and Sonia did not get to sleep easily that night. It was well after midnight before their long stressful day resolved itself into sleep. So it was not until 10AM that they were fully awake. They took their time checking out and it was well after lunch before they returned to the Polo in the Ibis Hotel car park. Ken carefully opened the driver's door of the Polo. The small piece of newspaper had gone. He was not surprised. Then they set off for somewhere to park for a long unobtrusive wait before taking up their place in *Heinegasse* to await the signal which would mark the opening of the final act of the elaborate plan to murder the European Humanitarian of the Year.

SEVENTEEN

During the long hours of waiting before their date with destiny, Ken and Sonia debated the strange turns their lives had taken and the desperate position they now found themselves in.

"Suppose the Countess is not like Selfridge and Harrod told us?" asked Sonia.

"I'd wondered about that. It's just possible that she is not a pot-smoking, boozed-up nymphomaniac."

"But all those newspaper hints about her. You know—'party queen', 'the Countess is smokin' hot'. You've read them."

"Yes, but they could equally have been planted by Harrod and his team. He did say that the papers will do what they are told."

"But if the Countess is not an embarrassment, sorry, an impediment, why go to all this trouble of rubbing her out?"

"Beats me. All I know is that if we chicken out of this job, it's us who will get rubbed out. I think we have to be a bit more professional. After all, it isn't a lot different than terminating some of the others. We did those with a clear conscience," Ken told her.

"I suppose the main difference is that when we terminated all those others, it was a public service, almost a public duty.

This is different. As far as I know, even if the Countess is an 'impediment', I don't see she has done anyone any great harm, unlike Tranley or Boyden or Bruce-Bubbson. It just seems immoral, somehow, to be eliminating someone for no discernible reason," Sonia replied.

"Oh, there's a reason all right," said Ken. "It's just that they haven't told us what it is. The real reason may be entirely different than what they told us."

By 5.30pm they had moved into their place in *Heinegasse*. They switched on the radio and searched the wavebands until they heard the cut-glass English of the Countess, interspersed with comments from the German presenter. At five to six, they switched off the car radio and started to listen for the signal that her car was on its way.

It came through at about ten minutes after the hour.

"A little later than expected," Ken said.

The next signal came through at twenty-five minutes after six. That meant that the Countess's car was now within two hundred metres. They switched on the engine of the Polo when they saw the grey Audi pass the end of the narrow lane. When they moved out into the traffic stream, there were three other cars between the Polo and the Audi. Skillfully, because they had learnt well the lessons about aggressive driving as taught to them by Sergeant Smith, they swiftly overtook first car, a large old Ford, and then the next vehicle, a white van, until finally only a single vehicle, a large top-of-the-range cream-coloured Mercedes, was between the Polo and the Countess's BMW.

Ken and Sonia flashed their headlights to request the driver to give way but he stolidly ignored them. Ken then realised that it was probably an escort vehicle for the Audi with orders not to let any other car come between them. But they were fast running out of road before it merged with the A5 autobahn. Something had to be done quickly.

All three cars were now speeding up and the distances between them were opening out.

"Hang on!" shouted Ken. "Time to see if the good sergeant knew what he was talking about!"

There was just enough space on the right of the two front cars for a very brave, or very stupid, driver to squeeze through. It would mean taking a chance that the grass verge, which sloped upwards, away from the road surface, would be firm enough to take the weight of the Polo. This was no time for careful risk analysis. There were now less than two hundred metres before the single file of traffic became the two-lane feeder into the autobahn. It had to be done now, or never at all.

Ken put his foot hard down on the accelerator and pulled out to the right. The drivers of both the Countess's Audi and the Mercedes behind it instantly recognised a threat and speeded up as well. But by acting quickly, Ken held the advantage and was suddenly ahead of the Audi with only five seconds left before the window of opportunity would be closed for good. He could spot, out of the corner of his eye, that the passenger in the front of the Mercedes had what looked like a gun.

"Get down!" he screamed at Sonia.

Then, right at the last possible moment, Ken swerved the Polo violently left into the front wheels of the Audi. The sudden loss of steering control caused the bigger car to pile into an oncoming sixty tonne articulated truck which could not have avoided driving over the Countess's car, even if the tired and slightly somnolent driver had been sufficiently alert to have tried to.

The rapid loss of speed by the Audi caused the driver of the following Mercedes to brake sharply as well and it was added to the multi-vehicle pile-up.

"BOGOF!" Ken shouted. "Buy one, get one free!"

"Do you think we killed the driver of the Mercedes as well?" asked Sonia.

"I don't know," Ken replied. "All I know is, the bugger was called Schmidt. As was his passenger, the heavy with the gun."

Fortunately, the Polo was still running, if a little crumpled. It was also having breathing troubles. But there was a fiery fate awaiting it and it would not be long for this world. The road ahead was clear and as they accelerated away from the scene of carnage behind them, there was no vehicle behind them either. By now cars to the left of them were braking hard to create what the Germans call a '*Stau*', a tailback.

Ken increased the speed of the Polo up to the hundred and twenty kph which is normal on the German autobahn, even at rush hour. It was only a half minute or so before they arrived at the *Zeppelinheim* slip road where the changeover car would be waiting.

"Can you open the window?" screamed Ken.

Sonia hit the window control but nothing happened.

"It's not working!"

Ken then tried his side. His window would not open either. It went through his mind then that the Smiths had out-thought them and they were going to be locked, or even entombed, in the Polo, now that they has served their purpose.

Ken pulled off the autobahn and drove down the narrow slip road and headed to where the Mercedes would be parked. At the end of the slip road, there was a country road with an arrow pointing to the small suburb of *Zeppelinheim*. He took this direction and stopped at the roadside. To his relief, his door opened. He reached over for the mobile phone and the detonator and threw them both as far and as hard as he could into the woodland. Then he got back into the car and drove, as fast as the poor battered old Polo could go, towards the village.

"What did you do that for?" asked Sonia.

"Sh!" Ken pointed to the dashboard and indicated by hand signals that they were being listened to.

"Do as I say!" Ken again mouthed the words.

They drove the kilometre into *Zeppelinheim* village and parked the car at the far end of the station car park where, Ken hoped, it would not be noticed.

Sonia leant into the car to get their overnight bags.

"Leave it!" said Ken.

"But . . ?"

"Don't worry, if everything goes OK, we will be fine." Ken said quietly, hoping that his words would not be picked up by the microphones sewn into their clothes.

They then ran up the steps of the small village train station to the platform for trains going back into central Frankfurt.

"What's going on?" Sonia was now nearly hysterical. "What do we do now?"

They could hear the screaming of police cars and emergency vehicles from the crash site a few kilometres away. As they got to the platform, they saw it was empty save for one man sitting on the bench. Beside him was a suitcase.

He came over to Ken and Sonia. Ken put his index finger to his lips.

"Sh!"

There was a brief handshake before the man reached into the suitcase and brought out two plastic bags. He handed one each to Ken and Sonia.

"Go into the ladies room and change!" Ken ordered Sonia. She obeyed immediately. They both dashed into the toilets and changed into the new clothes. The clothes they had been wearing were left inside the bags and deposited in the trash cans. Now they could speak freely.

"You old bugger! Is it good to see you!"

"Ken! Sonia! I never thought I'd see you again," said Lawson Baines, Senior Lecturer in Modern Languages at Upton Faldwell Community College.

"Sorry about all this cloak and dagger stuff," said Ken. "We couldn't speak. There were microphones inside our clothes."

They then bought three tickets from the ticket machine for the next train back into central Frankfurt. The suburban commuter train was nearly empty, going the wrong way at rush hour, so they easily found themselves a group of seats where they would not be overheard. Lawson took two other items out of his suitcase. These were new travel bags. He put the empty suitcase on to the luggage rack. It would no longer be needed.

"It's all there, just as you told me," said Lawson, handing one each of the bags to Ken and Sonia.

"Thank you for doing this for us," said Ken.

"Thank you for giving me your house," Lawson replied.

It was just as the train was pulling out of the little station at *Zeppelinheim* when they heard the explosion from the station car park as the now broken-down VW Polo was blown to smithereens.

"That was meant to be us," said Ken.

The train stopped and waited for about half a minute before it slowly moved forward.

"There was a bomb in the car!" Sonia cried, trying hard to keep the terror out of her voice. "And we drove around with it all day! How did you know it wouldn't go off? Why didn't it explode when we hit the Countess's car?" she said, her voice straining.

"Well, I only guessed," said Ken. "But I reckon our spooks would not want to leave traces at the scene just in case the Germans took exception. So the bomb would need an electronic detonator. Which is why I threw away the one they gave us. Although I guessed they would have a backup. My reading was that they wait until we had blown up the Polo and we were in the Mercedes. They would probably want us well on the way to Mannheim before the blew up the Merc. Eventually they would find out that we hadn't picked up the Mercedes. They would think we were still in the VW on our way to Stuttgart. So they would have to go for Plan B. Which was to blow up the Polo with us in it."

"How did you know there would be a bomb in the VW?"

"That was the little trick with the piece of paper. They opened the Polo overnight when we were at the Ibis Hotel. The paper was missing and the door was locked. So someone with a duplicate key got into it. The only reason they would want to do that would be to booby-trap the car."

"So why didn't they blow us up the moment we'd killed the Countess?"

"That was probably because they wanted us well away from the crime scene so that the *polizei* would not see any connection with the Countess. Hopefully, they're thinking that we were blown up in the Polo. With luck we should be out of the country by the time they realise their mistake."

"What I don't get," asked Sonia, "is why, if you knew there was a bomb in the car, you didn't try to disarm it?"

"Oh, that would have given the game away," replied Ken. "Most likely it would have exploded if we had touched it. Remember that first training course we went on?"

"What about the Mercedes we were supposed to get away in?" Sonia asked, a little calmer now.

"They'll probably be exploding it any time about now, I would think. Maybe even blown up already. Selfridge and Harrods and all the little Smiths are nothing if not thorough."

"So, whatever car we would have used, they were intending to get us?"

"Yes, we were down to be terminated," Ken told her. "But we're not out of the woods yet. We still have to get out of Germany. That's why Lawson here has been so valuable."

Lawson Baines had been listening to this exchange with barely suppressed amazement.

"Yes," he said. "In the travel bags you will find your old passports. Mr. Grassmann and Miss Lyttel, you are now back to your old identities! If the police are looking for a British couple, they will be looking for Jones and Robinson. In the bags are minimal disguises. A blond wig for you, Sonia, and some heavy specs for you, Ken. Oh and shave that beard off. Use this battery shaver at the Frankfurt *Hauptbahnhof*."

They arrived at the Frankfurt main station after a twenty minute trip. There was an air of tension about the place and a large number of police in their green and khaki uniforms, many of them carrying machine guns.

"Stay calm," Ken whispered to Sonia.

They made their way out into the plaza and found a small bar. The TV was on. It was carrying the news of the momentous events of the Frankfurt day.

Lawson translated for Ken and Sonia.

"It seems there's been a terrorist outrage," he told them. "They are saying that an Islamic fundamentalist cell has murdered the Countess and blown up a couple of cars. Apparently, so it says on the telly, there was a big car smash on the autobahn with several cars involved, including the Countess's. About five killed including her driver and two German security guards in the following car."

That made sense, getting the Islamicists blamed, thought Ken. Obviously the British end were only covering themselves. The Smiths had done them a real favour. It gave Ken and Sonia a chance to get out of Frankfurt.

Sonia was full of questions.

"What was all that business with Smith last Tuesday?" she asked first.

"Oh, that was so that he could slip microphones into the clothes in our bags. I even knew where mine were,—in the seams of my sweaters—but we couldn't take them out without tipping them off that we knew what they were up to. I couldn't even warn you. He was also checking that we were not taking our real passports."

"But wouldn't he know that we already had passports in our real names?"

"Yes he did. It was just a five minute job of checking at the passport office. But the Smiths never knew where they were. I hid them in college after the first visit from Scouse Bill of ERASED. Lawson picked them up for us."

"How did you two stay in touch?" asked Sonia, "The spooks were watching our every move. Our phones were tapped. We couldn't receive mail. Obviously our computers were hacked."

"Ha!" said Ken. "Do you remember the barman at the Queen Vic? The chap with the shirts? Well, he was our go-between. He took phone calls and mailed letters. He was very useful indeed."

"But you, Lawson, how do you feel about what we were doing?"

"Well," said Lawson Baines. "I was a bit, well, er, surprised at first. But after I got used to the idea of what you were up to before those spy types took you off, I started to admire you. Knocking off those dodgy estate agents and rotten politicians was just what they needed."

"Aren't you worried," asked Sonia, "that they may come after you? You have been aiding and abetting us."

"But I'm hardly a threat to the state, now am I? I'm sure they will keep an eye on me but who knows, they probably do that anyway. The way I see it, I'm just helping a couple of old friends with no knowledge of what you've been getting up to. If they take me in for questioning, I'll just be surprised. As far as I'm concerned, you are on academic leave in the States. I am here in Germany for, what, academic reasons—I do teach German, after all."

"But, the phone calls? The communications with Bob the Barman?"

"I never phoned from home. Always from the college. And I've burned all written evidence."

"How will you explain getting the house?"

"You sent me a letter from the States, saying you weren't coming back and did I want it? I have it here. It needs a signature and a letter giving power of attorney to your Faldwell lawyer. I need a few signatures on those as well. You're selling that lovely new apartment you never got much chance to use, I take it?"

"That's right. Sell the lot."

"Right," Lawson Baines went on. "To business. In your bags are the plane tickets. I've made all the bank transfers you requested. You can't carry too much cash. It's not safe. You have built up quite a nest-egg since you stopped teaching. I've been buying gold krugerrands bit by bit. They are all in this safe deposit box." He handed Ken an envelope. "Your money has been transferred to the National Arab Bank which has branches all over the world. Here are the details. Your plane tickets are for Mumbai. I've put five thousand dollars in cash inside each bag."

"We really appreciate you doing this, Lawson. Above and beyond the call of friendship."

"Like I said, thank you for giving me your house in Faldwell Upton. Rumour has it that there have been some dodgy people renting it. I'll let them stay there until their lease is up at Christmas. Then I may rent it out to students. I don't suppose we'll be seeing you back at the old place?"

"Well, no," said Sonia. "I don't think we are going to be very welcome in the UK any more. How are things at the college? Is it any different under Cloughie?"

"Dame Kathleen, if you don't mind."

"Is she difficult, then?"

"Well, she was already undergoing the usual transformation into Joseph Stalin even before she got damed. She was already turning into another Scregg, without the lechery, like they all do. Since she got her title she's no longer difficult, she's now unbearable. First thing she did when she got the thing was send us all a memo telling us that we had all earned the medal for her and would we please all call her 'Dame' Kathleen from now on. Otherwise things go on much as they have always done. As long as her dameship and the new management 'team' stay out of our hair, we can do our jobs well enough."

"Dame Kathleen, eh?" said Ken. "Well, I suppose it sounds better than 'Little Bitch'. I can put you in touch with Scouse Bill, if you like? He does a very nice line in problem eradication."

"I might consider that. Let's drink up and go to the airport." Lawson replied.

Lawson bought three tickets at the automatic ticket machine while Ken and Sonia disappeared into the toilets to change into their disguises. Then they got the first train out of the Frankfurt *Hauptbahnhof* to the airport. As an additional precaution, they sat apart and did not acknowledge each other. Fortunately the heavy police presence was looking for the sort of person who might join a *jihad*, not respectable English academic types. This sort of work was obviously a lot easier now that it become routine for the British Smiths to make sure the Muslims were always blamed, whatever skulduggery Selfridge and Harrod and their team might get up to.

Ken and Sonia had completely changed their appearances. Ken, now clean-shaven after months with a beard, had also shaved his head in the modern style. He had added the heavy black-framed spectacles which Lawson had brought him and he was now sporting a tweed jacket and bow-tie. He could have passed for an American professor or maybe a Wall Street finance manager. Sonia meanwhile, had exchanged her well-scrubbed English look for smart makeup, long blonde, false locks and Parisian designer chic.

The three got off the train at the airport and ascended the several levels of escalators until they reached the departure area.

Ken and Sonia said their goodbyes to Lawson discreetly. He immediately turned and went to the Lufthansa check-in desk for his return trip to the UK. They waved one last wave before he disappeared into airside security. Ken and Sonia would be getting the Gulfair flight to Bahrain where they would be changing to the plane for Mumbai. They would have three tense hours to wait before take-off.

After an hour, the Gulfair check-in was opened and they joined the line for first class. Lawson had not spared any expense. They were nervous. If their escape was going to be thwarted, now was the time when it would happen, when the security personnel would be under orders to be especially vigilant about people leaving the country. Fortunately, although there was an extra police presence on the desks and gates for flights to the middle east, Ken and Sonia were not the sort of people the police were looking for. The uniformed *polizei* would ask the occasional traveller from the line to step aside for further questioning behind a screen but every such man they identified was clearly non-European. It had not occurred to the logical German official mind that the revered English Countess might have been killed by two of her own countrymen.

After Ken and Sonia had successfully checked in, their bags, and their persons, were X-rayed. And although they did not spark off the electronic body alarm, they were still both needlessly fondled by those *frotteurs* who are employed to do the much sought-after job of groping airline passengers in the cause of that new world religion called 'security'.

But they were through. The next stage was passport control.

"Mr Grassmann, why are you going to Mumbai?"

Ken had his answer ready.

"Academic conference. I'm a college professor."

And he was through.

Similarly for Sonia, who told the security man she was going to her sister's wedding.

They met up next in the Gulfair first class lounge where snacks and drinks were on offer. They sat back-to-back on the benches.

"So far, so good."

"Fingers crossed."

They looked for all the world as if they were a couple who had just met for the first time and were beginning a travellers' flirtation.

They sat apart for the six-hour trip to Bahrain where the connecting Mumbai flight was due to take off at 11.00 AM the following morning. There would be a four hour stopover in Bahrain.

But they did not take the Mumbai flight. At Bahrain, they went out into the main booking arrivals hall and found their way to the departures hall where the check-in desks and tickets offices are to be found.

"Where to?" asked Ken.

"I thought we were supposed to be going to Mumbai?"

"Officially yes, that's where Lawson bought tickets for. I think we should go somewhere else."

"Why, don't you trust him? He's our friend." said Sonia.

"Yes, he is," agreed Ken. "But think. It's only a matter of time before the Smiths go through the computer records and see where he bought tickets for. They're probably searching his computer as we speak. The Smiths are probably going to be waiting for us in India. If we don't get the Mumbai plane, he will not be in any position to help them. We could be saving him a difficult interview with the British intelligence. Better for Lawson if he knows as little as necessary."

"So, we can't escape. If we buy tickets for somewhere else, they will find us eventually."

"No, darling, that's not how it works. What we need to do is cover as much of our tracks as possible. If we make it too difficult for them to follow us, then at some point they will give up on us because the effort stops being worth it. Other things will take over and they will slowly forget about us. We are not that important. Unless, of course, we went back into business."

"I think you're right. If they question Lawson too heavily, they will get it out of him that we are in India. I don't want him to get too much third degree grilling."

"Or," said Ken, "knowing Lawson, he might well have bought tickets for a place which needs a change of planes for that very reason. Not knowing where our final destination is going to be means that he will have nothing to tell them."

"Good thinking, said Sonia. "So where is it to be?"

They stood in the middle of the Bahrain Airport concourse and read off the names of the exotic countries which were actually only a short flight away. Like a travel agent laying out a menu for a rich client.

"So," Sonia read out, "Indonesia? China? Vietnam? The Philippines? Australia? There's so many."

"The Philippines. I've never been there. Nice warm climate. Speak English, Friendly people. Why not there?"

"Why not indeed?" Sonia agreed.

So they went over to the Gulfair desk.

"Can I change these first-class tickets for two one-way tickets to Manila, please."

"Certainly, sir," said the desk clerk. "First class, business class or economy?"

"First, I think," said Ken.

"There will be a surcharge." She consulted a price list at the side of her desk.

"There will be, let me see, less twenty-five percent for the Mumbai ticket returns, add the cost of the Manila tickets. A surcharge of four hundred and ten dollars each. Will it be credit card or cash?"

"Oh, cash. Yes, definitely cash."

"There are two first class seats on the flight to Manila departing at seventeen hundred this afternoon. Would that be OK?"

"Yes, please," Sonia and Ken said in unison.

Ken counted out eight hundred and twenty dollars and handed it over in exchange for the tickets.

"Check-in details will be on the board. Check-in begins at fifteen hundred. Enjoy your flight."

"Thank you!"

Ken and Sonia then returned to look for a couple of seats in the capacious transit lounge at Bahrain Airport. They found two beneath a palm tree where they snoozed until three o'clock in the afternoon and they could check into the Manila flight and spend the rest of their waiting time in the luxurious Gulfair first class lounge.

They slept most of the nine hours of the flight to The Philippines. After a good breakfast they were ready to greet their new home with optimism. It was already mid-morning when they landed and made their way to the Manila Airport immigration. There was even a band playing to welcome newcomers to the country.

"Mabuhay!!" read the sign over the immigration desks, in Tagalog, the local language.

And indeed, they did feel welcome.

EIGHTEEN

Ken and Sonia soon established themselves in The Philippines. They bought a secluded house at a beautiful place called Caylabne, about two hours drive south of the crowded city of Manila. Caylabne is a beach resort which boasts views across a wide bay out to the South China Sea. It lies far enough from the Manila City effluent that the sea there is clean and clear. Around the resort are tree-covered hills, protected as a wild life sanctuary. The soundtrack of this paradisiacal resort is the chatter of monkeys and the raucous squawks of parrots. There are monsoons from July until November when the heavy Pacific rain lashes down for an hour or so each day to restore a cleansing freshness to the landscape. When the rain subsides after a short time, it does so abruptly and the sky returns immediately to its intense tropical blue, cloudless and empty save for the wheeling of eagles.

Here they fell into a gentle lotus-eating life. Long days were spent in relaxing, reading, doing water-sports and making love. Once a week they would take their four-by-four truck to the supermarket five miles away and fill up with groceries and San Miguel beer, the last an essential in a country where 25 degrees Celsius is regarded as cool. The household chores were taken care of by Anni, an obliging Filipina maid who would earn a little for her family by doing the couple's laundry and cleaning.

After three or four months, they had put their old life as college lecturers and British state hitmen behind them and had begun to, as the English phrase has it, 'go native'. There was much to be said about a life free of ambition and western dissatisfactions. They had TV of course, and they could follow the stupidities and venalities of the important people of the so-called "developed" world via CNN. Little they saw there inclined them to question the new way of life which they had found for themselves.

By the end of their first year they could chat a little in Tagalog with the local residents and they found themselves completely immersed in their new environment. The fears they had first had when they had escaped from Germany had long since evaporated. If they thought about it, which they did from time to time, it was with a confidence that after so long, whatever trail they might have left would have gone completely cold and all those strange people in England—Marks, Spencer, Selfridge, Harrod, Tate, Lyle and all the Smiths—would have completely forgotten about them. By now, they confidently believed, the British intelligence community would have new worries beyond taking their revenge on two disobedient but harmless renegades.

Even the Earl, widower of the late lamented Countess, had moved on to where he was now being openly spoken of as the future husband of Princess Maria, heiress presumptive to the crown. The death of the Countess, European Humanitarian of the Year, sainted paragon of all feminine virtue, if you believed the daily press and dissolute embarrassment if you took the side of the Smiths in British intelligence, was, so the official line now had it, no longer down to some middle eastern religious fanatics but was now being officially ascribed to an error of judgement by a driver who had helped himself rather too liberally to the refreshments on offer at the complimentary bar of the *Kongresshaus* before he had taken the wheel to drive the Countess for their final mortal journey.

The subsequent theatrical extravaganza which had been her funeral had been the opportunity for the younger British to forsake the traditional dignified good taste of their elders in order to wallow in an excess of lachrymose sentimentality, learned second-hand from the down-market reality TV shows. When it was shown on Philippine television about one week after their arrival in Manila, Ken and Sonia watched the grotesque display with morbid fascination.

"We did all that," said Ken as they watched pictures of crowds of mourners, tears streaming down faces already wet from the London rain, their face-painted union jacks streaked and messy.

Whichever version of the Countess's character one inclined to, it is likely that the truth was somewhere in between, as it usually is. Ken and Sonia felt neither regret nor vindication at the way things had turned out. They were, they knew full well, merely tools in the hands of those who had calculatedly used them. And now, their usefulness ended, and having escaped termination themselves, they were planning a long and inconspicuous retirement at the other side of the world. For the past year they had worried decreasingly that they might be the victim of some freelance assassin doing a favour for the intelligence fellows from the British Embassy in Makati, where they had occasionally to report. But nothing happened and as time went by, they gradually lost their fear of going into the city and came to accept that they really had, at last, fallen below the spookish radar.

When the doorbell rang, late one afternoon, they were drinking beer on the terrace of their back garden.

"We're not expecting anyone, are we?" Sonia asked.

"Not that I know."

Ken opened the door. Two men were standing there. They had about them the unmistakable smell of 'official'. One was a middle-aged man dressed in a cheap tropical light-weight beige summer suit. His attire also included a Panama hat and incongruous black, highly-polished shoes. He was obviously uncomfortable to be dressed in these unfamiliar clothes because his appearance gave every impression that the suit was wearing him, instead of the other way around.

His younger companion was much better turned out. He wore his clothes, hand-made seersucker, with a swagger. His Gucci loafers were old and well-worn. His watch, Ken quickly took in, was a Patek Philippe. He had the unmistakable appearance of an upper middle class ex-public schoolboy.

Ken registered in a fraction of a second and before any of them had spoken, as any Englishman could, the entire social, economic and educational history of his two visitors. He also noted that neither man was sun-tanned, which meant that the two had come all the way from England to see him.

"Good afternoon, gentlemen," Ken began.

"You will remember me, will you not, Mr. Grassmann?"

"Indeed, I do! Inspector Fordham! What brings you all this way to The Philippines to see me?"

"May we come in?"

Ken opened the door to let the two men into his sitting room.

"Please sit down. Beer?"

"No, thank you," said Fordham. "This is business, not pleasure."

The two men sat at the table facing Ken.

"Sonia, love!" he called. "We have guests. You remember Inspector Fordham from Faldwell Upton, don't you?"

"Actually, it's Superintendent Fordham now," said Fordham with a slight emphasis on his new job title. Ken noticed that the tropical heat had already caused the armpits of his polyester suit to become stained with sweat.

"And this is Sergeant Thompson."

Thompson nodded.

"Are you sure you wouldn't like a beer?" Ken asked them again.

"Quite sure," said Fordham firmly. "Maybe some water."

"I'd love a beer," said Thompson, earning himself a black look from the superintendent.

"Actually," said Ken, "here in the tropics, you'll find that beer is a healthier way of staying hydrated than the water, which can be dodgy unless you buy the bottled stuff from a decent source."

Ken went to fetch the drinks and came back to the table with beer and water.

"So," he asked, "why, exactly, are you here?"

Fordham came straight to the point.

"We are here, Mr Grassmann, because we have not yet finished with you over the little matter of the death, nearly three years ago now, of one Morton Alamein Scregg, late Principal of Upton Faldwell Community College. A death which you, Mr Grassmann, as you very well know, were responsible for."

"Inspector, sorry, Superintendent, Fordham," Ken replied, "you know that was not my doing. The coroner gave his verdict. Scregg died accidentally. You should know. You were there at the inquest."

Fordham smiled a sly smile.

"You may think you've got away with it. But the case has been reopened at my request. The Crown Prosecution

Service will be appealing to have the coroner's verdict overturned."

Sonia was about to speak but Fordham held his hand up to silence her.

"If you don't mind, miss, we'll do it my way."

"I head up," Fordham continued, "a new national police department. It is called The National Criminal Research Office and it's based in Glasgow. It is our job to search through old cases to see if there are instances where a case has been closed but where they may have been some doubt about the fairness of the final outcome. And naturally, your name came out first, as the murderer of the late Mr Scregg."

"Alleged murderer. And only alleged by you, nobody else. According to the coroner, there was no murder. And, while we're about it, why exactly did you choose me? It couldn't have been because you are pursuing some sort of personal vendetta against me, could it?"

"Actually, Mr Grassmann, it just happens to be coincidence that we are investigating you first. But you have to admit that your actions have been, how shall we say, a little suspicious. For example . . ." said Fordham.

"For example, what?" retorted Ken.

"For example, shortly after Scregg was murdered."

"I keep telling you, he wasn't murdered!"

". . shortly after the death of Mr Scregg, you and Miss Lyttel here, suddenly upped sticks and moved away. No one knows where. We still have no knowledge of where you were for over two years between leaving Faldwell Upton and finding you here. Would you care to enlighten us?"

"Why should I? It's none of your business."

"You see, Mr Grassmann, that's exactly the sort of attitude which makes us suspicious. If a suspect is unwilling to co-operate with the rightful forces of law and order, it usually means they have something to hide."

"So, I'm a suspect now, am I?"

"You've always been a suspect, Mr Grassmann, ever since I first clapped eyes on you. Refusing to answer questions about your whereabouts this last two years looks very bad for you. Why not tell us and get it off your chest? If you've got nothing to hide, you've got nothing to fear."

"And if I refuse?" asked Ken.

"Then, if you refuse, Mr Grassmann, you will leave me with no alternative. I will have to arrest you on suspicion of murder and take you back with us to England, while we make further enquiries."

"Before I consider your kind offer," Ken asked, "how did you know we were here in The Philippines?"

"Just good old-fashioned coppering, that was. Records of flights, hotels, mobile phones. These days there is nowhere for criminals like you to hide. We will always find you, whatever you've done. It's the Internet. These days, we can track everybody every minute of the day. If you even fart, it's down on some computer somewhere and we officers of the law can find out about it."

"Well, then," said Ken, "I am going to refuse to answer any more of your ridiculous questions. Make a note in your book. I did not murder Scregg. I am not sorry that he died but I did not murder him. My defence will be that the coroner brought in a verdict of accidental death."

"Then I'm sorry," began Fordham. "I am arresting you on suspicion of the murder of Morton Alamein Scregg. You do not have . . ."

He got no further. Thompson, who had been sitting silently throughout the exchange between Ken and Fordham, was now standing up and was holding a small pistol, which was pointed directly at Fordham's head.

"What the hell is this?" expostulated Fordham. "Are you out of your mind? Sergeant Thompson, I order you, as your senior officer, to put that gun down right now, and sit down."

"Actually," said the Sergeant, "my name is not Thompson, it's Smith. And you are not my senior officer. In fact, I outrank you. By quite a long way, if you take a look at this ID."

Smith pulled an ID card from out of his inside pocket and waved it under Fordham's nose.

"Oh shit!" said Fordham. "I thought you were a bit iffy when they assigned you to me back in London. 'Just learning the job' they said. 'Fast track graduate trainee,' they said. Should have smelt a rat then. So what are you going to do?"

"You are going to get back inside the car waiting outside and tell the driver to take you straight back to Manila Airport. You will then get the next available flight back to the UK. When you get back to Glasgow, the case of Mr Grassmann and Miss Lyttel will be permanently closed and its contents destroyed. If anyone asks you about your trip here, you will say that it was a pleasure trip. You were here to meet the famous Filipina party girls."

"I'm still a senior police officer. I could arrest you for threatening behaviour with a lethal weapon." Fordham blustered.

"Don't forget," answered Smith, "that you're a very long way from home. Your authority doesn't count for very much out here. You could even disappear completely and I doubt if the locals would care very much unless Her Majesty's Government made a fuss about you. Which they won't. Because, well, any questions about what actually happened to you while you were away sunning yourself at taxpayers' expense will somehow never get to the top of the in-tray. No, Fordham, your best bet is to do exactly as you are told, like a good superintendent."

With that, Smith opened the door of the house and beckoned to the driver who was waiting in the car outside.

"Make sure this gentleman gets to the airport pronto," Smith ordered the driver.

Smith then came back into the house and closed the door behind him.

"I suppose you're here to settle the account. Wipe the slate clean? Tidy up loose ends?" Ken asked him.

"Whatever do you mean?" Smith replied, with feigned puzzlement.

"Aren't you here to kill us, now that you've found us?"

"Why do you think that?" Smith asked them.

"Well, we were obviously down for it when we escaped from Germany. Aren't you here to set the record straight? Aren't you going to finish the job you and the other Smiths weren't able to finish last year?"

"Oh no, you have me all wrong," Smith assured them. "I'm not here on some revenge mission to eliminate you. Whatever gave you that idea?"

"So why have you come looking for us now?" Sonia asked.

"Well," said Smith, "we'd been wondering what had happened to you after the big events in Frankfurt and how you managed to evade all those careful traps we set for you. We were all very impressed. Everyone agreed it was very clever of you, working it all out like that. The false trail to Stuttgart was a masterstroke. We did have a few words with your colleague from your old college. Baines? Yes, Baines. You didn't even tell him the full story. He thought you'd have lost yourselves in India. Had no idea where you could be if you didn't get off the plane in Mumbai. Which of course, you didn't. We checked the landing cards. We like the way you gave everyone just enough info to keep them happy but never quite enough to put all the pieces together and work out exactly where you were. Good thinking, that. Also a good learning curve for us too. Helps us plug a few holes here and there."

"So you're not going to erase us then?"

"Certainly not. You two have a real talent for the work. You showed clear thinking under pressure. You slipped through our net. You did everything we asked you to do. We certainly don't want to lose two top field operatives like you two. Just think of all that expensive training wasted!"

"But those fellows at Uxbridge, Selfridge and Harrod. They obviously wanted rid of us. What's changed?"

"Well, after the Frankfurt job, which you did perfectly, I have to say, there was quite a bit of diplomatic fallout."

"The Germans were a wee bit cross, perhaps, at losing two of their men?"

"Oh, no, nothing like that. The Jerries are always very understanding about collateral damage. We don't kick up when we lose one of ours in some German job. It's a sort of friendly European understanding we all have. No, the real problem was when our chaps at Uxbridge tried to blame it on the Muslims. Helluva row from the ethnic minority lobby. All sorts of accusations about racial stereotyping, convenient scape-goating, et bloody cetera, blah . . de . . blah. Anyway, the Prime Minister got it in the neck something rotten. Which is only fair, really, since it was his idea in the first place to blame it on our immigrant friends. Error of judgement on his part. Seems there's a lot of mosques in his constituency and, well, there's an election coming up as well. But someone had to take the blame for his blunder so there was a bit of a clear-out among the top brass at Uxbridge. New thinking is that you both actually did a fine job and you are still on the strength."

"But we understood the Countess would be our last job."

"I'm very sorry, Miss Lyttel, but I'm afraid we told you a little fib there. Still, not to worry, you have lots of back pay outstanding, pension rights restored, even some expenses due. We'll be in touch."

Smith got up to go.

"Just one thing," Sonia asked, "what was all that business about Fordham? Why was he trailing us?"

"He's never had anything to do with our side of things. He's what we, probably unfairly, call a 'woodentop'. Civilian police. A bit dim if you ask me, our Superintendent Fordham. Not to say completely unprofessional by our standards. Which are your standards too, of course, now that you've proved yourselves. For some reason, we can't understand why, the fellow has a bee in his bonnet about you and this Scregg chappie. Thinks you did him in. Got a bit of an obsession about it."

"And that's why he came all this way? To arrest us for the one job we didn't actually do? He doesn't know about all the others?" Sonia was incredulous.

"Yes, that's right. The minute he got his new job, it seems he spent all his time on the police computer tracking you down. Waste of time and money, if you ask me."

"So how did you find us?" asked Ken.

"Well," answered Smith, "we were always interested in where you'd actually ended up but we never did very much about it. Have far too much other work on our plates to search for you ourselves, so we just left it. But when we read on the police computer that Fordham was coming out here looking for you, I tagged along as his gopher. Pretended I was a police fast-track trainee. He was easily fooled."

"You hacked into the police computer?"

"Of course, text-book stuff. Quite routine. We go through everything they put on it, just in case they have anything we can use. When your names kept coming up, attached to requests from Fordham, we thought it worth a try to see what he'd got planned. Good job we did. Otherwise you'd be back on a plane to England right now. Which would mean a couple of nights in the cells before we got you out, then press, TV etc to be shut up before your names got out. A lot of unnecessary fuss. Big palaver. Better this way. English weather is pretty rotten right now."

"What will happen to Fordham?"

"Oh, nothing much. He'll be quietly warned to forget about you. He'll be told to explain away this trip by telling people he was taking a well-earned vacation. And, if he keeps his mouth shut, he can expect the Queen's Police Medal and promotion to Chief Constable in due course."

"And if he doesn't keep his mouth shut?"

"I'm surprised to hear you ask that, Mr Grassmann. You being a professional."